The Diary of Young Arthur Conan Doyle

Adventures in Russia, 1881

Edited

by

Dr. John Raffensperger & Richard Krevolin

Paperback ISBN 978-1-78705-153-9
ePub ISBN 978-1-78705-154-6
PDF ISBN 978-1-78705-155-3

Published in the UK by MX Publishing
335 Princess Park Manor, Royal Drive,
London, N11 3GX
www.mxpublishing.co.uk

Covers painted by Ewa Czarniecka,
graphic design Kyra Dunn, compilation Brian Belanger.

To our esteemed editor, Nancy Cohen, our wonderful agent, Paula Munier, Renee Braeunig, Melanie Jappy, Kathy Copas, Colleen Sell, Dr. Wally Duff, Dr. Glenn Shepard, John Haslett, Penny Macleod, Steve Callender, Katja Bressette, Katia Haddidian, Coach Bob Orgovan, and the Sanibel writing group four.

EDITORS' NOTE

In 1880, Arthur Conan Doyle wrote a diary of his adventures as a ship's surgeon on an Arctic whaler. It is a true story and that diary has been available to Sherlock Holmes fans for many years.

Until now, however, three of Doyle's other diaries about his international adventures had gone undiscovered. In a historic twist of fate, we were fortunate to recently find these three 'lost' diaries hidden in the compartment of a trunk purchased at auction and said to include some of the personal effects of Sir Arthur Conan Doyle.

The first diary contains stories from 1878 when Doyle was a nineteen-year-old student at the University of Edinburgh Medical School. These tales of high adventure begin with Conan Doyle's clerkship under the legendary Doctor Joseph Bell and follow the duo (and other well-known personalities) on their journey to America for a secret forensic mission to solve a string of grisly and mysterious murders.

The third, soon-to-be-published, diary in this trio of mayhem, murder, and medicine adventure stories, is a record of Doyle's experiences in 1883. It includes personal details from Doyle's second trip with Dr. Bell from Scotland to America, by which time he had become a doctor in his own right.

In the diary you now hold, the second of the 'lost' three, Doyle recorded his 1881 journey with Dr. Joseph Bell, this time to Russia, immediately following his graduation. It reveals how, despite initially being invited to teach the antiseptic technique at the medical school in St. Petersburg, the two became embroiled in nefarious conspiracies that could have engulfed Europe in a deadly war. If not for their abilities to discern all details and leave no stone unturned, we might have had a very different twentieth century…

We are including the following points of information with the hope that they offer some context and clarity about young Arthur Conan Doyle and these journeys.

- There is some controversy as to whether Bell was the inspiration for Sherlock Holmes, though a handwritten letter from Arthur Conan Doyle to Dr. Bell, which is housed in the archives [RS L1 Box B] of the Royal College of Surgeons in Edinburgh, states, "It is most certainly to you that I owe Sherlock Holmes."

- These three diaries indicate a somewhat thorny relationship between Dr. Joseph Bell and Arthur Conan Doyle. In his own words, Doyle was a mediocre medical student. But Bell observed in him talents that went beyond the usual student, hence his choice of Doyle to be his outpatient clerk. Dr. Bell, a third-generation Edinburgh surgeon and true medical aristocrat, could be hard on students. Doyle was acutely aware of his own humble background. His father was addicted to alcohol and his mother, whom he affectionately referred to as 'Mam,' took in lodgers to support the family. It is quite possible that, especially after the first trip to America, Doyle hoped Bell would become a replacement 'father figure,' but Bell continued to treat him as any other student. Doyle initially resented what he perceived as 'humiliation' by Bell. As his ability and confidence increased, a warmer relationship, based on mutual respect, grew between the two of them.

- These diaries demonstrate Dr. Bell's medical and surgical skills. He was one of the first to use Lister's antiseptic technique to prevent infection in wounds. Bell pioneered operations to save the limbs of children afflicted with tuberculosis of the bones and joints. He was in great demand to lecture and demonstrate his techniques to foreign surgeons. He was also an author, the first to support Nightingale nurses on his wards, and a forensic consultant to local police and Scotland Yard.

- While the diaries are also important because they document medical and surgical practices during the 19th century — when there were no X-rays, scans, or laboratory tests to guide doctors — this particular journal also explains Sherlock Holmes use of cocaine. At the time Doyle wrote this diary, many physicians, including Sigmund Freud, viewed cocaine as a panacea. It was also used as a powerful local anaesthetic. Surgeons who self-experimented with cocaine as a local anaesthetic quickly became addicted to the drug.

- Though he wrote in English, Arthur Conan Doyle was fluent in French and German and quickly learned basic Russian. Given that many of the entries in the diary appear to have been written during times of stress or several days after an event, and considering the great upheavals that have taken place in Russia since his visit, you may find an occasional minor variation in spelling. Additionally, in Great Britain (unlike in America or Russia), though physicians are called doctor, surgeons are referred to as mister. Because the 'lost' diaries traverse locales, you may notice the use of both titles depending upon who is addressing Doyle.

That said, it is with great joy that we now share with you, dear reader, the story of young Arthur Conan Doyle's adventures during those fateful months in 1881 as detailed in his second of three fabulously exciting 'lost journals.' We hope you enjoy the journey.

~ Dr. John Raffensperger and Richard Krevolin, Oxford, England, 9 October 2016.

7 June 1881

Despite my adventures in America with Dr. Joseph Bell, and even though I am a senior and will soon graduate, he continues to humiliate me in front of the entire class for my trivial errors in diagnosis. Professor Bell is a brilliant diagnostician and the most popular teacher in the medical school, but I sometimes feel like lashing out at him with curses and expletives.

Take today's Friday afternoon clinic: Dr. Bell walked in at exactly two o'clock sharp. Sun streamed through the sooty windows of the great surgical amphitheatre of the Royal Edinburgh Infirmary. Medical students filled tiers of hard-backed seats overlooking the 'cockpit,' which doubled as operating theater, as well as Bell's clinic.

I had recently finished my term as Dr. Bell's clerk, and now, another poor, trembling third year student, Josiah Weeks, was in my place, organizing patients to see the professor. I pitied poor Weeks and did not envy his position, although I could sorely use the extra funds from the measly salary that accompanies the post.

There was a sprinkling of visiting doctors from all of Europe, as well as America, to observe Dr. Bell's brilliant operating skills and his diagnostic acumen. Dmitry Gorchakov of the St. Petersburg faculty of Medicine and Surgery, a great bear of a man with a bushy, black beard, had taken notes during clinics and operating sessions for the past week. He was especially interested in Dr. Bell's operation for joint excision in cases of tuberculosis and injuries. The Russian spoke broken English with a thick, guttural accent, but I suspected he understood our language better than he let on.

Meanwhile, I was idly thinking about Miss Jean McGill, a pretty new nurse who was sitting a few rows back, when Dr. Bell turned his keen gaze upon me. "Mr. Doyle, if you please, what causes Mrs. Connor's cough?"

Mrs. Connor, the patient in a plain, black skirt, black coat, black hat, and black, ankle-high shoes, was spare and stooped with a sad, sharp, lined face and nearly-white hair. She had walked haltingly, resting on the arm of Weeks, the third year clerk, to a chair in front of us students. Connor could have been anyone's grandmother. Weeks, a nervous boy of perhaps nineteen years, had stammered out the information that Mrs. Connor's cough had resisted all treatment for the past half-decade.

For the life of me, I couldn't think of a plausible diagnosis. Aye, I had seen several coal miners with such a cough, but never a woman. The patient hung her head and seemed to gaze at the floor, when she took a rag from her handbag, covered her mouth, and coughed out a gob of bloody phlegm.

I mumbled, "Well, sir, um, eh, she could have tuberculosis or chronic bronchitis?"

"Indeed, Mr. Doyle." He paused for a painful moment. "I'd recommend visiting the bursar's office this afternoon," he advised.

"Why, sir?"

"Well, laddie, the bursar can issue a refund of your tuition, since it appears as if you have yet to learn how to truly examine a patient after four years of medical school."

The other students burst out in raucous laughter. I flared with anger, my cheeks grew red, and I was barely able to hold my tongue.

Dr. Bell's fierce, probing eyes twinkled with pleasure. After our trip to America a few years ago, I felt a close kinship with him. Being that my father was a worthless drunkard, when I was admitted to Edinburgh, I had hoped that Bell would fill his shoes as the sober authority figure and a mentor. Alas, upon our return, he seemed to coldly withdraw and resume a formal teacher/student relationship.

Nay, he was not truly malicious; but neither was he kind and forgiving. I looked up at him and Bell leaned back in his chair. "Doyle, how many years have you been under my tutelage?"

"Several, sir."

"And what is the single most important precept I have taught you?"

"Never assume anything. Look at every situation with fresh eyes, observe fully, and then deduce properly."

"Aye. 'Tis good to know that at least your ears work . . . Now, let us begin again." Dr. Bell folded his hands over his chest and stretched out his long legs as he questioned the patient. "Good afternoon, Mrs. Connor. Did you have a good trip from Lancashire?"

"Yissir, but for the childer was after giving me cheek on the train. I coulda give 'em a smackin'. "

At the sound of her lilting voice, Dr. Bell rose from his chair, went to the patient, and gently touched her cheek, then carefully examined, one by one, her fingers.

"You left Connacht during the famine?"

"Yissir, when me poor ma and pa passed on for lack of food."

"When did Mr. Connor die in the mines?"

"It was twenty years ago, near time when our only boy passed on. The mine caved in."

As cutting and cruel as he was, I still couldn't help but be filled with awe and respect as he unraveled a patient's history; keenly observing telling, minute attributes, weaving them together in his mind, and then using this web of seemingly disconnected information as the basis for an accurate diagnosis.

As he rubbed his chin, my classmates had become quiet as so many mice. Bell now had their attention; this promised to be one of his better performances and those rough-hewn boys were overcome by the woman's sad, but gentle, visage.

"Hmm. Aye... Mr. Doyle, bring that shiny new stethoscope of yours and please give a listen to Mrs. Connor's lungs."

I turned her chair away from the students, and after she loosened the front of her

blouse, I applied the stethoscope to the apex and then the base of her lungs. Her chest was filled with mysterious crackles, bubbling, and wheezing.

"Well, Mr. Doyle, tell us, what did you hear?"

"She has rales and wheezing, sir."

"Do you still think the diagnosis is tuberculosis?"

"It is possible, but I don't know anymore, sir," I answered.

Dr. Bell dictated two prescriptions to his clerk. "Mrs. Connor, each morning, burn a quarter cup of the leaves of Jimson weed and inhale the smoke. In the evening, put a teaspoon of dried sage and fifteen drops of oil of eucalyptus in a cup of boiling water and drink the tea. You will feel much better." The good doctor gave Mrs. Connor his arm and personally helped her to the anteroom.

There was a stir amongst the students until Dr. Bell returned, drew a hand across his pure white hair, and spoke. "Gentlemen, this is one of the more simple cases we have seen today and yet, not a one of you made the necessary observations. I regret to say that it is a result of your innate presumptions and prejudices. Never let them get in the way of a proper diagnosis. Observe, deduce, and diagnose with a clear mind and open eyes."

What was he getting at? I was confused and stupefied.

"Dr. Bell?"

"Did you, Mr. Doyle, or anyone, note the slip of paper pinned on her coat? It was yellow, the color of tickets for the Lancashire line. She has the dialect of West Ireland, and many of the poor Irish were forced to work in the coal mines of Scotland after the great famine. Coal dust is still embedded in her skin. When evaluating the lungs, carefully examine the finger nails. Mrs. Connor's nails are slightly blue, pitted, and down-curved, a sure sign of chronic oxygen deprivation caused by long-standing lung disease. The diagnosis is silicosis, better known as 'miner's lung.' The word, silicosis, as you surely know, is derived from the Latin, *silex*, or flint. When miner's inhale dust in the mines, the silica becomes imbedded in the alveoli of the lung. Any questions?"

We students remained perfectly mute. Not a one of us stirred, overcome by Dr. Bell's great powers of observation and his quick wit. One student finally raised his hand.

"Aye," Dr. Bell said, pointing to the student.

"Sir, that makes sense for a man who toiled in the mines, but how does that apply to a woman?"

"Don't assume anything just because she's a woman… Ah, one of the great tragedies of Scotland. I would venture to say that when her husband died, she was forced to labor in the mines to support herself. Next patient, please."

He was a ten-year-old boy whose flushed, feverish face was contorted by pain. The clerk rolled him into the amphitheatre on a cart. "Jamie McLeod here has a pain in his stomach," he said. At the poor boy's side was his mother — a poorly dressed, tearful, young woman twisting a handkerchief with both hands.

Dr. Bell did not question and harass us students in his usual way. Instead, he went to the cart and immediately put his finger on the boy's pulse. There came over his face a look of intense concern. He closed his eyes and pursed his lips. "Now, mother, how long has your boy been ill?"

"He's been down with pain in his belly these five days, sir."

"Can he keep down his food?"

"No sir. He throws out every mouthful and hasn't had even a drop of water this past day."

"Have his bowels moved?"

"No sir."

The professor loosened the boy's trousers and gently ran his hand over the abdomen. The child winced and cried out when he touched the right lower quadrant.

Dr. Bell absently stroked his chin. "In the past, we would have diagnosed your son with a severe case of inflammation of the bowels, but these days, there are physicians in America who would posit that your son is suffering from a disease of the vermiform appendix. However, we would have to do exploratory surgery to know for certain."

"Do whatever you need to, sir. Just ease his pain."

"Mr. Doyle, fetch my instrument case, please," Dr. Bell instructed.

The appendix? There was nothing in our textbooks about the appendix. Aye, my anatomy professor had mentioned it in passing, calling it a useless organ with no known function. We all murmured and twisted in our seats, not sure what to make of Bell's diagnosis. Meanwhile, the Russian sitting behind me leaned forward, straining to understand every word.

When all was ready, the junior clerk dripped chloroform on a mask over the boy's face. When he was asleep, Dr. Bell swabbed the abdomen with carbolic, attached a trocar to the syringe and, after a moment's hesitation, plunged the sharp steel probe into the boy's abdomen. We all held our breath. He pulled back the plunger, and the syringe filled with yellow, creamy pus.

"By Jove, the Americans are on to something," Dr. Bell said and then looked at Weeks. "Take this young man and his mother straight to the Royal Hospital. Find Dr. John Hetherington and tell him that I said that this lad needs to have his appendix surgically removed immediately."

As Weeks led the boy — still groggy from the chloroform anaesthetic — and his mother out of the theater, there was a great clatter of horse's hooves and a jangling of bells on Lauriston Street. An agitated police officer burst into the amphitheatre. "There's been an accident at the quarry!"

In the next instant, two burly orderlies carried a groaning, bleeding, bearded man on a crimson-stained stretcher into the amphitheatre. Something about him was familiar, but I could not place him nor was he in any condition to identify himself. Who was he and why did I feel like I knew him?

His legs below the knee were a jumble of bloody boots, mangled skin, and muscle, with white, jagged bone protruding from his torn trousers. Bright red blood bubbled up from lacerated arteries. His right hand was a scarlet mess.

In a flash, Dr. Bell with his two assistants cut away the man's clothing and applied tourniquets above his knees. The furiously spurting blood slowed to a trickle; a great sigh of relief went up from the students.

Dr. Bell removed his coat and rolled up his sleeves. "Mr. Doyle, please administer the anaesthetic," he said. I adjusted a cloth mask over the poor man's nose and mouth and poured a few drops of chloroform. His moaning soon ceased and his clenched jaw relaxed.

For a moment, I thought he was dead, but there was a faint pulse at his neck. The gentleman wore a fine tweed jacket, but at the time, I was too busy with the anaesthetic to wonder at his clothing.

Dr. Bell and his assistants scrubbed their hands, then swabbed the patient's legs with a solution of carbolic, while the clerk arranged the instruments on a clean towel. There was a sense of great urgency as he cut through the skin and layers of muscle, sawed bone, ligated arteries, and stitched up the skin. He amputated both legs just above the knees within twenty minutes of the time the patient had entered the room.

I stopped the chloroform, but the poor man remained unconscious. We worked furiously to save his life. Dr. Bell ordered coffee enemas, and we attempted to force brandy down his throat, but to no avail. He sank lower and lower.

Suddenly, he stirred, opened his eyes, and murmured with a slight Irish accent. "It was no accident. No accident." Damn! I couldn't determine his identity. His voice was familiar, but a beard and scars covered his face.

Bell hovered over him as his bloody hand rose and he uttered a few words. He seemed to be saying, "Proof... Dr. Hutton correct... No God... End of the old regime."

With that effort, his entire body seemed to shrink into itself. His chest rose in a great sigh as he gave a shout with his last breath. "Tsar must die!"

The students and observers had left, but the Russian surgeon had stood by Dr. Bell's elbow. Now, he stepped back as if struck. "No, no, no..." he murmured. "We will save the tsar. We have blood. Blood for transfusion." All of a sudden, the Russian grabbed his notebook and stomped out of the amphitheatre.

Proof? Blood? The tsar?

What did it all mean? I was lost, and needless to say, no matter who our patient was, Dr. Bell and I were both upset at not being able to save him. We were the only ones left. "Doyle, please clean the corpse," Dr. Bell said.

As I did, I opened his clenched hands and found a scrap of paper. A clue. Was this his proof?

Dr. Bell, who had been slumped in his chair in utter defeat, took the paper, spread it flat on the sink, and gently mopped away some clotted blood, which had dropped on it. On one side was a sketch of a small animal, somewhat like a lizard, and on the other was an address: 41 Maitland Park Road.

The professor then minutely examined the corpse, muttering all the time. "Well-tanned, a once-handsome man, and a fine tweed jacket; this is no ordinary quarryman." He then delicately sponged away the blood from the dead hand. Two fingers had been blown away, and in the middle of his hand was a dark, thick scar from an old wound — one that penetrated through the palm of the hand. There was an identical scar in the center of the palm of his left hand.

"Sir, what was that about the tsar?" I asked.

"Doyle, when was the last time you read a newspaper?"

"It's been a while, sir, with studying for my examinations and all …"

"If you were aware of current events, you'd know that anarchists assassinated Tsar Alexander II three months ago, on March the first."

"Aye, I may have heard about that."

"This is a case for Scotland Yard," he said. "Now, Doyle, go home, get some rest, and meet me in the morgue tomorrow morning."

While walking home, the words "No God" and "Tsar must die" kept reverberating in my mind.

Who was that injured man?

Why did he seem so familiar?

8 June 1881

I was busy with a cadaver, tracing the optic nerve from the eye through its foramen to the brain, when the two men interrupted my work. They were from London and had the bearing of military men.

Indeed, the short bull of a man, with greying red hair that poked in clumps from under his derby, introduced himself as such. "Sergeant James O'Grady of her Queen's Own Rifles at your service, sir." He had bright blue eyes and a freckled face that was toughened from years in the sun. His broad girth and strong musculature was such that I would have liked to have him on my rugby team.

The second man was nearly six feet tall and elegantly dressed in fawn-colored trousers, a black frock coat, and a grey jacket. I immediately recognized the ribbon of the Victoria Cross on his lapel and, almost as a reflex, stood at full attention. He did not offer to shake hands. His lips barely moved as he introduced himself, displaying the finest example of the British stiff upper lip I had ever witnessed. "Colonel Sir Cameron Beachy-Edwards." I judged him to be at least sixty years of age. He was pale and slender, almost to the point of emaciation, as if he had suffered some terrible disease, such as typhus or dysentery.

The colonel didn't waste time or words. "Conduct us to the morgue."

I nodded. "Follow me," I said. We immediately set off down the corridor to a flight of wooden stairs, then through a door, smudgy with many hands that had handled body parts, into the cold, damp basement morgue. It was no surprise to see Dr. Bell already folding back the sheet that covered our deceased patient. I studied the bearded and scarred face once again. Who was it?

Sergeant O'Grady took up station by the door while the colonel stood with his hands clasped, staring at the dead face. Then, he minutely examined the dense scars on the man's face and the palms of the dead man's hands.

"Oh, dear God, it's Foley."

13

Foley?! I staggered back, away from that dreadfully maimed body. Was that why he seemed so familiar? Could he be Declan Foley? Foley is not an uncommon name, but my mam was a Foley and said Declan was a relative, perhaps a distant cousin. When he was stationed in Edinburgh, he often came to our house for Mam's cooking. One Christmas he brought a huge ham with sauces and a dessert. I was very young at the time and clung to him like he was my real father. I would run all the way to the castle to watch when he drilled the troops for the noon gun ceremony. I called him 'uncle' and loved it when he tossed me into the air and always caught me on the way down. He took me on long walks and to the museum, where told me the names of all the stuffed animals and where they were from. He was an amateur scientist as well as a soldier. When I last saw Uncle Declan, he wore his red officer's coat and a sword. He was off to the war in Afghanistan. I had often dreamed of him, gallantly slashing the heathen with his sword for the Queen and country. When pa was away on a drunken spree, I would frequently yearn for Uncle Declan's strong protective arms. The last we had heard, the poor man had died during a battle. This couldn't be . . .

The colonel wiped his eyes, seemed to be overcome by emotion, but gathered himself. "He was a lieutenant in command of a troop of Gurkha border guards while gathering intelligence in Baluchistan when he was captured by the Russians. Recently, we learned that the fiends turned him over to Moslem women who pinned him to the ground with stakes driven through his hands then propped his jaws open with a stick. Those sadistic women took turns squatting over his face and urinating into his mouth. Most men drown during this bizarre ritual, but Lt. Foley and another intelligence officer survived. Foley did not return to his regiment. Little is known about the other man, but we think he killed an officer of the Okhrana, took his identity, and disappeared into Russia," Colonel Beachy-Edwards said.

"What a horrible story! What happened to poor Foley?" I asked.

"He wandered around Eastern Europe. Recently, we learned that he came home and entered Cambridge under a pseudonym to study geology. Needless to say, Declan was a changed man as a result of the torture," the colonel said.

I studied the dead man's features. "Oh, my God! It is Uncle Declan!" I exclaimed.

"You knew this man?"

"My mother's relative, Declan Foley, was reported missing in action a few years ago. We assumed he was dead."

"As we did, too."

"But surely, he would've contacted us once he returned from . . ."

"Actually, Declan avoided family and old friends once he returned, changed his name, and dedicated himself to his study of geology. As I said, he was a changed man."

"I still can't believe . . ."

Dr. Bell cleared his throat. "Come here, laddie, and take another look."

"Aye." I studied the bearded, well-tanned face of the corpse. It was much more wrinkled and leathery than I remembered. There were new scars, but I saw the resemblance to my mam.

Aye, it was definitely him. He had the high cheek bones and the grey eyes of a Foley. He even had the same heart-shaped face as my mam. We had failed to save him. My eyes wandered to the stumps of his legs. Tears came to my eyes.

Dr. Bell saw I was deeply affected. "Tis him, aye?" he asked.

"Aye." I answered. "Dr. Bell, what did we do wrong? Why couldn't we save him?"

"We tried, laddie. We did everything in our power. There is no reason to feel shame."

I felt as if my uncle had been delivered to me for a reason. I swore I would — I must — find his assassin to redeem myself for our failure to save his life. The best surgeon in Scotland had been unable to save him. My years of study seemed futile. I would try to honor him. "Dr. Bell, we must discover his killer," I said.

"Aye." Dr. Bell said, "We will try... I am sorry, laddie. Were you and Declan close?"

"My father . . . Well, you know about my father. When I was a young lad, Declan was like a father to me, and I called him 'uncle.' Mam and I always looked forward to his visits. Oh, how my mam's face lit up when he appeared in the doorway. She loved him so."

"Then, we shall do everything in our power to solve his murder."

"Aye, thank you, sir." I brushed away my tears.

Dr. Bell, touched by my emotion, gently held my shoulder. "There, there, laddie. There, there."

"Thank you, sir. Sorry about that."

"Don't mention it. But remember, you are a physician; buck up and keep a professional demeanor." Dr. Bell replaced the sheet covering the corpse. "Let us adjourn to more comfortable surroundings. My cook makes an excellent breakfast tea."

It was in this moment when I most appreciated Dr. Bell and felt guilty that I complained about his abuse.

At Dr. Bell's house, O'Grady and I wolfed down boiled eggs, buttered toast with jam, and a rasher of bacon, while Dr. Bell and the colonel sipped tea. The colonel lit a cigar. "Who is Dr. Hutton?" he asked.

Dr. Bell took down from his bookshelf a heavy volume, *Theory of the Earth* by Dr. James Hutton. "Dr. Hutton was trained as a physician, but spent his entire life studying geology to prove that the earth was made over millions of years, not in the biblical six days."

"Balderdash. Sounds like one of those Darwinians. That goes against all authority."

O'Grady lifted his hand. "Sir, if I may be so bold. Lieutenant Foley was born a Roman Catholic, but, ever in search of the truth, he became an atheist and often talked about inciting the peasants to overthrow the Russian tsar if he could prove to them that the tsar's power was not derived from God."

"Perhaps Foley found something at the quarry that proved Dr. Hutton's theory," Dr. Bell said. He blew a cloud of pipe smoke and leaped from his chair. "Let us go there. Doyle, call James to bring up the landau," said Bell. He also took a telescope in a long case and one of his fine English shotguns. "We may see grouse on the moor," he muttered, while stuffing cartridges into a pocket. It was not the season for bird shooting.

The day was overcast with a fine mist but not enough rain to put up the folding top of the chaise. We spun along in fine style to the abandoned quarry, three miles outside of Edinburgh. "James, stop here," Dr. Bell commanded. We were perhaps two hundred yards from the granite face of the open quarry.

He intently scrutinized the exposed rock with the telescope. After a few moments, he passed the instrument to the colonel. "See the horizontal lines of the granite overlying the vertical lines of limestone. According to Dr. Hutton, the granite was formed over millions of years by upheaval of the earth on top of the limestone."

"Doesn't prove a damn thing," the colonel said, handing the telescope to me.

I trained the instrument, first on the granite, then on the underlying limestone. After a bit of focusing, I saw the tracing of a lizard-like animal, exactly like that of the sketch in Foley's clenched fist. "There, a fossil. I'd like to take a closer look," I said, and began moving towards the face of the cliff. The others followed, stumbling over rocks and uneven ground.

I was nearly fifty yards away when the entire cliff face dissolved in a terrific explosion. The force of the blast sent us to the ground beneath a rain of pebbles and clouds of dust.

I was still dazed when I heard Dr. Bell. "After him!" he shouted.

A figure ran for all he was worth high atop the cliff. O'Grady went off like a scared hare and disappeared among the trees on the hill. The colonel followed but after a few steps, slowed and sank to the ground.

I followed the professor around the hill towards the road. It seemed longer, but in a matter of minutes, we met O'Grady and glimpsed a dark figure on a dappled, light grey horse pounding away towards the city. Dr. Bell fired two shots after the man, but the distance was too great for his light loads of bird shot.

I trained the telescope on the retreating figure. "There is something wrong with the animal's right rear leg!" I shouted.

We criss-crossed the rough ground until Dr. Bell found hoof prints. "Aha! Here is a perfect print. Doyle, you are correct. The shoe in this print has a loose nail. We will find our man and I will wager that he is in the theology department."

Colonel Beachy-Edwards limped back to the chaise while the three of us explored the blasted rock face of the old quarry. Except for a faint imprint of a fish's tail, there was no sign of the fossil that my poor uncle had sketched.

After we presented our findings to the local police, the colonel and O'Grady took the next train to London. "You fellows have things well in hand," the colonel said as he waved goodbye.

Dr. Bell's close friend, Detective Willie McGregor found the dappled, grey horse with a sore right rear hoof at the second farrier he visited. He sent a message to say it was, as Bell had predicted, owned by Ian Stewart, an anti-Darwinian professor of theology.

Upon receiving the detective's message, we hurried to meet him at the professor's door. There was no response to our knock, but after butting the door open with my shoulder, we found Stewart attempting to escape by the back window of his flat.

He was wild-eyed and, at first, denied all knowledge of the explosion or of Foley.

"Hold his hands, please, Mr. Doyle." Dr. Bell said. I grabbed Stewart's hands. Under the careful gaze of detective McGregor, Bell scraped beneath the nail of Stewart's index finger with the blade of his penknife. He soon collected grains of powder on a slip of paper. "There," he said. "Gun powder of the type used for blasting."

The man wilted and admitted that Foley had come to him asking for the whereabouts of Dr. Hutton's cliff, with evidence that the world was millions of years old.

"He was clearly mad — mad as a hatter. He planned to take proof that God didn't make the world in six days to that atheist Karl Marx. In doing so, he aimed to give Marx the proof he needed to destroy the divine right of kings and emperors to rule. He wanted nothing less than to shake up all of Europe, dethrone the royals, and start a revolution."

My God! I thought to myself. This was not the Uncle Declan I knew. He had changed into a truly dangerous man; it was no wonder he was murdered.

Detective McGregor questioned Stewart further until the man admitted to the deliberate murder of Lt. Foley to "…save the world from these godless communist lunatics."

21 June 1881

It has been close to two weeks since the incident with Declan and the arrest of Stewart. Things have been uneventful. I have not mentioned a word to mam because she thought he died a few years ago, and bringing up these sordid affairs would only hurt her further.

Yet, with that said, the events surrounding my uncle were troublesome; I wanted to discover more about his past. Today, after morning ward rounds, Dr. Bell took me aside. "Doyle, I have been invited to St. Petersburg, Russia and will need an assistant."

I almost died several times on my trip to America in 1878 with Dr. Bell, so needless to say, I was a bit hesitant. When I did not eagerly reply in the affirmative, Dr. Bell showed me a letter.

"It might be in your best interest to accompany me, laddie."

"How so?" I asked.

"Well, you might be able to learn the truth about your deceased relative, Declan. Here, read this." He handed me the letter, which was written in English on heavy parchment. The handsome, embossed letterhead consisted of an open book beneath a gold, double-headed eagle.

Dear Professor Bell,
The faculty of medicine and surgery would be honored if you would consent to give a series of lectures and demonstrations of the antiseptic technique of surgery with special emphasis on your treatment of joints infected with tuberculosis. The Academy will pay all expenses for you and an assistant. There will be formal receptions and private consultations. We would especially value your assistance in training a special corps of surgeons to treat victims of attempted assassinations.
Sincerely, and gratefully yours,
Aleksey Sechenov, Professor of Physiology
St. Petersburg Academy of Medicine and Surgery

Dr. Bell must have known how troubled I was about Uncle Declan. His last words referenced the tsar, so perhaps the answer did lie in Russia. Furthermore, in another week, I would graduate with a bachelor of medicine and master of surgery; sadly, there were no prospects for work for me, so there seemed to be few other options open to me. "Does it pay well?" I asked.

"Aye, lad, you will be remunerated handsomely for your time, that I assure you."

"Well, then, yes sir, I would welcome the opportunity."

"In that case, come to my home at seven o'clock tomorrow evening to discuss the details."

22 June 1881

I arrived at seven o'clock. Dr. Bell had started on a bottle of good Madeira and a round of cheese when his man, Willum, escorted me into the small study. The professor rose from his desk and took my hand in a firm grip.

"Doyle, good of you to come." He was as excited as a school boy as he pushed aside the bottle. "On August the sixth, the *Servia*, a Baltic-American liner, arrives in Liverpool to take on coal and passengers on her way from America to Copenhagen and St. Petersburg. We will have first-class accommodations. This is especially fortuitous in that it coincides nicely with your graduation."

"Aye, the timing is perfect. I will graduate in a few days and then celebrate with a journey to Russia," I said. "May I ask, sir . . . Is Russia still dangerous? It is not so long since the war in Afghanistan and there is still considerable anti-British sentiment there, aye?"

"Doyle, sometimes you can be a right numpty, laddie." He slashed the air with a stout cane and pressed a hidden button on the silver mounted knob. A wicked steel blade sprung out of the cane. He parried, slashed, then, quicker than my eye could see, he held the point of the blade against my neck. "Be an old stick in the mud, or join me for a bloody good adventure."

"Sir, I can't think with that blade at my neck."

He lowered the cane sword. "So, what do ye say?"

"I have read about the Russian government's purchase of the new Colt revolvers from America. Your sword cane will not prevail over a six-shooter."

"Ah yes." He slid a drawer out of his built-in gun case and selected a Webley .455 calibre army pistol. "This, as you may recall, fits nicely in a corner of my instrument case."

"Sir, you fired at the notorious Captain Hook with a British Bulldog, a smaller revolver. I don't believe the Webley will fit in your case."

"You may be correct. No matter. I shall adjust the case to take the Webley. Now, Doyle, this is the maiden voyage of the

Servia. It is built for the comfort of the rich and famous. According to this brochure, first-class passengers are expected to dress for dinner, and in Russia, there will be formal receptions and perhaps a ball or two."

"First class, sir?"

"Aye, Doyle, we will be traveling in grand style."

"But I no longer have a formal suit."

"Angus Duncan gave you a tidy bit of reward money for your part in saving the American President from an early demise. I presume you still have some of it."

I was deeply embarrassed to admit that most of the money had gone to provide care for my father in the asylum and to my mam for my brothers and sisters. "No. Um, well, actually, I don't have any left ..." I stammered.

"Lad, you need to be more careful with your savings. Here." He handed me several pounds. "Armstrong's on Grassmarket Street will tailor a dinner suit for you."

I was preparing to leave when there was a knock at the door. Willum brought a middle-aged man into the study. "You might remember me as Sergeant O'Grady," he said."

I hardly recognized the man with black hair, dressed as a gentleman's valet, who only vaguely resembled O'Grady. "I am to be Dr. Bell's personal valet on your trip to Russia," he said.

"I have no need of a personal valet," Dr. Bell said.

"I suggest you read this before you decide whether you truly need me or not." O'Grady took a folded letter from his wallet. "You are to burn it immediately after reading the message."

I unfolded the paper. ***The carrier of this letter is a special agent of Her Majesty's Secret Service. He will accompany you on your journey to Russia***. The slashing signature was merely, 'Roberts' — none other than General Roberts, hero of the legendary march from Kandahar to Kabul that ended hostilities in the second Anglo-Afghan war.

Clearly, there was more to this humble-appearing sergeant than met the eye. "My apologies, Sergeant O'Grady. I'd be honored to have you as my valet." Dr. Bell said with a wink.

O'Grady replied with a soft grunt, cleared his throat, and spoke, not as a tough sergeant but as a refined gentleman's servant. "Hereafter, sir, refer to me as Mr. Lionel Tatum."

Dr. Bell poured a double measure of single malt whiskey for each of us and fed the letter into the fire. "Tatum, you had better move your things into the house so we can become better acquainted."

Armstrong's Men's Haberdashery on Grassmarket Street was shadowed by the palace. When I stepped through the door a bell tinkled far away in a dim back room. The floor creaked, and it took a moment to become accustomed to the gloom. My mam had stitched or knitted most all of my clothing, and I had been to a haberdashery only once before, when I traveled to America with Dr. Bell. "Kin I help you, sir?" the proprietor asked.

"I am traveling to Russia and need a formal white tie dinner suit," I said.

Mr. Armstrong, a pallid, old bloke with wire-rimmed glasses, looked me over as if he was an undertaker sizing me for a casket.

"Ah, sir, it will be a pleasure to provide you with suitable attire." He began with a measuring tape and a mouthful of pins, muttering about the amount of cloth needed to cover the breadth of my shoulders and height of nearly six feet two inches. He also measured me for a bespoke formal shirt and recommended a set of studs.

"Mr. Doyle, the climate is quite warm in Russia at this time of year. May I suggest an additional lightweight suit?"

My only jacket was of heavy tweed and hardly suitable for warm weather. I selected light grey linen for the new suit and left hoping I would have enough dosh to pay the bill.

6 August 1881

The great day of our departure has finally arrived. I have graduated and am now officially a doctor, but I have no job, no money, and few prospects for gainful employment upon my return. I have vowed to worry about such matters later and, for now, focus on solving the mystery of my uncle's untimely demise.

Beyond that, life at home has been filled with sorrow and woe. I couldn't keep my secret and had told my mam about Uncle Declan because she should know the truth. She cried for days and grieved even more about my trip to Russia. Sometimes, I have now come to believe, the truth is not the best medicine.

Aye, time and again, she begged me to stay home, but I convinced her that this experience would be an important part of my medical training and would provide me with the seed money I most sorely needed to start my practice. Finally, she reluctantly gave me her blessing.

Meanwhile, Da is still in the asylum. He is not drinking but is no better. I try to visit him every day, but it is always uncomfortable. On most of my visits, he does not recognize me and, when he does, he speaks of sprites and faeries.

And then yesterday, we started to argue. As our disagreement grew, he had a fit and the attendants asked me to leave. I could not tell if he had epilepsy or delirium tremens. It was horrible to see the man I once worshipped now demented, frail, and sickly.

Da's one saving grace is his art, and thankfully, he is drawing again. One day, I picked up one of his sketchbooks and marveled at his stunning images of faerie folk. If only he hadn't been cursed with a penchant for whiskey, he might have made these fantastic images years ago. He could have become a famous and well-paid artist like his brothers, and we wouldn't have had to live in squalor for all those years...

If only...

It is now time to stop daydreaming and to look forward.

Truth be told, I'm rather relieved to be departing Edinburgh for another adventure, but I will miss the Auld Reekie. I always do when I go away. Maybe I will even meet my future wife in the land of the tsars. Who knows?

Either way, I will now look like a proper gentleman because my new suits were completed yesterday. So, as I write this, I am decked out with a white tie, white shirt with a winged collar, silk stockings, and shiny, pointed shoes. It is all splendid beyond my wildest dreams.

Aye, I am now ready to taste life amongst the upper crust and could imagine squiring Jean the pretty lassie, to a great ball at the Edinburgh Palace. Yet, as I packed my things, I fingered my life savings, the measly sum of one shilling and six pence that remained from what Dr. Bell had given me. Oh, how it made me yearn for the day when I will be a famous surgeon with grand sums of money.

When we arrived in Liverpool, the yellow waters of the Mersey were covered with steamships and sailing vessels bound for every port in the world. Tug boats chugged back and forth while stevedores hooted, shouted, and unloaded cargo amidst a tangle of horses and wagons.

The *Servia* had only that morning arrived from Boston. And it was now moored to the Prince's Dock at the foot of Bath Street. She towered majestically above other vessels. The stars and stripes of the United States and the Baltic-American line pennant fluttered at her stern. Sailors wearing smart, white, duck trousers, and blouses lined her deck. The captain, with yards of gold braid on his sleeve, and surrounded by the ship's officers, waved goodbye to disembarking first-class passengers. With trumpets flashing in the sun, the band played a rousing version of "Rule Britannia" in deference to arriving British passengers.

Drawn by a prancing, chestnut mare, our cab pulled up amidst carriages and broughams carrying what appeared to the glittering royalty of England. Aye, this was the maiden voyage of a new steamship, pioneering a route from America to the Baltic states and Russia, and I wagered that many of its passengers would be of royal blood or important political figures or captains of industry. We waited for the passengers from America to disembark, and then, we began to make our way up the gangway.

Lionel Tatum, now completely at home as a manservant, passed Dr. Bell's trunks and my lone Gladstone bag to the stevedores. Dr. Bell insisted that I carry his precious instrument case, the lantern slides, and the projector.

I was at his side, toiling up the gangplank, feeling shabby in my hot, heavy tweed jacket when I caught the scent of orange blossoms. Next thing I knew, an absolute confection of young womanhood with the most magnificent, curly, chestnut-colored hair I had ever seen, brushed my arm as she regally extended her hand to the ship's captain. I was instantly smitten. Could this be the future Mrs. Arthur Conan Doyle? I would readily spend my life with her and envisioned sharing romantic days and evenings together in our bedroom.

I tried to appear uninterested and gave her an innocent, sidelong glance. Was it my imagination, or did she favour me with a smile and a whimsical toss of her head?

I lost her in the crowd when immaculately clad waiters bowed and offered glasses of champagne to us first-class passengers. I chugged my glass of the bubbly, and a smartly-clad steward led us up a paneled staircase to our stateroom on the upper deck, just aft of the landing and the library.

Dr. Bell handed him a gold guinea while 'Mr. Tatum' unpacked our bags before discretely withdrawing to his own less sumptuous cabin on a lower deck.

At Dr. Bell's suggestion, I chewed ginger root to guard against the *mal de mer* I had suffered during our passage to America. We were on deck while tugs pushed the *Servia* away from her dock. The band struck up "Heart of Oak" and then the "Navy Hymn." We spent the splendid afternoon watching the flats and low hills of Liverpool Harbor slip by until the ship passed Anglesey Island and headed through the Irish Sea to the St. George's Channel and Cape Cornwall.

As the sun set, we were back in our quarters. I was struggling with the studs and tie of my new outfit when Dr. Bell appeared from the dressing room, resplendent in a dress blue kilt with black and green stripes, a velvet Barathea jacket with silver buttons, and a tartan waistcoat. He had a dirk and silver, mounted, sealskin sporran with the crest of Clan Bell, a hand holding a dagger. Mr. Tatum straightened the Professor's black tie and adjusted the silk flashes on his plaid stockings then helped me with the studs and made a trifling adjustment to my tie. "Doyle, you are now a doctor and graduate of Edinburgh, the greatest medical school in the world. Hold your head high and bow to no man, whether he be an English lord, German baron or Russian count," said Dr. Bell.

All heads turned in our direction when we marched, side by side, into the splendid paneled dining room, bright with the new Edison incandescent electric lights glowing from a great chandelier. A small orchestra played dinner music while a crowd of perhaps two hundred smartly-clad passengers milled about sipping chilled wine.

The lovely lass who had brushed my arm on the gangplank was across the room, clinging to a devilishly handsome man with a long scar on his cheek. He appeared to be in his late twenties and wore red trousers with a silver-buttoned, dark blue tunic. She was stunning in a long, flounced, light green dress with a plunging neckline. Her hair was piled high on her head with soft ringlets framing her angelic face.

Before I could push through the crowd to reach her side and introduce myself, the ship's captain struck a bell and announced dinner. We found our places at a long table covered with white damask, set with bone porcelain plates and highly polished silverware. My gaze was still fastened on the captain's table, where the lovely creature was engaged in animated conversation with her dinner companion. The cad's leer was riveted on the glorious pink flesh of her upper bosom. Damn him for ogling my future wife!

Dr. Bell, seated at the head of the table, engaged in a discussion with a Russian count on the surgical aspects of the recent assassination attempt on James Garfield, the American president. I was next to a stout American who guzzled glass after glass of wine. After smacking his lips, he nudged my elbow. "What's your game, fella?" He asked.

"Oh, a bit of rugby and I've been known to box."

"Nah, sorry 'bout that. What I meant was — what'ya do for a living? In other words, how do you make enough filthy lucre to pay to travel first-class?"

It was a rude question, typical of an American. I was a bit short with him, hoping he would leave me alone. "I am a physician."

"Oh, I see, doc." He applied himself to the wine for a minute or so, then spoke with slurred speech. "My name is Adam Gritz. Electric boats are my game. By God, the world will take notice when we teach those Russkies not to kill our president."

"Excuse me?"

"Everybody knows the Russians killed Garfield."

"Sorry, but the papers here in Scotland claimed an American citizen of French descent named Charles Guiteau killed him," I said.

"Ah yes, that was the papers said. In truth, his real name was Gitorski and he was part of an intricate Russkie plot. All those damn Russians want our gold in Alaska."

I did not challenge the American and assumed his conspiracy theory was the drunken meandering of a deluded fool.

I love a sumptuous meal, especially while traveling, and I was famished. For the next two hours, I consumed oysters, consommé, salmon with mousseline sauce, creamed peas with roast sirloin, curried chicken, a gargantuan portion of squab with cress, guinea fowl baked in a delicious dressing, a black currant sorbet, buttered new potatoes, a double lamb chop, fresh asparagus, pâté de foie gras, and at last, peaches in jelly with a chocolate éclair.

The waiters served Turkish coffee in tiny china cups while sailors cleared an area in the center of the room beneath the glittering chandelier. Captain Veery struck a bell to get everyone's attention. "Ladies and gentlemen, the ship's company will now offer real seafaring entertainment. I present, for your pleasure, Billy and the Horn Pipers," said the captain.

The seven sailors wore identical, tight-fitting, white, duck trousers, singlets and black, hard-soled brogues. They launched into a merry tune with a tin whistle, a fiddle, and a squeeze box.

Suddenly, a young, sandy-haired lad with bright white teeth danced to the front of the stage. With arms tight to his chest and

29

with legs kicking and stomping, he danced a hornpipe while singing "Blow the man down," "Maid of Amsterdam," and "Paddy lay you back."

The music became slower and solemn while Billy, in the very image of a captain, scowled, shaded his eyes, peered through an imaginary telescope, and then began to chant.

"Captain Bligh, that silly man
Was master in command.
He was growling day and night
An answer for his complaints."

Billy turned toward the three chanters.

"I flogged the men, flogged the men," he sang, with his arms flailing.

"He flogged his men, OH,
Captain Bligh, he flogged his men, OH," the chanters answered.

As sweat soaked the muscular frame under his singlet, Billy gracefully bowed to the audience and the program came to an end. There were cheers and much stamping of feet. Ladies crowded about the performers, and more than one opened her purse and dropped golden guineas into the hands of the sailors.

Later, after an hour or so in the smoking room with a fine cigar and more than one brandy, I wobbled, unsteadily, out on deck and leaned against the railing for a breath of salt air. I couldn't have been there for more than a few seconds, when, much to my surprise, I sniffed orange blossoms and was immediately enveloped in a dark cloak and pushed against the deckhouse.

At first I struggled to get free, but she pressed her lips over my mouth. I felt her soft flesh and was filled with pleasure until she forced the cold muzzle of a pistol into my ribs. "If you cry out, I'll put a bullet in your spleen," she whispered.

More than thinking about any threat, I was caught up in the pleasant sensation of soft lips on my skin and even softer breasts pushing against my chest. So, I grunted and kissed her again. She responded with passion, and after a moment, she whispered breathily with her lips delicately brushing my ear. "Look carefully. Who is on the deck?"

For the first time, I became aware of two men at the railing perhaps thirty or forty feet down the deck. Their heads were together as if in earnest conversation, but in the mist and dark, they were barely visible.

"I can hardly make them out." I replied. She adjusted her hips, so we were pressed together, full length, toe to nose. The pistol was probably a fake, and the sensation was quite delicious.

"Damn you! Pay close attention," she chided.

I squinted and whispered. "It could be Gritz, an American engineer. The other may be your dinner companion."

Her lips, with her mouth slightly opened, returned to mine, and the hand with the pistol went around my neck. We snuggled like lovers for another moment, until she pushed me off balance and silently ran aft, away from the men at the railing.

I was totally mystified, slightly dizzy, and more than a bit aroused from the whole affair. I remained frozen in place, savoring the lingering scent of orange blossoms. Who was this woman? What was she after? Why wouldn't she stay with me? Why did she have a gun?

I remained by the rail for a few more minutes, eagerly hoping for her to return, but she never did. I reluctantly went to my berth just aft on the same deck, my head still swimming with her citrus scent and the lovely soft sensation of her voluptuous body pressing against me.

7 August 1881

Sun was streaming through the porthole when Dr. Bell, rather more roughly than necessary, shook me awake. I had a pounding headache and my stomach was queasy, although the ship was hardly rolling.

"Laddie, you can't sleep all day. Up, up. Time for breakfast."

I rolled out of the bunk, dressed, and made it to the nearly-empty dining room. I did not have much appetite, but after several cups of tea, I managed to put away a rasher of bacon, several fried eggs, and toast with marmalade.

A short nap was in order, but when I returned to our cabin, the stunning young lady who smelled of orange blossoms was there, sitting with crossed legs on a comfortable chair. She wore a tight-fitting purple dress with a bit of lace around her neck. As she swung her foot back and forth, I could not take my eyes away from her elegant lower leg and slender ankle. She opened a large purse and withdrew a yellow, tin box marked 'Kyriazi Freres' and selected a cigarette.

I was taken aback at her behavior, and Dr. Bell pursed his lips with disapproval. She held the cigarette to her lips between her index and middle fingers and smiled. "Well ..." she said. I fumbled for a lucifer and lit her cigarette. She drew in a lungful of smoke, expelled the cloud through her perfect nostrils, and turned her luminous eyes on Dr. Bell.

"Colonel Sir Cameron Beachy-Edwards informed me that you attended Declan Foley when he was fatally injured. I am anxious to learn about his last moments and what, if anything, he found at Hutton's quarry. What were his last words?" she asked.

"What was your relationship with Lt. Foley?" Dr. Bell asked.

"Lieutenant Foley was my husband."

Jings! I could hardly believe it. Last night, I had been kissing — my 'aunt'?!!

Dr. Bell raised an eyebrow, "Aye, and you are?"

"Penelope Walshingham of the Norfolk Walshinghams. My father is the fourth Earl of Leicester. I was one of the few women to study at Cambridge." She paused to dab her eyes, sniffed, and went on. "Lieutenant Declan was the only man who showed me kindness. My parents disapproved of his lowly birth, but I am a free thinker and we wed in secret a few weeks before his death."

She gave no sign that we had met — not only met, but feverishly kissed one another — the night before. I was stunned.

How could this elegant, sophisticated lady have been married to Uncle Declan? I remembered his great beard, his face ravaged by scars and suffering. How could she have been drawn to him? Aye, she said that he showed her kindness, but none of it seemed to make sense.

I have to admit, this mystery only added to her allure. I felt as if I was being drawn into a whirlpool of emotion and, well, lust, if not love. It made no difference that this stunning creature was actually my relative through marriage. Now that Uncle Declan was dead, she would need someone to take care of her and I most certainly could be the one. Uncle Declan … I had no idea that he had remained alive the last couple of years, never mind taken on a bride.

I could hold my tongue no longer. "Excuse me, Miss Walshingham, or should I call you Mrs. Foley?" I asked.

"Since our marriage was secret, and seeing that he is no longer alive, I prefer to be referred to as Miss Walshingham."

"Aye, then answer me this, ma'am. When did Declan decide to take a bride?"

She glared and tossed her head. "Dear child, that is none of your business."

"Oh, but it is my business," I answered, angry that she had referred to me as a child. "I am Arthur Conan Doyle. My mother is Mary Foley and Declan was our relative."

"Oh my! Declan never spoke of any family. It is only recently that I discovered his real name was Declan Foley. Please, give a poor widow a moment." She began sobbing and removed a lorgnette from her bosom, placed it on her delicate nose, and looked me up and down. She gave no sign that she remembered our ardent embrace only a few hours before.

She finally stopped weeping. "How are you associated with Dr. Bell?" she asked.

Dr. Bell answered for me. "Mr. Doyle is a recent graduate of the Edinburgh University Medical School, as well as my assistant."

"I see. And my dearly departed was your relative."

"Well, aye… I called him 'uncle.' "

"So, you, like me, must also be devastated by his loss."

"Aye, and I will do everything in my power to assist you in ensuring his murderer is brought to justice."

"Good. Please, tell me about his last moments."

I told her everything and remembered his final words, "A tsar will die."

"Ah, poor Declan was horribly abused by the Russians during the war but didn't blame the people. He vowed vengeance on the tsar and his foul government."

With that, she tossed her head and ground out the cigarette in an empty teacup. I was torn between a desire to take her in my arms and a yearning to slap her for her appalling behavior. Abruptly, tears drizzled down her lovely cheeks again.

I couldn't help it. In that moment, I was overcome for sympathy for her. What I would've given in that moment to kiss away those dear droplets.

And then, I thought — *is it appropriate to have feelings for the woman who was my 'aunt'? Or at least had been my aunt until Uncle Declan was killed …?*

At that moment, there was a knock. I leaped from my chair and opened the door. The first officer saluted rather stiffly. "Dr. Bell, Captain Veery requests your assistance. A passenger has died," he said.

The stateroom of the deceased was a few doors away from our own and not far from where Penelope had so pleasantly accosted me a few hours ago. We crowded into the room. Surprisingly, Penelope followed us. The captain and the ship's doctor, a middle-aged gentleman, were staring glumly at the corpse. The dead man, stretched on his back across the bed, had silvery-grey hair, was fully dressed, and appeared to be about sixty years of age. "This is all that remains of Lord Asquith," said the captain.

Asquith's fine features and neatly trimmed mustache marked him as definitely upper-class. The first officer swished at a common housefly twitching its wings on the man's upper lip and was about to close the man's eyes.

"Please, don't touch a thing," Dr. Bell warned, rather sharply.

The officer shrank away from the corpse and wiped his lips with a white handkerchief.

"Sorry," he muttered. "It's like he is staring right at us."

"Doyle, can you make a diagnosis?" Dr. Bell asked.

"It appears as if Lord Asquith has suffered a sudden heart attack or a lethal brain hemorrhage."

"Yes, that is what we are supposed to believe. But look carefully. His fingernails and skin are dead white, as if he lost a great deal of blood."

"But, there are no signs of blood loss, lacerations, or bleeding." I said.

Dr. Bell put a hand on the body. "He has been dead for no more than six hours."

"If it wasn't a natural death, then what?" asked first officer.

"I can't say as of yet."

The Professor ran his fingers through the corpse's hair, peered into his eyes, nose, and ears, gently pulled down the lower lip, and sniffed at the mouth. "He smoked Cuban cigars." Bell examined the hands and fingernails and, with some difficulty, opened the left, clenched fist. He minutely examined the fingers and nails with a small magnifying glass.

"There are no signs that he fought an assailant." He then directed us to remove clothing from the corpse and, much to my great surprise, inspected the abdomen and thumped the chest as if examining the lungs of a live patient.

"Ah, dull to percussion. There is blood or fluid in his left chest. Turn him over, very carefully, so his left side is up, please."

He adjusted the light and, with his hand lens, minutely observed every inch of the chest. "Ah ... Here it is."

He had discovered a tiny wound, just lateral to the vertebrae, that was hardly larger than a needle prick.

"Oh, please, that little pin prick could not possibly have killed the man," the captain said.

"Death was due to a slow, but massive, hemorrhage into his thoracic cavity from a small wound in his aorta, the largest blood vessel in the body. I would wager that the weapon was a slender needle or even a hat pin. I trust that an autopsy will prove me correct. Only a highly trained assassin would know exactly where to insert his weapon in order to fatally penetrate the thoracic aorta," Dr. Bell said.

The ship's medical officer spoke. "We don't have the facilities for a proper autopsy."

"I will not disturb the passengers," Captain Veery said.

"Sir, you have a murderer on board your ship. We need every bit of information possible in order to find the man."

Dr. Bell stooped and commenced a minute examination of the floor and the furniture, then went into the adjacent bathroom. There, he sniffed the air like a bloodhound on a scent.

"Doyle, now is a grand opportunity for you to use your keen, young senses. Please identify that odor."

I inhaled a nose full of air and sensed, first, a lingering odor of brandy, cigar smoke, and something else, something rather sweet that I could not name.

"Brandy and cigar smoke," I said. "And something else, but I can't seem to put my finger on it."

"Very good. Asquith drank a quantity of brandy after dinner and then he smoked at least one Cuban cigar. There is something more ..." He sniffed again, *Papaver somniferum*, better known as opium."

"Opium is in so many common medicines that it probably means nothing," said I.

"Laddie, it means that either Asquith or his assailant used opium, perhaps combined with tobacco," Dr. Bell said.

It was not my place to argue with the professor, but the faint odor reminded me of a long distant pleasant memory. I couldn't put my finger on it, but I knew that it was certainly not opium. Bell paced back and forth for several minutes, hands clenched behind his back, with his eyes darting around the room from the corpse to the floor to the walls.

"Here is what took place . . . The murderer waited for Asquith, knowing that he had consumed a quantity of alcohol. He was in this room, perhaps crouched beside the bed or in the bathroom. He waited until Lord Asquith turned his back and then inserted the weapon. Asquith would have ignored the faint pinprick and slowly bled to death over the course of several hours."

"Ahem." Captain Veery cleared his throat for attention. "How ridiculous. Mere speculation," he spluttered.

"I think not! An autopsy will prove that I am quite correct. Asquith was a British citizen and his murderer is on this ship," said Dr. Bell.

"Damn your impertinence, Dr. Bell! I will have none of this. My master-at-arms will investigate. There will be no autopsy, and the body will be handed over to the British Consulate when we dock in Copenhagen!" shouted the captain.

"Nay, sir. By then, the body may be decomposed and the murderer will escape. Doyle, fetch my instrument case and ask Mr. Tatum to join us, if you please."

Tatum and I arrived at Asquith's room the same time as the chief master-at-arms, the ship's police officer.

Dr. Bell unlatched the case, slid out a separate compartment, and removed a revolver. "Mr. Tatum, I presume you know how to use a Webley .455."

"Yes, sir, that I do." Tatum admired the well-oiled, gleaming weapon and checked to see that the cylinder was loaded with bullets.

"Mr. Tatum, use force, if necessary. The ship's officers are to line up against the far wall and witness my findings."

Tatum thrust out his chest and sucked in his belly. "Over there, lads. As the Dr. ordered. Against the wall!" he boomed, in a voice suitable for the drill field.

The master-at-arms clenched his fists and growled. "No damn lackey gives orders to my captain!"

With a calloused thumb, Mr. Tatum pulled back the pistol's hammer and aimed at the master-at-arms. The captain's face was violaceous, and an artery throbbed at his forehead. "Obey the man," he said. The ship's officers formed a ragged line with their backs to the wall.

Bell then took command of the room. "Gentlemen, what you are about to witness is not for the faint-hearted; I urge all of you to pay the utmost of attention. Mr. Doyle, my scalpel, forceps, and scissors. Oh, and please fetch a stack of towels."

I did as he asked. Then, with a few deft strokes of the knife, the professor sliced through the chest wall and cut away the anterior portion of a half-dozen ribs, opening the left chest. "A-hah! There, gentlemen — the left thoracic cavity is filled with blood and clots." "My word!" the ship's doctor gasped.

The first officer wilted into an unconscious heap on the floor.

I was feeling a bit queasy. "Mop the blood, Mr. Doyle. Make yourself useful," Dr. Bell said in a slightly mocking voice.

I clenched my teeth, held my tongue, and did as I was told. Dr. Bell assumed his accustomed role as a medical school professor. "Now, gentlemen, please, one at a time observe the thoracic aorta, the largest blood vessel in the body. It courses from top to bottom of the chest cavity. The hole was in the upper portion, where the aorta hugs the thoracic vertebra. The defect, at first, was no larger than a pinhole, but just as the flow of water enlarges a small leak in a dike, cardiac contractions forced more and more blood to enlarge the pinhole. Gentlemen, this is a case of cold-blooded murder. The perpetrator is a skilled assassin with a good knowledge of human anatomy," said Dr. Bell.

"Confound it! Our passengers will not stand for interrogations," Captain Veery said.

"Perhaps, that won't be necessary. Please allow me to see your passenger list."

"Come to my cabin within the hour," the captain replied.

Without thinking, I blurted out a statement of confession. "Sir, I was with Miss Walshingham, just outside this stateroom late last night. Two men were not far away."

"Eh, what is that you say?" the captain asked. I repeated my statement, adding that Miss Walshingham was on the deck prior to my arrival.

The captain was annoyed and simply dismissed my comment. "Humph. Coincidence, nothing but coincidence," he said.

Mr. Tatum, with elaborate courtesy, turned to Penelope and offered her the crook of his arm. "Miss Walshingham, please join us for tea." We returned to our stateroom. Dr. Bell rang for tea.

"Miss Walshingham, what is your role in this affair?" he rather pleasantly asked.

My dear Penelope rolled her eyes, and large tears coursed down her cheeks.

"I am not at liberty to discuss the matter."

"Were you having a romantic liaison with Asquith?"

"Of course not. I scarcely knew him. And, ahem, sir, I am a grieving widow."

"Then why were you outside his room at about the time of his death? Perhaps you stuck him with a hat pin in a moment of passion."

Her eyes blazed, hot with anger. "Damn you! I am a courier for Naval Intelligence and had a message for Lord Asquith. My instructions were to deliver a letter to him on our first night at sea. The entertainment went on so long I didn't go to his stateroom until nearly three o'clock in the morning."

"Aye, so you say," Dr. Bell said. "Did you enter the room?"

Penelope selected a cigarette from the tin box. I leaped up with a fresh lucifer and lit the cigarette. She exhaled a cloud of smoke before speaking. "The door was ajar. I entered, but he was reclining on the bed, sound asleep. I did not disturb him and turned to leave, only to be accosted by . . . him." She jerked her hand towards me.

Damn, I thought, *is this an act?* Her entire performance only added to her air of mystery and my desire.

"The message, please," Dr. Bell said. She hesitated, but Mr. Tatum prodded her with a sharp look. She removed a pale blue, unmarked envelope, sealed with a blob of red wax from her handbag.

The professor slit open the envelope with a penknife and unfolded a sheet of heavy, blue paper.

Dear Percy,
I am praying that you have a pleasant and rewarding journey to St. Petersburg.
Give my fondest regards to Alexi.
Sincerely,
A.V.

Penelope was so close to me that, as we read the letter over Dr. Bell's shoulder, I thought I distinctly felt her pressing into my side. Sadly though, she took no notice of me and, instead, stared at the letter with intense interest.

Dr. Bell frowned, lit his pipe, and puffed clouds of smoke while carefully perusing the letter.

"Note the strong downward strokes of a modern fountain pen. A small blob of ink escaped when she dotted the "i" in *rewarding*. Alexi must be the new tsar, Alexander the third.

"Who is A.V.? I asked.

"Doyle, you should be ashamed of yourself to ask such a thing," Dr. Bell said.

"Why? What does it stand for?"

"The Queen used the name Alexandria Victoria before her coronation," Penelope said. "How could you call yourself a Scot and not recognize the initials of our Queen?"

"There must be more." Bell held the paper up to the porthole. "Ah-ha, look at this." Faint marks became visible as he moved the page in the sunlight.

"I do believe there is an additional message," Dr. Bell said. He struck another lucifer and held the flame beneath the letter. Nothing appeared.

"Some forms of invisible ink require a chemical to become visible. I will wager the chemical is in Lord Asquith's cabin."

"The captain has sealed Asquith's room." Penelope said.

"There are alternative ways into a room," said Dr. Bell, as he selected a delicate chisel from his instrument case. "Aye, this will do nicely."

Penelope and I shielded the doctor as he inserted the thin metal between the door and casing. There was a faint *click*, and he was in the room, leaving us on guard. I was glad that, once again, we were alone together, and I reached out for Penelope's hand. "We must provide a distraction. Shall we re-enact last night's dalliance?" I whispered to her.

"I say – you're cheeky, but I like that. That's the Foley in you." Penelope leaned against the door, clutched me to her bosom, and planted her lovely lips on mine. She may have been play-acting, but I passionately returned her embrace and kisses.

Suddenly, there were footsteps on the deck, and through a half-opened eye, I made out a couple who hurried past while averting their gaze. In hardly any time at all, certainly not long enough to satisfy my hot-blooded, rampant lust, Dr. Bell appeared at the threshold of the door.

Penelope pushed me away and smacked my face with her opened hand. "How dare you!" she said.

"My heavens!" Dr. Bell blushed. "What has gotten into you, laddie? She's your bloody aunt!" He shook his head as if reprimanding a child.

Before I could explain, he held up a small bottle labeled 'tincture of iodine.' "It was in his shaving kit," he said.

Back in our room, Dr. Bell poured a few drops of the iodine on a bit of cloth and gently swabbed the letter.

ODQB C RSNOY ZKDBW LTRS MATO VHKKHD HR LHRBGOUHNUR VHKK AD SQNTAKD

Penelope snatched the letter. "This is my responsibility."

"Not unless you can break the cipher," Bell said as he pulled it back from her.

"Damn you! Give it to me!" she shouted.

Tatum's big hand closed on her wrist. "Leave it be, Miss. Your only job was to deliver the message."

Penelope's face hardened. "You are hurting me." Tatum released her.

"The letter is useless unless we break the code. Dr. Bell has assisted the Secret Service in other cases. I suggest we leave the letter with him and get on to the captain's cabin."

"I am going with you," Penelope said.

"The letter can wait. I, too, will attend to the Captain," said Bell.

The captain's quarters were richly furnished with teak chairs, a desk, and a table. A Persian carpet and paintings of maritime scenes completed the picture of a man at the peak of his career in command of the greatest passenger ship ever launched.

I felt decidedly out of place. The chief master-at-arms and Billy, the handsome, horn-piping sailor, put the passenger manifest at our disposal. Most were American citizens, Swedes, Norwegians, Poles, and a Finn or two returning to visit their homeland.

Bell paused, his finger on the name of a lone Japanese passenger. "The Japanese have plans to annex Russian territory and would be more likely to assassinate the tsar than a British diplomat." There were a large group of American names, including the engineer, Adam Gritz. "Doyle, use your charm to mix with the other passengers and learn more about the Americans. Some of them still hate Britain."

I jotted down a list of names. "Right, sir."

Bell paused over a name. "Is Count Carl von Wittenberg — a Prussian?"

Penelope blushed. "He is from Berlin — a naval architect and great friend of Wilhelm II."

"Wilhelm II will be the next emperor of Germany. The man hates both England and Russia," Bell said.

"He is the grandson of Queen Victoria," Penelope said.

"True, but his father, Frederick is ill, possibly with cancer. Wilhelm will ascend to the throne within a decade. He blames the English for his deformed arm and the woman he loved has married a Russian prince."

Bell paused and stared at the captain. "So much for the passengers. What about your crew?"

"My men are the finest sailors in the world, Americans and Danes, one or two Norwegians. They are above reproach."

"Doyle, if you please, socialize with the passengers. See what you can learn and later meet me for tea," Bell said.

I sunk ankle-deep into a lush Persian carpet in the lounge and gazed with wonder at oil paintings and the array of bottles in front of a mirror behind the bar. The lounge was an elegant enough place to commence my investigations.

I nursed a pint of ale while listening to jovial American doctors discussing their plans for study in Vienna and Berlin. They were above suspicion, but another group of Americans, clustered about a table and talking in low tones, aroused my interest.

I moved to an empty chair and heard only snatches of their conversation, which was mainly about the shooting of President Garfield. They had, it seemed, served under Garfield while he was an officer in the union army and were on a commission to improve the U.S. Navy. Their destination was Germany. There seemed to be no reason to suspect their involvement in Asquith's murder.

I was about to leave when a tall, stringy fellow with a long, pointy mustache, wearing high leather boots and a large brimmed cowboy hat, jostled my arm, spilling a bit of my ale. He laughed. "Pardon me, partna.' This damn ship rocks worse than a painted pinto being gelded." He held out his hand. "Howdy. Cowboy Bill, at your service."

He already had a few too many ales, but he was friendly enough. I'd met my fair share of eccentric characters in America and I'd always enjoyed their company. I figured it was worth befriending this gregarious bloke and hearing what he had to say. "Pleasure to make your acquaintance, Bill. Let me guess — you're an American."

"Yessir! Born in West Virginia and, as of late, a resident of the great lone star state of Texas. Yee ha!"

I loved his energy and couldn't resist bragging a bit about my time in America, "Have you ever heard of the notorious James Gang?"

"Hell yeah! Those damn bastards wanted me to partner up with them and be in their gang." With my mate, Carl, I'd escaped near-death by that gang when Dr. Bell and I were in America. So, although I wasn't exactly sure how much was true and how much was the ale speaking, I decided to let him keep talking. "You see, back way yonder, when I was merely a stripling poking cows, them boys wanted me to help wrangle a few thousand head of steer, but I plum refused. Where'd you say you're from?" the American asked.

"I'm from Scotland. The name's Doyle, Arthur Doyle."

"Well, Artie, good to meet ya. Most of you limeys are usually too snooty to shoot the breeze with old Cowboy Bill, but you seem to be cut of a different cloth — maybe a Scottish tartan, eh?"

"Bill, what brings you on board this vessel?"

"I shouldn't tell you this, but you seem like a good hombre and so I'll spill the beans." He lowered his voice to a whisper. "I'll be damned if I ain't bringin' a whole cage full of Texas rattlesnakes to them hifulatin' Russkies."

"What?" I whispered.

He spoke louder. "You got cotton in your ears, boy? I got me a whole mess of rattlers in my quarters. Lassoed them critters behind the head and stuffed 'em in a feed sack. If you see any mice on board, tell me, since those critters will soon be needing some vittles."

"Why do the Russians want rattlesnakes?"

"I was told they're gonna be used for medical 'speriments. I don't really care as long as they pay… Now don't mean to be rude, but rumor has it that there are some poker games and dancing painted ladies below deck, so I'll be seeing you around." And with that, he was off…

I surveyed the other passengers, who seemed totally innocent, and departed from the lounge. Once I got out on the deck, the ship was in the Channel crashing against heavy seas and a north wind. I struggled on the pitching vessel to reach our stateroom, when, just ahead, a fellow who had been leaning against the guard rail fell to the deck.

I grabbed his coat just in time to prevent him from rolling into the sea. His legs beat up and down on the deck and his jaws were so tightly clenched, he was scarcely breathing. He looked to be around sixty years old.

I had seen the same symptoms of epilepsy in my father and immediately wrapped my fingers in a handkerchief. His jaws were tightly clenched, but with difficulty, I forced his mouth open. He took in a great deep breath.

Soon after, he relaxed but was confused. He was small and fragile as a chipmunk with a high, bald forehead and a great, black beard. I helped him to his feet. "Come to the lounge. You could use a tot of brandy," I said.

"Brandy, no. Vodka, yes." he said.

After downing half a glass of the clear, fiery liquor, he offered his hand and spoke a decent English with a strong Russian accent. "Bah. Damn London doctors could not cure my illness. Who are you, boy?"

"Arthur Doyle."

"*Dobry den*. I am Fyodor . . . Fyodor Dostoevsky."

"The great author?"

"Hah, yes, I have heard of that man. He's not so great these days . . . These days, the mediocre Dostoevsky is only great at one thing – drinking."

"And when you aren't drinking?"

"I gamble."

"And when you aren't gambling?"

"I write drivel to pay for my drinking and gambling."

"I would give up medicine if I could write drivel as well as you."

He lit a cigarette and coughed up a gob of phlegm. "Writing's a fool's folly. I would've been better off if I never put pen to paper. It only leads to poverty, suffering and prison," he said.

"Maybe so. But, still, I'd like to try my hand at it one day. At university, our French professor had us read French translations of your dark and brooding stories. They are brilliant psychological tales. All about suffering…"

"Suffering is the key to our redemption. And redemption is nigh impossible. So, in the end, life is a folly, and it is only through drink that one might find momentary escape."

"Well then, sir, may I buy you another drink?"

45

"No, it is my turn. You saved me from falling into the sea. Tonight, be my guest on the steerage deck for vodka, discussion, and entertainment. And then, we shall see if you are truly cut out for the life of an author."

With that, Dostoevsky left and I made my way to Bell's stateroom. After the ale and vodka, and with the ship's erratic movement, I could hardly wobble. I gratefully sunk into an armchair, accepted a cup of tea, and reported my observations of the passengers. Penelope was sitting primly as a nun with pinched lips and a cold, fixed expression on her darling face.

Dr. Bell listened to my recital of the passengers with his chin resting on his hand.

"None of them sound like a killer. Meanwhile, I've made progress. The cipher is a simple transposition of letters."

Percy, stop D. Alex must live. Willie is mischievous and will cause trouble.

"We believe the Queen chose Asquith to protect Alexander III from a secret assassin," Mr. Tatum said.

"Wait, who is Willie?" I asked.

"The very same Wilhelm of Germany we discussed earlier."

"Then, who is D?"

"David." It was a soft, almost involuntary, answer. "Poor, poor David." Penelope wiped her tears and turned away.

Dr. Bell put a comforting hand on her shoulder. "There, there, lassie…"

"Who is David?" I asked.

She cleared her throat. "Captain David Campbell was my husband's best friend. After they escaped from the Russians, they found their way to a field hospital in Kabul. My husband recovered from his injuries and, after resigning his commission, bounced around Eastern Europe before going to Cambridge for geology. They say David was a brilliant linguist and a student of the Russian people but never regained his health. In his delirium, he vowed to kill the tsar."

Penelope paused to sip tea. "Captain David Campbell escaped from the hospital and disappeared. He is thought to be somewhere in Russia," she said, in a flat, dead voice.

"If Campbell kills Tsar Alexander III, there will be a major war between England and Russia. The Queen's intelligence agents must know of his intentions and sent Asquith to prevent a murder and international conflict." Mr. Tatum paced the room and continued talking. "He has had time to reach St. Petersburg. It is up to us to stop him. In the years ahead, England needs Russia as an ally."

"We still don't know who killed Lord Asquith. Who would have the most to gain by the tsar's assassination? Doyle, do you suspect any of the Americans?"

"An American at dinner swore revenge on the Russians for killing their president but seemed to be a harmless drunk. I don't trust that Count von Wittenberg."

"Penelope, tell us more about this German fellow."

Was it accidental? On purpose? Penelope spilled her tea and then rubbed the dark stain on her dress. "I hardly know him. He is just a casual acquaintance."

Dr. Bell sat up straighter and fiddled with his pipe. "He is German and probably an enemy of Russia. Surely, Miss Walshingham, you can learn more."

"We should also consider the Russian students in steerage. I have made a new friend who invited me to a party," I said.

"Good. Do look in on them this evening."

An hour later, Penelope and I met Dostoevsky. He was still pale and walked with a stumbling, feeble gait. I held his arm as we descended stairs into the depths of the ship. The air grew dank with the smell of cooking and unwashed bodies in the crowded steerage compartment. At the lowest level, we entered a cramped, ill-lit room. A dozen plainly dressed men and women, all about my age, were smoking and drinking. As we entered, their animated conversation stopped and hostile faces turned our way.

Dostoevsky gestured toward us. "Mes amis."

I felt suspicion mingled with curiosity, despite Dostoevsky's introduction. The hostility broke when, to my great surprise, Penelope rattled off what must have been a joke, in Russian. They laughed and offered drinks. She went off with three men to a table in the corner. They greeted her with what seemed an easy familiarity. Could they have been students at Cambridge? It didn't seem likely.

"They are elitists, radical students who have studied with Marx in London and want to overthrow the tsar," Dostoevsky whispered.

Perhaps, it was my Irish half that hated authority, but I sympathized with the students. As I looked around the group, I was drawn to a buxom young woman with a long braid of blonde hair that hung down over her back. She caught my eye and smiled. "I am Vera Nayechev," she said, in good English.

I took her hand. "Dr. Arthur Conan Doyle."

"Ah, how delightful. I am a medical student."

"I am with Dr. Joseph Bell who is to give a series of lectures. Perhaps, you will attend his demonstrations in St. Petersburg. So, why were you in England?"

"We studied with Karl Marx in London. Our task is to teach the peasants and make them understand the tsar is not their 'little father,' but their oppressor."

Before I could gather my wits to answer, a bulky fellow with red hair and beard pulled her aside and gave me a fierce scowl.

Dostoevsky raised his hand for silence. "Calm yourselves, please. The new tsar is more kind and generous. Revolution will only lead to anarchy and the death of us all. We must support all Slavs and bring peace to Russia."

Vera Nayechev pulled me closer. "He is sick and old and should not speak like this. Nicholas I put him in prison and sentenced him to death, but at the last minute, he commuted the death sentence and sent him to Siberia. He should be anti-tsarist, but he has sympathy with our oppressors," she said.

The author left after his speech. Vera, rather stealthily, rubbed the inside of my wrist with her hand. Was it just an absent Russian gesture or an invitation? While I dallied with Vera, I kept an eye on Penelope. She didn't touch a drop of alcohol and remained in deep conversation with the Russians.

I had more vodka and dozed off but awakened when two white uniformed sailors placed a cauldron of beet soup and a platter of dark bread with a round of cheese on the table. Was it my imagination, or was there a whiff of that same sweetish odor that Dr. Bell thought was opium? Almost always, Bell is correct, but in this case, I thought he was definitely wrong. Yet, I could not place the odor. What was it?

The party broke up in the wee hours of the morning and I took Penelope to her room, expecting at least a long, goodnight kiss. Instead, she rather rudely pushed me away without even a friendly squeeze. Had I done something to offend her? Might she have been upset that I was sitting with Vera?

8 August 1881

In the wee hours of the morning, as I lay in bed trying to sleep, a pleasant memory returned. The sweetish odor was associated with food, but what kind of food? It reminded me of a special meal, but what was it?

I dozed off and dreamed of our traditional family Christmas dinner and my mother's lovely, glazed, baked ham, studded with cloves. When I awoke, I knew, instantly, that the faint odor in Lord Asquith's room had not been opium, but, rather, was cloves.

Over breakfast, I told Dr. Bell of my theory. He listened with rising excitement. "Very good, lad. Very good." He struck his forehead. "Yes, of course, cloves … I should have known. In the Far East, natives smoke cloves mixed with tobacco instead of opium. Someone on this ship smokes clove cigarettes. Doyle, see if you can learn more."

I was on deck, idling along, when I ran into Billy, the horn piper, scrubbing the deck. "Morning sir," he said.

"Billy, have you been with the ship for long?"

"Since she was commissioned, sir."

"Do you know of a crewmember who smokes clove cigarettes?"

"No, sir, I don't."

I slipped him an American silver dollar. "I am curious. It is a pleasant smoke. Let me know if you find a man who mixes cloves and tobacco."

Billy smiled. "I shall make inquiries."

He returned to his work. I poked into the crew's quarters and sniffed the air, but found nothing. By the end of the evening, Billy had not reported back. This struck me as strange but I was tired, so I came to my room to get some sleep.

9 August 1881

We were at breakfast when the first officer approached us. "Excuse me for interrupting your breakfast, but the doctor requests your immediate assistance in the sick bay," he whispered.

He could have been asleep on the sick bay examining table, but the body of Billy the sailor was in the first stage of rigor mortis. A stoker had found his body crumpled in a passageway forward of the crew's quarters. Fortunately, the officers and masters-at-arms had whisked the body away to the sick bay before the passengers were up and about.

Billy had been the picture of health. His body was tall and athletic — a blue-eyed, blonde Viking. Who could have struck down this man and why?

I was dumbfounded and guilty. Was I responsible for his death because I set him to discover the user of clove cigarettes? It was with great trepidation that I told Bell of my involvement.

Dr. Bell flicked open his pocket magnifying glass and commenced a minute examination; first the head and neck, then hands and arms, and on down the body to the feet. There were no marks of violence, no bruises, no hair or skin beneath the fingernails suggesting a scuffle. There was the odor of beer in his mouth, but nothing else. He searched the skin for a tell-tale pin prick — a place where an assailant could have inserted a long needle into the brain or the chest.

"A mirror and a light, please," he said.

Bell adjusted the gaslight, bent the head back, and I shined reflected light from the mirror while he examined the interior of the nasal cavity with a speculum.

"Well, well, look at this."

There, high in the back of the nose, were a few drops of blood. "Very clever. The assailant grabbed Billy from behind, bent back his head, and inserted a long needle into his nose. The assailant knows human anatomy well enough to stab through the thin base of the skull and on into the brain. Billy was instantly paralyzed and died within minutes."

Neither the ship's doctor nor Captain Veery argued against an autopsy. Dr. Bell, rather casually, assigned to me the task of slicing through the scalp and sawing off the skull cap while he took his usual morning stroll on deck. He returned, an hour later, just as I was lifting the brain from the base of the skull.

"There, a needle track. Doyle, hold the lens while I dissect." The faint needle went from the base of the brain upward through the vital respiratory center.

He put down the scalpel and wiped his hands. "Aye, indeed, our Billy did find the murderer. Unfortunately, before he could bring the villain to justice, he became one of his victims," he said, almost to himself.

I felt awful for being involved in sending him to his untimely demise, and when the autopsy was complete, I returned to our cabin and sulked for a bit.

That afternoon, the ship disembarked passengers at Copenhagen, but none of the crew left the ship. After another long dinner, I couldn't sleep and prowled the deck until quite late. We had entered the Baltic Sea and now had a strong wind on our stern. The ship rushed through the waves. There were fleeting glimpses of the Big Dipper and the North Star through ragged clouds.

It was peculiar that we were on a southern course, rather than east to St. Petersburg. I stopped to light a smoke and noticed a figure in a long, dark cloak forward of the bridge. As I watched, I became more and more convinced it was Penelope. What was she doing, alone on deck at this time of night?

I caught up with her. It was indeed Penelope. I immediately hoped for another passionate embrace or a little snuggle, but she drew back into the folds of her dark cloak.

"Are you following me?"

"No, I chanced to be on deck, and there you were. Would you care for a drink in the lounge?"

"Leave me alone."

"But, there is a murderer about. You might be in danger. I will not leave until you are safely in your room."

It seemed like a calculated move, rather than a romantic impulse. She flung her arms around my neck and offered her lips for another passionate kiss. "Help me," she breathed. "Come along and be of some use." As if under a spell, I followed without a word. She led the way forward to a hatch cover. "Lift it," she said.

I followed her down a steel ladder forty or fifty feet deep into the very bowels of the ship. It was a cavernous space, as dark as a black, tropical night. She fumbled in a voluminous purse, found a lucifer, and lit a small bulldog lantern. In the flare of the light, I could see three large crates in the center of a cargo hold.

"This is supposed to be a passenger ship. Why is it carrying cargo?" I asked.

"Don't ask questions. Stay on guard," she hissed.

Penelope shined the lantern about the cavernous space and focused on three huge wooden crates chained to bolts. The words 'Brooklyn Navy Yard' were printed in large, black letters on the center crate.

I clung to the ladder for support against the rolling ship and felt, as much as heard, the relentless crashing of waves against the bow. Penelope moved about, probing here and there with a folding knife until she disappeared on the far side of the crates. I was left alone in pitch dark, clinging to the ladder and feeling more and more sea sick from the pitching and rolling of the ship. Hot acid rose in my throat.

I spit foul saliva onto the steel floor and swallowed. What was she looking for? Seconds lengthened to minutes. Except for occasional flashes of light from her lantern, the hold was chill and completely dark. I shivered when the thought of a tomb crossed my mind. Was it my heightened imagination, or was there a faint tremor in the ladder? I heard the faintest scrape of shoe leather against a steel rung and I thought it was the killer with his lethal needle coming to murder both of us.

In the darkened hold, the figure descending the ladder was invisible, but his raspy breathing and the scrape of his shoe came closer and closer. Where should I go? How could I stay alive? I was close to panic. We were in a trap and the killer had us at his mercy.

I didn't dare call out to alert Penelope but braced myself for an attack. At the very moment the figure reached the bottom rung, Penelope emerged from behind the crates. She shined the lantern

53

directly on me, and in an instant, a small revolver appeared in her other hand. Was it my imagination? Was she aiming the gun at me or the intruder?

The *click* of another revolver was only a foot or so from my ear. I lashed out at the shadowy figure by the ladder with a fist and struck solid bone. His gun went off with a tremendous roar, but the killer went down without a sound.

In an instant, I had him in a choke-hold, yet he was already unconscious from my blow to his head. I twisted the revolver from his inert hand just as Penelope cried out. "For God's sakes … Don't kill him!"

"Penelope, are you hurt?" I screamed.

Did anger flare in her eyes? For an instant, I had the feeling she had expected the intruder and that I had interrupted a secret meeting. Then, her demeanor seemed to change and Penelope almost cooed. "I'm fine, shaken but unhurt. You're as dashing a young man as your uncle. Bravo. I owe you a kiss."

My anger drained away. She shined her lantern on the intruder's face. He was the American engineer, Gritz, unconscious but still breathing. Penelope went through his pockets and found nothing, then searched the inside of his waistcoat. There was only a thick wallet, but she wasn't interested in the contents. "Damn. Oh, damn," she muttered. "It isn't here."

"What are you looking for?"

She flashed another hard look. "Nothing, nothing at all… Now, Arthur, sweetheart, listen to me. This has to look like an accident."

"How?"

"We must take him to the deck and you report to the ship's officers. Please, Arthur, if you care for me, say nothing about this incident. I cannot tell you more, but you must trust me. It is part of my secret work as a spy for the Crown."

She believed in me to help make things right for her. My suspicions melted away. It was impossible to refuse this beautiful woman, and besides, she was practically a relative, even though Uncle Declan was dead. However, I also knew the body would be too heavy for me to carry on my own. "Sorry, Penelope. I want to help, but his body is dead weight and there is no way I can carry him straight up that ladder," I said.

Penelope swept the revolver from the floor and leveled it at my chest.

"Fine, I can kill you and give him another good rap on the head. You will both be dead. It will look like you killed each other."

"But why would you do that?"

"Your uncle is dead, so what if another Foley joins him?"

What a ghastly creature! I half-wondered if she was joking, but realized she was serious, clearly mad, and without any scruples. Though I wanted to abandon her right then, I still enjoyed the thought of her passionate kisses and, if I wanted to live, I could not resist her gun, her steely eye, and the tension of her finger on the trigger. "Aye, then. Let us give it a try," I sighed.

"That's a good lad." She smiled. "I would not want to harm you."

"You always get your way."

"That I do."

It was a long and weary task. With great difficulty, I hoisted the man's dead weight on my back with his arms crossed in front of my chest. There was a ripping sound as Penelope tore strips from her dress, which she twisted into ropes.

She then bound his arms across my chest so I could carry him with my hands free to grasp the ladder. Up we went, rung by each painful rung, as I dragged two hundred extra pounds on my back. I was near exhaustion when I reached the closed hatch. It was dogged down and wouldn't budge.

I couldn't let go of the ladder to turn the locking handle. The man on my back moaned and feebly moved, as if he was waking up. It was a devilish situation. I could have dropped the bastard. "Goddamnit! We are trapped!" I gasped.

"Idiot! God knows how you made it through medical school. Let me by," hissed Penelope, who was still below on the ladder.

By moving aside only a few inches, Penelope was just able to climb by. She angrily bumped me as she went up the ladder and released the locking handle, opening the hatch. The engineer moaned as I moved through the hatch and collapsed on deck. He opened his eyes and began to move once again, but Penelope smashed the butt of the revolver against his head and he went back out cold for a second time.

"What? Woman, are you completely insane?"

"It was nothing."

"Nothing? You could've killed him!"

"I didn't hit him that hard. He has to be unconscious long enough for us to get away. Report him to the officers and take him to sick bay."

The third officer and the master-at-arms believed my story of finding the victim passed out on the deck during an evening stroll. The American engineer was unconscious, but breathing regularly. The ship's doctor examined him in sick bay.

"I would wager the fellow had a bit to drink and fell on deck; happens all the time," he said.

"I will be happy to stay with him," I said.

"That would be kind of you. It's getting late and I want to retire for the night."

"I'll sit with him until he comes around," said I.

"Fine. And if you'd lock up when you go, it would be much appreciated."

I nodded and the ship's doctor departed. Penelope arrived in less than an hour wearing a stunning new evening dress. She tucked the cleaned and reloaded revolver and his fat wallet into the engineer's waistcoat pocket. When the fellow woke up, there would be nothing missing. She was very clever, but what was behind her actions? Did she really spy for the Crown, or could she be some sort of double or triple agent?

When the fellow woke up, he was disoriented and amnesic. I offered to walk him back to his quarters, but he refused and shakily left the sick bay. After locking up, I went on deck for fresh air and a bit of a walk. I stretched my back and shoulders, which ached from carrying the damn engineer. I wearily sat in the shadow of a lifeboat to have a smoke.

The ship was entering a narrow channel that led to a brightly-lit naval shipyard in the city of Kiel. A tugboat guided the

Servia alongside a long embankment with a huge steam-driven crane ablaze with gas lights.

The passengers were still sleeping off another large dinner, but to my amazement, the German, Count von Wittenberg, accompanied by the Americans, appeared on deck.

"Where is Mr. Gritz?" the count asked.

"Don't know. We haven't seen him since dinner," one American said.

The count spat on the deck. "*Mein lieber gott*! Damn imbeciles! Find him."

German workers swarmed onto the deck, opened the forward hatch, and led massive cables down into the hold. In less than half an hour, the three large crates were lifted out and deposited on the embankment. The crane then rolled away, and another machine with a long conveyer belt poured coal into the hold.

The Americans appeared, assisting the wobbly engineer, now a familiar figure, out of the darkness. At the same time, Penelope, shrouded in a cloak, glided to Count von Wittenberg. There was a moment's conversation, then she disappeared as silently as she had arrived. The entire affair was most mysterious. The pouring of the coal appeared to be a cover to hide the unloading of the secret cargo.

So then, the question remained — what was the secret cargo? What was in those three huge crates, and why was Penelope involved with the German, as well as the Americans? Why was she so cozy with the Russian students? Was I really in love with her, or was this another one of my infatuations? My poor head whirled with these contradictory thoughts.

Dawn was breaking as the ship churned into the Baltic Sea. I returned to my cabin and rolled into my bunk without even undressing.

10 August 1881

My rest was short-lived. It seemed as if it was only minutes after I had gone to bed that I was awakened by Mr. Tatum, who entered our cabin with a pot of strong tea, cups, milk, and sugar on a tray. Even thought it was quite early in the morning, Dr. Bell was already at his writing desk.

I roused and splashed water from the basin over my face.

"Well, Doyle, what were you up to last night?" Dr. Bell asked.

I toweled off the water and gratefully accepted a cup of tea from Mr. Tatum. "I was with Miss Walshingham and aided an unconscious passenger who fell on deck," I said.

"Were you up and about when the ship stopped in Kiel?" Mr. Tatum asked. How did he know? I didn't want to be caught out in another lie. "Yes," I answered.

Mr. Tatum did not seem the least bit surprised. "Miss Walshingham will join us following breakfast," he said.

Penelope entered our quarters. "What is the meaning of this?" she imperiously asked.

"If you, as you say, are a courier for the Royal Navy, explain your relationship with Count von Wittenburg and your interest in the cargo that was unloaded in a German port." Mr. Tatum said.

"The count is an old family friend." Penelope tossed her head as if in contempt of Mr. Tatum. "We were merely admiring the sky when the ship stopped in Kiel."

"Surely, the count confided in you about the contents of the crates from America?" Mr. Tatum asked.

"I wouldn't know."

"Miss Walshingham, do you have anything further to say about this matter?"

My heart melted when she inclined her head with a toss of her lovely hair. "No, nothing. Nothing at all," she barely murmured, before turning on her heels and walking out of the cabin.

By that afternoon, we were in the Gulf of Finland and still had not discovered the murderer. The captain reluctantly agreed to Bell's request to search the crew's possessions.

We followed the tall, surly master-at-arms through the crew's quarters. There was the usual grumbling over the confiscation of alcohol, knives, and a small Smith & Wesson pistol. However, the officers found nothing that could have been the murder weapon.

Dr. Bell followed, rather nonchalantly swinging his cane and puffing his pipe, yet, he intently inspected each man's possessions, which were laid out on the bunks.

We came, at last, to the galley. Much to our surprise, one of the cooks looked to be Chinese.

"You assured us that your crew was made up entirely of Americans and Scandinavians, did you not?" Dr. Bell asked.

"We don't count the cooks as crew," Captain Veery gruffly responded. "See here, this man is harmless." The captain took a step towards the Chinese cook, and then, suddenly, all hell broke loose.

The Chinaman spun about, threw a pot of boiling water at the huge master-at-arms, who ducked, but the Cook came on and, with a violent, skull-crushing kick, felled the master-at-arms. "English dogs!" shouted the Chinaman, as he spun about and smashed a two-handed blow to the abdomen of the second officer.

He let out a loud "Hee-yah!" with each blow.

I went in for a tackle, lost my balance, but was close enough to see the yellowish tints in his eyes and sweat dripping off his chin. "Death to English! Hee-yah!"

His long, high-pitched scream ended when he whipped a long knife from the back of his belt. In an instant, he held the long, curved blade to the captain's throat. "Release me in St. Petersburg or the captain dies!" he shouted.

I stood, frozen, incredulous at the Chinaman's impressive martial arts skills. Dr. Bell, however, remained cool as ever. "Damn you. Unhand him," he said.

"No. I will kill him first."

With a mere twitch of his hand, Dr. Bell flicked out the blade of his cane and drove it through the Chinaman's right arm.

"Ahh!" Spittle streamed from his lips as he dropped the knife and writhed on the deck in great pain, his right hand paralyzed and useless. Bell had severed the median nerve.

The master-at-arms and the first officer subdued the howling Chinaman and tied his hands behind his back.

Meanwhile, Bell examined the cook's seaman's bag and found a carved wooden box, which contained a beautiful set of slender steel needles varying in size from one to eight inches in length. I had never seen anything like them, but it was clear that they were the murder weapons. Dr. Bell continued his search and withdrew a fifty pound note tucked beneath the lining of the box. "Captain Veery, is this not a lot of money for a cook?"

"Indeed, the man must have been a thief as well as a killer," the captain said. "I will place it in the crew's fund."

Dr. Bell slipped the brand new note into his wallet and, with a clever sleight of hand, gave the captain a different bill. In the excitement, the episode slipped my mind until much later.

An hour later, Penelope, rather breathlessly, joined Bell and me in our stateroom. Dr. Bell blew a cloud of smoke. "He was a practitioner of acupuncture, one of the most ancient of the healing arts, and for reasons yet to be known, he used his knowledge to commit murder. It is even more puzzling because, according to the first mate, the cook was educated by British missionaries in Hong Kong."

Penelope put down her cup. "Lord Asquith's last assignment was Chairman of the British Committee on Opium in Shanghai. The missionaries bitterly opposed the British practice of selling opium to the Chinese."

"Indeed, you are a knowledgeable young woman. Selling opium and enslaving a nation with a heinous addiction is inexcusable, yet murder is never a solution." Bell pressed his fingers together. "Ah, the fifty pound note. Now, there is a mystery," he mused.

Her face contorted into a featureless mask and Penelope rose abruptly. "I must pack," she said. Penelope swished out the door of our cabin while Dr. Bell watched her lovely retreat with amusement, or was it a speculative look? Did he believe the darling girl?

Later, Penelope and I went on deck to see the Russian Baltic fleet at anchor off the Kronstadt naval base on Kotlin Island. The *Servia* gave three long blasts of the ship's horn and dipped the U.S. flag as we steamed past cruisers, destroyers, and torpedo boats.

"Your friend, the German count, is taking a great interest in the Russian fleet," I said.

"He is to be the naval attaché to the German Embassy," Penelope answered.

Merchant ships from all over the world were anchored in the harbor, and a small trim yawl wound through the huge anchorage. Two tugs nudged the *Servia* alongside the long, stone-covered embankment at the passenger port on the west end of Vasilievsky Island. Once the *Servia* reached its slip, the crew let down the gangplanks with a great clatter of chain.

Armed guards from the British and American embassies came aboard and conducted a grim procession off the ship with the shrouded bodies on stretchers followed by the chained and manacled Chinese cook. He was docile as the guards dragged him across the deck, but in front of Penelope, the Chinaman jerked to a halt. Hatred spilled from his eyes as he spit a glob of mucous at her feet. Her face went dead-white but she said nothing.

The British soldiers roughly hauled at his chains. He followed, docile as a whipped dog, but on the gangplank, midway between the ship and shore, he shrieked, wrenched free, and jumped to his death in the frigid water. The passengers gasped and fled the 'bad luck' ship to waiting carriages.

When we were disembarking, I had hoped for a kiss, or at least a fond farewell, but Penelope left the ship arm in arm with the German, Count von Wittenberg. She never so much as glanced my way. Was it my imagination, or was she being coerced?

As the couple neared the line of waiting carriages, a black phaeton, drawn by a pair of fine-looking horses, drew up across the street. Penelope appeared to be confused, twisted her arm from the German's grip, and seemed to recognize the two men in dark suits and derby hats who rushed from the phaeton. Count von Wittenberg threw an arm around her shoulder and tried to push her into his carriage. Then, just as the carriage door was about to close, the two men wrenched her free. Had she intended to go with the count? Were the strangers abducting Penelope?

I flung open the instrument case and fumbled for the secret compartment. In an instant, I had the Webley revolver out and held in wobbly hands. Though I had fired a gun before, I still felt nervous. My intention was to fire a warning shot, but Mr. Tatum roughly restrained my arm and took the gun. "No, Doyle. Don't!" he said, in his Sergeant-Major voice. "Don't interfere."

I slumped, utterly defeated, and watched helplessly as the wretches tumbled Penelope into the light carriage and sped away towards the city.

I was still reeling from her apparent abduction, when, in the tumult on the dock, Dr. Aleksey Sechenov, our host at the medical school, arrived in a sumptuous blue and white carriage drawn by matching grey horses.

Two liveried footmen whisked our baggage to the boot while my new friend, Cowboy Bill, directed two stevedores to carry a stout cage containing a mass of hissing, writhing rattlesnakes to a waiting wagon. "Ah my limey friend, young Doyle. Did you have a good voyage?" asked Cowboy Bill.

"It was certainly unusual and eventful."

"Come visit me and my snakes if you have time in St. Pete."

"I will."

"And speaking of snakes, hope you kept yours in your pants the whole trip, eh pardner?" he asked, with a wink.

Before I could answer, a footman handed me into the carriage. I sat on a plush velvet seat across from Professor Sechenov who was elegantly turned out in fawn-colored tight breeches and a grey coat. "Is St. Petersburg safe these days?" I asked, still a bit shaken and unsure of the meaning of Penelope's abduction.

"Oui. There have been a few problems with student anarchist groups, but I trust that you will be as safe as in Edinburgh."

Sechenov's soft voice soothed my frazzled nerves. He explained how Peter the Great had built this city on marshland with slave labor. I was soon lost in wonder as we sped past wide canals with granite embankments, magnificent brick and stone buildings with white trim, then down a wide avenue along the Neva River. Magnificent buildings and cathedrals with blue, onion-shaped domes glowed in the soft golden afternoon light.

"How beautiful!" I pointed to a long building with two columns. "What is that?"

Professor Sechenov answered in impeccable French, which I learned was the language of the Russian nobility and intelligentsia. "The stock exchange."

Within a few minutes, we turned onto another broad street, Bolshoi Prospekt, and then into the driveway of his home, our quarters during our stay in St. Petersburg.

An obsequious footman led us through a drawing room — well-lit with gold chandeliers and filled with dark, well-upholstered furniture — and then up a curving staircase to the second floor. Dr. Bell enjoyed a bedroom with an adjoining sitting room, while I had a simple, but adequate room overlooking a garden and the buildings of the university.

After a bit of discussion, our host found a room for Mr. Tatum on our floor, rather than in the servant's quarters. A few minutes' exploration revealed a small rear stairway that led to a pantry, the servants' quarters, or the kitchen. Another possible exit was from the balcony down a convenient rain pipe to the garden. I was nicely settled when it was time to dress for dinner.

The guests assembled in the dining room consisted of St. Petersburg's leading physicians, government officials, aristocrats, and Dr. Piragoff, a high-ranking military officer and surgeon known for his work with the wounded of both sides during the Crimean war. There were toasts to the tsar and the Queen, then to Dr. Bell, the guest of honor.

When they learned that I was neither a nobleman nor a professor, but little more than a peasant, I was soon ignored and left to my own devices to enjoy the caviar, champagne, and to overhear the somber undertones of the guests.

I soon learned that the royal family, in mortal fear for their lives, was in virtual isolation at Anichkof Palace. The secret police were scouring the city for anarchists, terrorists, and members of the intelligentsia who were suspected of plotting to kill the new tsar.

I suddenly thought of Penelope. Was she in the hands of the secret police because of her relationship with Uncle Declan and Captain David Campbell? Or did British agents take her to the British ambassador with the message? Would she search for the officer who, crazed by vengeance, would kill the tsar and throw all of Europe into war?

I could not know the answer, but I was certain that our stay here in St. Petersburg would be filled with danger and intrigue. It was sometime after two in the morning, when the party broke up and I stumbled, dazed by drink, to my room. Waiting at the door, the porter passed an envelope into my hand.

Dr. Doyle,
If you will, please join me with a group of fellow students for lunch at The Beranger at noon tomorrow.
Vera Nayechev

I was intrigued and planned to join them at noon. The rest of the day was uneventful. The bed with a down filled mattress felt wonderful.

11 August 1881

The Beranger, a coffee house, was evidently a favourite meeting place for university students. Dark and musty, it was packed with young people drinking and smoking. There were no empty tables and no Vera.

Then, I made my way through thick tobacco smoke to the stairs and up to the second floor. There she was, at a table overlooking Nevsky Prospekt, St. Petersburg's main street. Vera looked as she did that night when I was with Dostoevsky on the ship, but she was calmer and more refined. She was with three men, one of whom was the sour, stocky, red-headed fellow with the beard whom I had met on the *Servia*.

"Ah, Dr. Doyle. Welcome. Please, sit... Are you enjoying your stay in our fair city?" she asked.

"Yes, I love the architecture. Reminds me of Paris," I answered.

"Ah, so have you spent a lot of time in Paris?"

"No, but I have read a great deal about Paris, and St. Petersburg reminds me of what I think it would look like."

"Peter the Great yearned for this city to rival Paris in its beauty. If only the modern tsars were as enlightened as Peter."

I had only a moment to order tea when the red-bearded one fixed me with piercing, green eyes. "You were present when Foley died, yes?" he asked.

"Yes."

"What were his last words?"

I had to think for a moment, and then remembered his words. "He said something very strange. He mentioned a Dr. Hutton and no God and the end of the old regime."

"He said this?"

"Yes, but his final words were, 'Tsar die.' "

Red relaxed for a moment. "He was one of us."

"Silence!" Another student, a slight, owlish fellow with round, dark glasses, raised his hand. "How do we know we can trust this damned Englishman?"

Vera interjected on my behalf. "He saved Dostoevsky's life."

"Bah. That old man can write, but sometimes I question his loyalties, too."

"And this boy's people, the Irish, were persecuted by the English Crown. He has a natural sympathy with our cause," Vera said, as she put her hand on top of mine.

"Aye, I have Irish blood, and aye, I am a friend of anyone who befriended my Uncle Declan." I said.

"I like this Irishman! I am Sviazhky. Welcome to Russia. Lt. Foley was your relative?"

"Aye."

"Any relative of Foley is a friend of mine." Red embraced me with a bear hug. "I had a good feeling about you since I first laid eyes upon you. Your uncle was studying our Russian people and intended to go among the peasants, disguised as a priest, to explain Darwin's theory, debunk God, and stir up the serfs against the church and the tsar."

I was more perplexed than ever. "But he was an English military officer who fought against your country in Afghanistan. I don't understand."

"He knew he was fighting the tsar and the nobility, not the people. He swore vengeance and joined our group in London."

"What exactly does your group believe?"

"For our revolution to succeed, we must break the peasants of their habit of obeisance to the church and the tsar. They actually believe that he is anointed by God and this belief must be destroyed."

I nodded and glanced at my watch.

"I apologize. Dr. Bell is giving a demonstration at two," I said. "Sorry, but it will not look good if I am late. I should go, but hopefully, I will see you there."

When I arrived at the medical school lecture hall, distinguished physicians and the school's faculty were seated in the front row. Sun poured in from a skylight and lit the space. The walls were whitewashed and the tile floor showed old blood stains. Glass-fronted cabinets held surgical instruments and rolls of gauze. As in

Edinburgh, the room was both a lecture hall and operating theater. What seats were still open rapidly filled with excited students, as motley a bunch as my Edinburgh classmates. Vera and her group sat down near the center, surrounded by roughly-clad young men from the country. Furthest in the back were rather elegant, bored, young aristocrats.

I sat with Dr. Bell in the front row, still at somewhat of a loss to explain my encounter with the young anarchists. Professor Sechenov stood behind a podium and spoke in French. In fact, all the students and faculty spoke French in class.

Sechenov removed his pince-nez and peered at the audience. "Our first patient is paralyzed by a spinal cord tumor. I have invited Dr. Joseph Bell, an esteemed Professor of Surgery at Edinburgh Medical College, to perform the operation. Dr. Bell, if you will . . ."

Dr. Bell went into the cockpit. I followed to assist or give the anaesthetic, but was immediately anxious. Operations for spinal cord tumors were rarely, if ever, successful. Was this a cunning Russian trap to make a foreign doctor look bad? I had thought Dr. Bell would teach and maybe see some patients, but I had no idea we were about to engage in major surgery.

The patient, on the wheeled stretcher, was an attractive woman of perhaps thirty years. She was on her back, covered with a sheet. Dr. Bell was clearly not prepared for surgery, and I wondered how he was going to handle this unusual situation.

"Good afternoon. May I have your name, please?" Dr. Bell asked.

"Lydia Sorokina," she answered in a low-pitched, barely audible voice.

"Miss Sorokina, how long have you been paralyzed?"

"Almost three weeks."

The professor drew back the sheet, exposing her muscular legs. He examined the soles of her feet and barely touched a callous on her great toe.

"You are a ballerina?"

"Yes, I danced with the Bolshoi," she whispered. Her eyes filled with tears. "Today, I can no longer dance, and that is why I am here. It is my dream to dance again."

The professor palpated the muscles in her thighs and calves and struck the patellar tendon at the knee with a reflex hammer. The lower leg responded normally with a jump. Next, he held her ankle and tapped the Achilles tendon. At each tap of the hammer, a muscle contracted and her ankle flexed. He stroked the sole of her foot; the great toe turned down, a normal Babinski reflex.

He then checked her sensation with a long needle. There was no response to a light pinprick or even when he drove the needle a half-centimeter into her skin. She did not flinch.

"Dr. Doyle, would you determine the level of sensory loss?"

I hesitated, then pulled the sheet below her waist, exposing her breasts. The young students in the gallery whistled and made lewd remarks. Professor Sechenov silenced them angrily. "Enough of that, please!"

I overcame my timidity and, commencing at her thighs, first touched her skin with a wisp of cotton, then with a sharp pin. She made no response until, at the level of her umbilicus, she winced at the prick of pin. She had no sensation below the level of her umbilicus. The level of sensory loss had no connection to the nervous innervation but was in a perfect ring around her body and, seemingly, bore no relation to her muscle paralysis. I was completely confused.

Dr. Bell watched her responses with lowered eyelids while a mere hint of a smile played over his lips. It was then that I knew he was up to one of his old tricks.

Suddenly, he upended the stretcher. "Dance again, young lady," he said.

Had Dr. Bell lost his mind? The students and faculty sucked in their breath as the surprised young woman slid off the stretcher and landed on her feet.

For a second, there was silence. Then, she gathered the sheet about her breasts and shook her fist at the professor. "Damn you!" she shouted.

She walked out on her own two feet and left by the side door. There was much chatter amongst the audience. "Gentlemen, please, quiet down. This is a case of hysterical paralysis. Clearly, there was no need for an operation."

Many of the students clapped and cheered. Dr. Bell had done it again. Under pressure in a foreign city, he had displayed his mastery of the entire field of medicine and, indeed, the science of psychology.

The professors in the front row were silent until Sechenov stammered a few words. "How did you make that diagnosis?" he asked.

Bell cleared his throat and raised his hand to his chin. "In cases of spinal cord injury or tumor, the deep tendon reflexes of the legs, mediated by the lumbar and sacral nerves, should be absent. Her reflexes were hyperactive, suggesting an emotional state. The loss of sensation to the level of the umbilicus, as demonstrated by my associate, Dr. Doyle, bore no relationship to the normal patterns of the thoracic nerves. Gentlemen, if you enquire closely, I wager you will find a psychological reason to explain why the patient cannot dance."

Dr. Sechenov tapped the lens of his glasses against his thigh. "Yes, she was dismissed from the Bolshoi a day prior to the onset of symptoms."

Sechenov restored order with a glance and cleared his throat. "Next, Dr. Bell has been so kind to agree to demonstrate the anatomy of his operation for joint excision on a fresh cadaver."

Surgeons have often practiced and demonstrated operations on cadavers because it is easier to identify bones, nerves and tendons without the constant flow of blood to obscure the anatomy. This corpse was covered with a shroud, except for his ankles and feet. With a great sense of self-importance, I opened the instrument case on a table and arranged the scalpels, chisels, hammers, probes, and forceps, as if for a real operation. It struck me as unusual that the skin of the 'patient's' feet did not exhibit the usual lividity of death, but was absolutely dead white. I was not sure what to make of the strange pallor.

The professor removed his coat, rolled up his sleeves, and, rather dramatically, took up the razor-sharp, steel scalpel in his right hand.

"If this was an operation, instead of an anatomical dissection, we would first prepare the skin and all instruments with a solution of carbolic. However, since this man is deceased, it is not necessary."

He then applied the knife and incised the skin from the lateral malleolus of the ankle down the lateral side of the foot. There was an immediate muffled groan, and then a piercing shriek as the 'patient's' foot lifted from the table.

"Good God!" Dr. Bell stepped back and, with a single motion, applied the scalpel to the cloth and opened the shroud. He exposed the face and torso of a strongly-built, middle-aged man. His colorless lips were drawn back in a rictus of terror.

"Heavens, the man is alive!" Dr. Bell shouted. "What is the meaning of this? Is this some type of prank?"

"No, no, no. I apologize." Professor Sechenov's face went livid. He turned to his assistant. "Pavlov, this is an outrage. What is going on?"

"He was the subject for this morning's experiment, we removed all his blood. He should be dead. Dead!" Pavlov exclaimed.

With that declaration, the patient's head jerked up and down. His eyes closed. He shuddered and then became completely still. His skin was white as fresh snow, and his lips were colorless. If he was not dead when he was wheeled in, he was truly dead now.

"I am appalled." Dr. Bell lifted the right arm of the deceased. "What is this?" There was a long incision down the medial side of the arm and the brachial artery was severed. Bell sniffed at the man's mouth. "It appears as if some damned criminal performed surgery on this man without anaesthesia. What in heaven's name is going on here? This is barbaric!"

"Let me explain." Dr. Pavlov was perfectly at ease. "I am a doctor and not a criminal. I injected cocaine into the skin this morning. The operation was completely pain free. I drained blood from the artery for my work on blood coagulation. This man was found guilty of plotting against the tsar; he chose to be an experimental subject, rather than face torture and a military firing squad."

In an instant, Dr. Bell's rage gave way to his keen scientific interest. "Wait, did you anaesthetize the skin, rather than administer ether or chloroform?"

"Exactly! German chemists have isolated the active ingredient of the South American coca leaf." Pavlov held out a small container of a white powder. "Test a bit on your tongue. Your entire mouth will go perfectly numb."

Dr. Bell applied his index finger to the powder, then placed it on his tongue. "Yes, by God, my tongue is completely numb!" he exclaimed, after a moment. He bit down and drew blood from his tongue. "By Jove, Doyle, we must try this new drug. It will revolutionize surgery!"

Pavlov shook with excitement. "Simply dissolve the powder in water and inject the solution into the skin. The patient will feel nothing." Pavlov gave the container of cocaine to Dr. Bell. "Here, Doctor. Test it."

Dr. Bell placed the vial in his jacket pocket and then appeared as if all was normal. I thought, for sure, he would refuse to continue a sham operation on this newly-deceased man, but Bell didn't think twice about going ahead.

"Well, gentleman, since our subject is now truly dead, we will proceed," Dr. Bell said. And, just like that, he continued.

Dr. Bell was a church deacon and highly ethical. This was totally out of character for the professor. Had the cocaine affected his judgement?

It seemed as if his love of science blotted out his finer instincts. Had his moral principles had suddenly deserted him? He lectured as he dissected and demonstrated the anatomy of the foot and ankle with unusual brilliance.

I was horrified and repelled by Bell's display, but the others were taken in by his charisma and brilliance. The audience was truly captivated.

At the end of the demonstration, in late afternoon, Bell was mobbed by professors and doctors from all of St. Petersburg who excitedly begged him to dinners and to see their patients in consultation.

I was sickened. The more I watched these great men of science, the less I wanted to be a doctor. I had worked my whole life to become a man of medicine, but here was the heartlessness of pure science. I wanted no part of it.

12 August 1881

This morning, I couldn't shake my sick feeling about my fellow scientists. I was thinking that I should go home, give up medicine, and focus on my dream of becoming a writer. After further inner debate, though, I decided that, alas, I was too desperately poor to try anything else, especially a riskier career such as writing, so there was no alternative for me but the practice of medicine.

Thus, this morning, I dragged myself through the streets of St. Petersburg to attend lectures on chemistry and bacteriology given by two scientists with German accents. I understood most of the lectures and tried not to fall asleep.

At noon, I met Vera Nayechev for lunch. "Fyodor has spoken of your kindness to him and wishes to consult with you about his lung congestion," she said, while we ate delicious small pancakes, called blini, topped with caviar and hot soup.

I did a bit of sightseeing and, at four o'clock, reached Dostoevsky's small flat. I opened the door to the odor of decay and sickness mingled with stale beer and cabbage. A subdued group of students, writers, and a publisher was eating and drinking. Sviazhky, with the red beard, gave me an immense bear hug. He wore a grave expression on his face. "Fyodor's health is deteriorating. He is near the end," he said.

"When I saw him on the *Servia*, he appeared to have epilepsy," I said.

"It all started when he was arrested, then shackled hand and foot in the St. Peter and Paul fortress years ago. For months, he ate nothing but stale crusts of bread."

"What was his crime?"

"There was no crime. The secret police accused him of plotting against the tsar and sentenced him to death by firing squad. A priest insisted he confess his sins and kiss the cross as they led him into Semyonovsky Square. The tsar's men put a hood over his head and tied his hands, but at the last minute, Tsar Nicholas I commuted his sentence to eight years in Siberia."

"How terrible."

"Yes, and his story is not uncommon. That is why so many people want to see the end of the tsars."

After perhaps a half-hour of pleasant conversation and drinking vodka, Sviazhky flung his arms around a middle-aged man who appeared from an adjacent room. "Doyle, this is Golovinsky, the son of a man who was in Siberia with Fyodor. He is now one of Fyodor's most trusted friends."

Golovinsky gestured to me. "He is ready for you."

He took my arm and led the way into the author's small study. Dostoevsky, reclining on a chaise lounge, raised himself and languidly offered a thin, pale hand, criss-crossed by blue veins. "Ah, my young Scottish doctor. Welcome to St. Petersburg. I am glad to see you."

His face was pallid, with just a hint of freckles over his cheeks, and his beard was matted with a yellowish scum. He lay back on the lounge, covering his mouth with a soiled, blood-stained handkerchief and was convulsed with a moist, gurgling cough.

I spent a moment looking at the shelves of his books. I could not read Cyrillic but recognized many of his novels and stories. He had lived a writer's life, a life I had always dreamed about but never had the courage to pursue. This man was pure bravery, yet look at where it had gotten him — frail and sickly and dying in a hovel.

I vowed to do whatever I could with my limited skills and the meager supply of medicines in my instrument bag. Several students crowded into the room, as if expecting a miracle from the foreign doctor. There was no way that I, a recent graduate, could meet their expectations. I tried to comfort him by putting my hand on his shoulder. "So Fyodor, tell me how you are feeling."

"My cough has become insufferable and my doctors can do nothing."

"I will try to alleviate your suffering."

With my best, assumed, professional manner, I counted his pulse at the wrist. The beats were rapid and erratic, not a good sign. He had another paroxysm of coughing while I removed his shirt to percuss and auscultate his lungs. His thin chest was sunken and the ribs were prominent. There was no subcutaneous fat and only a few strands of muscle. I placed the middle finger of my left hand on his chest wall and tapped it with my right index finger. The percussion note sounded like a hammer striking an empty drum, except at the apex, where the note was flat and dull.

This was a sign of a fluid-filled cavity. One hardly needed a stethoscope to hear the gurgling rales in both lungs. I surmised that Dostoevsky was in the end stage of pulmonary tuberculosis, aggravated by years of smoking cigarettes, poor diet, and general ill health. I guessed his ailment originated in the ordeal of imprisonment and Siberian exile while he was a young man. There was little to be done except to palliate his symptoms. I poured a strong dose of laudanum into his bedside cup and wrote a prescription for menthol.

"Take as much laudanum as you wish to decrease the cough, and get this from your chemist. Place a tablespoonful in a kettle of boiling water, and inhale the steam with a towel or blanket over your head twice a day."

It was a useless nostrum, but I had learned from Dr. Bell to always prescribe something to give the patient hope — no matter what.

Dostoevsky thanked me. I lingered a while, talking with Golovinsky and Vera at the window as a half-dozen students from the flat sauntered toward the main street. Suddenly, a troop of mounted police, the Okhrana, cantered into Kuznechney Alley and, with no warning, began to beat the students with their rifle butts. "Disperse, disperse! No meetings allowed!" the policemen barked.

Two students fell with bleeding heads. Others cowed under the blows and meekly submitted to the shackles and chains. An older, stout woman — what the Russians called a babushka — showed great courage and dashed her handbag in the face of one of the officers who was beating a frail young man on the ground.

She attempted to run, but to my horror, the captain of the troop took deliberate aim with his pistol and brought the fleeing woman down with one shot. Blood spurted from her chest as she lay on the cobblestones. Then, the police dragged the shackled students away, leaving the dead woman under a dispersing cloud of gun smoke.

"This happens every day," Vera whispered. "It is the great tragedy of our lives. These horrible Okhrana round up suspects and take them away to the fortress — the ones that they have not already killed, that is."

"Is there no justice in this forsaken place?" I shouted, without thought of my hosts.

Dostoevsky finished a wracking, gurgling coughing spasm. "Watch out, my young Scottish doctor. This is not Edinburgh. If you are too loud, they will come for you, too," he said.

"Thank you, my friend," I answered.

Then, with a glance to Golovinsky, I thought I heard Dostoevsky speak. "Only one more, then I will be at peace. Now go," he whispered.

Vera took both of my hands with a firm grip. "Doyle, we should leave, but be very careful, please. I don't want you to come to harm. Keep your eyes open and your mouth shut."

I thanked her for the advice, which sounded like what Dr. Bell had said all through medical school.

It was near dusk when we left Dostoevsky's flat. Bright red sprays of light reflected from western clouds but the day had turned gloomy. Vera tucked her arm through mine and we cautiously walked out onto the street. Ah, I felt a growing warmth for this strange, but delicious young woman who was concerned for my well-being.

"Come, Dr. Doyle, we will not allow the secret police to spoil our day."

She held me so close that an observer might have thought we were lovers. Was she, like Penelope, playing me for another purpose? She was a sensuous, full-bodied woman with a scent of roses. I was attracted to her bosom thrusting against a thin blouse.

We lingered at the Bronze Horseman — the bigger than life statue of Peter the Great astride a magnificent horse — and watched the Neva peacefully flow into the Gulf. I loved the way she thrust herself against my body and enjoyed inhaling her scent.

She pulled me towards her. "I must leave, but let us meet again at the Beranger, let us say, at three o'clock," she said. The brush of my mouth on her face soon turned into a very satisfactory lip-bruising kiss.

"Yes, tomorrow at three o'clock."

Upon my return, Bell was jittery, nervous, and poised with a syringe and a needle over his bared left arm. "Ah, good! Doyle, you are just in time to witness a great surgical advance. I shall inject three cubic centimeters of cocaine and water into my skin."

He inserted the needle, depressed the plunger, and immediately relaxed.

"Now Doyle, plunge the point of your penknife into the area of injection."

"Sir, I couldn't do that. The pain would be intense."

"Nonsense. Cocaine renders the area pain free. Think what this means to the future of surgery."

With that, he stabbed the needle deep into his arm. "Look, there is no pain."

I was worried and perplexed. Since he first tried cocaine at the lecture, Dr. Bell's behavior had alternated between bouts of euphoric hyperactivity and dreamy lethargy. I was sorry about his use of cocaine and yearned for the old caustic, cutting Bell.

I excused myself and went to my room to study and mull over the day's events. My thoughts, as they seemed to inevitably do, soon turned to Penelope. Where was she now? Was she in the clutches of the secret police in some horrid prison cell? What was the role of our mysterious Mr. Tatum? He posed as our valet, but went off on mysterious errands, and once, I heard him speak of the 'embassy men.' Was he watching over us or pursuing his own affairs?

13 August 1881

In the morning, Dr. Bell ate a good breakfast and seemed to be his usual self. We accompanied Professor Sechenov to the morgue. Dr. Bell was to demonstrate a point of anatomy involved in excision of the wrist joint, an operation used in the treatment of tuberculosis.

All morgues are dismal, but this fetid, ill-lit place was more dungeon than anatomical laboratory. We passed the mutilated victims of the secret police on the way into the dissection room where the pathologist, in his rubber apron, waited by the body of an elderly man. "No one claimed the body."

"What do you know about him?" Dr. Bell queried.

"The police found him in Semyonovsky Square with his hands shackled and his mouth stuffed with dried bread," the pathologist said.

Bell paced around the table and minutely scrutinized the body. "There is no doubt about the cause of death. There are five bullet wounds to his chest and the back of his head is blown away. It appears to be an execution."

"I agree."

"Wait." He pointed at his lower arm. "What is this? There seems to be some sort of note tied to his wrist."

The pathologist pulled the note and translated in stilted English. "I am a ridiculous man." The words made no impression on the others, but I recognized the first line from a story by Dostoevsky. But what did they mean? Why would a murderer quote Dostoevsky?

"Why would anyone kill an old, harmless man?" Sechenov asked.

"Wait, this reminds me of another peculiar message." The pathologist rummaged around on a desk littered with scraps of paper, bottles of specimens, and soiled instruments. "Ah, here it is — from the body of another elderly man with identical wounds."

He read from a soiled slip of paper. "I am a sick man, a spiteful man."

Dr. Bell dissected the metacarpal bones and the flexor tendons at the wrist with more than his usual enthusiasm and skill while lecturing in rapid-fire French.

Meanwhile, I pondered the words, *I am a sick man, a spiteful man.*

Aye, they comprised the opening line from another short story by Fyodor Dostoevsky. There had to be a connection between the notes with the quotes on them and the strange deaths of these elderly men, but what was it?

By now, I had lost interest in the anatomy lecture and I wanted to think more about the notes, so I decided on a walk to the Beranger. I must admit, I was also hoping that, as I walked, I might see Vera, even though it was before three o'clock. Why did I always become infatuated with the latest good-looking woman to cross my path? Aye, the delicious Jean, the nurse, was a mere distant flicker of my imagination. Penelope? *Well,* I thought, *she is a darling girl, but she is perhaps too prickly for me.* I was in luck. Aye, Vera was already there, sipping tea alone at a table overlooking Nevsky Prospekt. I was worried that the Russian students might be jealous of my excessive attentions to her, but they shared everything; food, drink — and even their women.

We sipped our tea and ate small cakes while Vera, in an undertone, told me about the disappearance of another student.

"Dear God, is there no justice here? How can people be treated that way?" I asked.

She gripped my arm so hard the muscle ached, while a tempestuous light came into her dark, slightly-upturned eyes. There was a hint of a wild Mongolian ancestry in her high cheekbones and the tiniest of slants of her eyes. "My dearest Doyle, please come with me tonight and you will see real Russian justice."

I could not say no; we arranged to meet at midnight.

We wore dark cloaks against the light rain and huddled in the misty shadows of the old regimental headquarters overlooking Semyonovsky Square. I grew sleepy and would have been happy to leave, but Vera clutched my arm and insisted that we stay, even through the night, if necessary. To keep me from falling asleep, she gave me kisses and rubbed my back. Her attention was so lovely that I would have happily stayed with her for the whole night.

Shortly after the clock struck three, the gentle clip-clop of approaching hooves could be heard, and soon, two darkened carriages entered the square. We scarcely breathed while two men jumped from one of the carriages and erected a small platform with a sturdy pole in the center of the square.

I heard a piteous, stifled cry from the second carriage, then, two men dragged a struggling victim to the platform and bound him to the pole. His face was, for a moment, bathed in the light of a hooded lantern. A small, hunched, feeble figure then emerged from the first carriage and slowly approached the platform. "It is him."

The hunched man held a large silver cross to the victim's lips. "Damn you. Kiss the cross." The victims head inclined and his lips touched the cross. There was a long, gurgling cough and five muffled shots. I was horrified by it all. How could they call this barbarity justice?

The man's body sagged against the pole.

Then, a final shot rang out — the *coup de grace* — to end the victim's suffering. The two carriages vanished as quickly as they had arrived. A moment later, the square was silent. It didn't seem possible that six shots would not arouse the neighbors.

"Why haven't the shots stirred anyone?"

"Our people are afraid. Gunfire usually means the secret police, and no one wants to create trouble," Vera whispered.

"He may be alive. We must help that poor man."

"No. Leave him alone."

Heedless of Vera's warnings, I set off toward the victim. "It is our duty."

Vera followed me. "Dr. Doyle, stop. No."

I reached the poor man and I struck a lucifer. His eyes were filmed over by death. The lifeless lips barely touched a large crucifix hanging around his neck and resting on his chest. The dead man wore the vestments of an old priest.

There was nothing to be done; Vera dragged me away. No one appeared — not the secret police or any citizens — and we were lucky to escape without any problems. We walked along the river, thankful for the darkened, misty night. My confused thoughts would make nothing of Vera. Was she a vicious anarchist, bent on murder, or, as I had once hoped, a medical student who valued and saved lives? How could justice be cruelty and revenge? Most of all, I missed Edinburgh and my old life…

18 August 1881

I haven't had a moment to put down my thoughts in days, so I am glad to finally have time to write.

First, the day after I last saw him, Fyodor Dostoevsky died of a massive lung hemorrhage. He had said goodbye to his family and friends and seemed to have been ready to pass to the other world. A huge gathering of almost forty thousand people came to see the funeral in the Alexander Nevsky Square. Many great men spoke of how his stories had changed and inspired their lives. He had a deep understanding of the human heart and mind that few others had expressed. I suspect that he will be translated into English soon and become known as one of the world's greatest novelists.

Otherwise, we have begun a grueling routine. Dr. Bell visits hospitals and demonstrates surgery while I attend Professor Sechenov's lectures to improve my knowledge of anatomy and physiology.

Although the students in Vera Nayechev's small circle welcomed my presence and are interested in my thoughts, the better-dressed upper-class students either take no notice of me or go out of their way to elbow me aside. So, my experience with the Russian people has been mixed. Some seem to adore my accent and habits while others disdain me.

After a lecture on the circulation of blood and cardiac function yesterday morning, the same seedy fellow with a patched coat and a scraggly beard — who had been in charge of the first demonstration — approached me as we were leaving the lecture hall. He spoke in heavily-accented French. "I am Ivan Pavlov, assistant to the professor. You are Dr. Bell's assistant, yes?

"Aye."

"Would you like to visit our laboratory?"

I hesitated. Would there be live patients — experimental subjects — in his laboratory? I was repelled as well as fascinated. "Yes, of course. I would enjoy seeing your work," I said, solely out of curiosity.

"Excellent. Please follow me." We walked through a maze of university lecture halls and classrooms to a new building on the outskirts of the campus. As we talked, I became aware of his brilliant, but one-track, mind. Pavlov was not interested in medicine to benefit sick patients, but in learning how the nervous system functioned.

I was on the verge of asking about Cowboy Bill and the rattlesnakes when Pavlov spoke first. "There is another project. Our beloved tsar has ordered a study of blood coagulation."

"Ah, yes. On our very first day, one of your subjects was not quite dead when he was used in Dr. Bell's lecture."

"Yes, that was an unfortunate error. Science can sometimes be difficult. But when you get to the lab, you will see that we are doing important, groundbreaking work that will help all of mankind."

I heard whining and an occasional bark even before we entered the laboratory where a half-dozen pitiful dogs were in the center of the room. Heavy ropes immobilized each animal to a wooden frame, and rubber tubes connected their mouths to an apparatus that collected and measured their excretion of saliva. Another tube led from their stomachs to a similar apparatus. As a dog lover, my first instinct was to release the poor animals but it was not my lab.

"Once you see our experiments, you will understand how they will change the way we live." Pavlov said. "My experiments demonstrate psychic salivation and gastric stimulation in response to a secondary stimulus."

He blew a whistle; the dogs howled and whined, and within a few moments, saliva and gastric juice flowed into the measuring glasses.

"These dogs have learned that the sound of a whistle is often accompanied by food. I have named the phenomena 'conditioned reflex.' "

"Igor, turn on the generator." An elderly man — with a long, white beard and wearing a soiled smock with dark pants stuffed into knee-high boots — put down a broom and shuffled to a large box mounted on wheels.

Pavlov held a two-pronged stick that carried heavy wires from the box, which, evidently, was an electric generator.

"Igor, turn the crank."

The professor then touched the wires to a large, black and tan hound who was salivating copiously in anticipation of food. A spark jumped from the wires to the dog. The poor animal stiffened and let out a piteous, low moan. The flow of saliva and gastric juice stopped almost instantly.

Pavlov's eyes glowed with satisfaction. "A noxious counter-stimulation overcomes the animal's anticipation of food. Just think … with a combination of pleasurable and noxious stimuli, we can control the masses. If every prison in the world had such a mechanism we could end crime."

On the surface, it seemed promising, but I was deeply disturbed about the idea of conditioning people to please authority. In the wrong hands, this science had the potential to become truly dark and terrifying.

Ivanov, the student with the dark-rimmed, owlish glasses, was at a table anaesthetizing a dog with drops of chloroform. I smiled and nodded, but he ignored my gesture and continued working.

When the dog was asleep, Pavlov took a scalpel from a tray of dirty instruments and slashed open the dog's neck. There was none of the practiced grace of a surgeon, but his straightforwardness was effective, and within minutes, he opened the carotid sheath and isolated the vagus nerve.

"Igor, the wires."

With a few shuffling steps, the old man brought the generator and handed Pavlov the wires which he wrapped around the nerve.

I was mystified by the procedure, especially when Ivanov attached a rubber diaphragm to the dog's leg. A tube led to a stylus that moved on a revolving drum of smoked paper. It was a kymograph, a German invention that recorded physiologic observations.

"Start recording," Pavlov ordered.

Ivanov flicked a switch, and the spring loaded drum rotated, while the stylus moved up and down recording the animal's heart beats.

"Igor, turn the crank slowly."

The dog convulsed at the electric shock.

"Igor, you fool. I said turn the crank SLOWLY."

It was cruel. I wanted to scream, but held my tongue and vowed to rescue at least one of these poor creatures from this fate.

The elderly man hunched, and I swear there were tears in his eyes. He turned the crank several slow revolutions. The low current to the nerve slowed the heart rate. It was a brilliant demonstration of how the brain could, through the vagus nerve, control the heart.

"I am determined to unravel the mysteries of the brain and its control over the body," he said. "Igor, have you cleaned the cages?"

Igor stroked his matted beard, mumbled in Russian, picked up his broom and a bucket, and shuffled off to the next room. He had no sooner gone through the door when he emitted a terrible scream of terror and pain.

I immediately rushed to his side. The snakes were out of their cage and Igor had already collapsed into the writhing, hissing nightmare of slithering rattlers.

I seized the broom and struck at a huge rattlesnake coiled around his arm, its head only inches from his face. There were already fang marks on his hand, and the old man's eyes were insane with fear.

I batted at another huge reptile within striking distance of my own leg. I jumped back, but the fangs penetrated my thick woolen trousers. I struck out at the writhing snake again and again, but the blows only made it more viciously determined to sink its needle-like fangs into my flesh.

The old man screamed and howled in pain and fear.

Time stood still as I wildly flailed to keep them off poor Igor while defending myself. I was weakening when Ivanov appeared with the generator. He furiously turned the crank and jammed the wooden stick with bare wires into the mass of snakes. They writhed with increased rage but turned away from Igor and the electricity. They hissed and struck at the wires but retreated to the cages.

"Don't hurt them! The snakes belong to the tsar! If they die, he will have us killed!" Pavlov shouted.

He blew a long blast on his whistle and tossed a box containing live, white mice into the cage. The hissing, coiling mass of snakes, in a fury of blood and snapping jaws, devoured the mice.

I crouched beside old Igor and, with my penknife, slashed double X's across fang marks on his upper arm, then with my lips attempted to draw out the poison. Hot blood gushed into my mouth at first, but soon, the blood flow slowed to a trickle.

It was no use. He stopped breathing, and even as I held my hand over his chest, his heart made its last feeble thump.

"Damn! The old fool. I warned him one hundred times about those snakes and he never listened. Ivanov, find another caretaker without delay," Pavlov said.

The whole experience had left me shaken and deeply upset. I was troubled by Pavlov's cruel experiments and his inhumanity to poor Igor.

"Dr. Pavlov, I have medical duties to attend to. Please excuse me."

"Ivanov, show him out," said Pavlov.

Ivanov walked with me until we stopped in front of a small cage which held a shivering pup. "His mother died during an experiment," Ivanov said.

The pitiable beast was mostly brown but he had an appealing white patch around one of his sad eyes. He wriggled when I lifted him from the cage and hid him under my coat. Ivanov chuckled while we made our way to a dimly-lit worker's café tucked away on a refuse-strewn alley. The place smelled of stale beer and cooking. Ivanov ordered vodka. My nerves settled after I tossed down two glasses.

The pup was content to stay in my arms. He whimpered and shivered until Ivanov shared a bit of sausage and I fed him boiled potatoes.

"My oldest sister lives on a farm. She has room for another dog and will give him a good home," Ivanov said. He improvised a leash with his belt. "Doyle, you are a brave man, risking your life for poor old Igor."

"Anyone would have done the same."

"Pavlov gave Igor the job for food and a place to sleep. For that little bit, Igor loved Pavlov. It was more than most of the landowners give their serfs." Ivanov slammed his fist on the table. "No one cares a shit for the poor in Russia!"

"It is not much different from the way the English treat my Irish cousins," I said.

"Are you interested in justice for the poor?"

I paused, wondering where this would lead. "Of course. But, tell me, please, why is Dr. Pavlov interested in snakes and what do they have to do with the tsar?"

"The tsar is deathly afraid he will bleed to death after an attempted assassination, and there is a bleeding disease that kills infants born to every royal family in Europe. He gave a small fortune to the university to find a cure for bleeding. Pavlov took on the task because he is one of those fools who worship the tsar."

He paused and drained a glass. "Ho there, more vodka." The waiter refilled our glasses.

"Aye, I understand, but why use snakes in the research? They are extraordinarily expensive and extremely dangerous."

"For their venom. You see, he injects a small amount of venom into convicted criminals to cause uncontrolled hemorrhage. Then, he tries to cure the bleeding with blood transfusions from other criminals. It is all part of a grand experiment for the tsar."

Before he continued, a stranger slid into the seat next to Ivanov. "Dobry den," he said, before continuing to speak to him in Russian.

Ivanov responded in Russian.

I had learned enough Russian to understand 'Good afternoon' (*Dobry den*), but I was unable to understand their conversation and wondered why they didn't speak French or German like most students or members of the elite in St. Petersburg.

The newcomer was not old, but a mass of uncut, white hair stuck out from under his soft cap. His beard was flecked with grey, and there were heavy lines around his deep-set, watchful eyes. He spoke and dressed like a typical worker, but all the same, there was something not quite right about him.

"Doyle, meet my friend, Dmitri."

We shook hands. The stranger's rough, callused hand was clearly accustomed to hard work; my doubts about the man faded as I watched him speak with Ivanov. He appeared to be a good-hearted soul.

"Dmitri needs work. I will recommend him to Dr. Pavlov for Igor's job."

I felt left out when Ivanov and the new man continued to converse in Russian and used a dinner date I had with Vera as an excuse to leave. My meeting with Vera did not go well. She seemed distracted and paid little attention to me. After dinner, we walked along the Neva, but Vera barely spoke. Though it could have been a romantic date in the pleasing yellow glow of the fading evening sun, she was cold and distant. It felt, instead, like an evening with a stranger, a distracted stranger. After a chaste, unsatisfactory kiss, she suddenly turned and hurried away.

It was perplexing and disappointing; I went to my room to read about the blood's circulation through the cerebrum, when Dr. Bell banged on the door.

"Ah, Doyle, there you are. Come quickly! An emergency … Bring my medical bag. Professor Sechenov has requested an immediate consultation on one of his private cases. He is already with the patient. The situation is dire."

He seemed to be his old self, and I hoped that he had stopped the cocaine injections.

"Mr. Tatum, hail a cab, this instant!" he shouted.

Tatum was waiting with a hack and off we went at a brisk trot.

"Who is the patient?" I asked.

"Count Michael Ignatov," Bell said.

"He is the interior minister and directs the secret police, the tsar's right hand man." Mr. Tatum said.

The minister's grand house had lights in every window, and the curving driveway was lined with footmen carrying flaming torches. An elegantly dressed young woman, wringing her hands, met us at the door. "Oh, hurry, please hurry! My dear husband is desperately ill."

An agitated footman in full livery led us through the waiting room and up a flight of gilded stairs to a room where Professor Sechenov rocked back and forth on a chair, with his hands to his face. "It is too late. He is dead," Sechenov said, between moans.

The rather corpulent man, dressed in a fine silk dressing gown, was face down on a thick Turkish rug. His hands were stretched towards the casement of a floor-to-ceiling window that overlooked the Neva River.

While Dr. Bell knelt by the dead man, I took in the beautifully-furnished room. A table set up for chess was by the marble-faced fireplace. The ashes were warm. A decanter of port with a single glass stood on a second table. The room was filled with books, trinkets, and souvenirs from far countries. Portraits of men in military uniform looked down from the walls.

From the positions of the ivory and ebony chess pieces, it appeared that play had been in progress. If that was the case, then why was there only one chair at the table, on the white side of the board? The second chair, with a pillow on the seat, was off to one side.

"Except for a touch of gout he was perfectly healthy until this evening, but he had many enemies and feared for his life. He sent a message that he couldn't urinate and felt strange. I arrived within an hour. He was already beyond help," Professor Sechenov said.

Dr. Bell inspected and sniffed the body. It appeared that Ignatov had been struck by a sudden attack of angina or a cerebral fit. When satisfied with his minute inspection, he turned the body onto its back. Ignatov's face was bright red, the eyes were open, and his lips were drawn back, almost in a smile.

"Doyle, can you identify the cause of death?"

"From the color of his face, I should think he had an attack of apoplexy brought on by the excesses of drink and rich food," I said.

"I don't think so. Professor Sechenov, what do you think?" Dr. Bell asked.

"I suspect foul play. It appears that he had a visitor — a chess player, perhaps an agent provocateur – most likely, the killer."

"Nay, I think he was alone at the time of death."

"Why?"

"My dear professor, the white bishop is poised to attack black's f-seven position when the white knight moves to g-five. It is the classic Philidor attack that can be blocked by any novice. The second chair was not for a player, but arranged so the count could place his gouty foot on a pillow. The count was studying moves to overcome the attack and was alone when he died." Bell said.

"No, I respectfully disagree. It is quite possible that a killer entered the room, throttled him, and left unseen. This is a matter for the police," Sechenov said.

"I don't think so; please observe his eyes."

Sechenov looked as Bell had requested. "What about them?" he asked.

"Doyle, your turn to make a diagnosis."

I went down on hands and knees and peered into two deep, black holes. "Sir, the pupils are widely dilated."

"And what does that mean?"

"The stroke affected the optic center in his brain."

"Dammit, Doyle! Don't be such a simpleton! Have you never heard of *belladonna*, from the Italian words for a beautiful woman? At one time, women used eye drops of belladonna to dilate their pupils so they would appear more seductive. Another name for belladonna is 'deadly nightshade,' a potent poison. This is a clear case of death by poison."

"Yes, that's it. I agree. And I would wager that he was poisoned by those damn terrorists. This is a police matter. By God, we must find the culprits before there is another assassination!" Sechenov shouted.

I immediately thought of the medical students. Any one of them could have prepared the poison, but, how could they have administered the drug? The police would think along the same lines and would suspect Vera and her radical friends. Though she had all but ignored me during our date, I did not want to see her imprisoned.

"That is unnecessary. Please refrain from calling the authorities. The police will find nothing," Bell said. "Professor, you said he called for help with urinary retention. That is another symptom of belladonna toxicity and suggests a slow onset, rather than an acute ingestion. In other words, this process has been going on for some time. Doyle, please remove the bandage from his right foot."

As I unrolled the bandage to reveal his swollen, gouty great toe, a sticky, greenish ointment smeared over my hands. Meanwhile, Dr. Bell hunched over the corpse, rubbing his chin while deep in thought. I wondered about his thought processes and gradually felt a slight giddiness, a pounding headache, an increase in heart rate, and my skin was hot.

"Sir, I don't feel so well."

"Doyle, your face has gone bright red. For God's sakes, lad, wipe your hands before the stuff kills you."

I became lightheaded, dizzy, and felt like flying out the window to soar over the Neva. Though he said it could kill me, it was a wonderful sensation. Dr. Bell dragged me away from the window, seized the decanter of Port wine, and with a handkerchief, vigorously wiped the ointment from my hands.

Sometime later, I awoke, stretched on a couch. An attractive house maid dabbed cold water on my face. I was giddy, with blurred eyes. The drug must have affected my moral senses because I lightly caressed her bosom; she giggled and gently kissed my forehead until two footmen carried me away to a carriage.

Later, with Mr. Tatum's assistance, I fell into my own bed. In the morning, I awoke with a headache. Was the episode real or a hallucination?

It was nearly ten o'clock when I made my way to the kitchen. After two cups of strong, sweet Turkish coffee, I felt like myself again.

Dr. Bell greeted me. "Laddie, you had a close call."

"What happened?"

"The ointment contained belladonna, a hellish brew derived from nightshade. It can be a useful remedy in small doses, but deadly poison in higher doses. During the fifteenth century, it was used in an ointment by witches to produce the sensation of flying."

"But, did the count apply the ointment to his own foot?"

"Aye, there were traces of the ointment beneath his fingernails. He was suffering great pain and sent his butler with a note to his apothecary for the strongest pain-relieving medicine possible. The chemist compounded a belladonna ointment with directions to apply no more than a quarter teaspoon to his gouty foot. He foolishly used the whole batch at once."

"Ah, so he accidently killed himself."

"Aye. He made a fatal mistake."

21 August 1881

Recent events have left me with frightening, disorienting flashes of memory. Am I going insane?

I am not even certain of the date, since the Russians use the old Julian calendar that is some twelve days behind our European calculations of time. If it wasn't for Mr. Tatum, I would no longer be keeping this diary for fear the secret police will discover its contents and send us all to prison or worse.

Days after the belladonna episode and my futile attempt to save Old Igor, I went with Dr. Bell to his rounds and lectures. It was at one of these lectures that Vera invited me to attend a student meeting. She asked if I could explain the theories of Darwin to the workers in order to wean them from the Church. Even with my scientific education, I was uncertain, but Tatum made it clear that I should mingle with the students. There might also be an opportunity to be alone with Vera, and I had the wild thought that Penelope might be there.

I hailed a droshky, a two-wheeled cab. The grubby driver understood my poor attempt at Russian when I asked him to take me to the Imperial Library. He beat his tired nag and we went across the Nikolaevsky Bridge, then along the embankment to Nevsky Prospekt. I handed the driver five kopecks, but he wanted more. Money was in short supply, so I gave him another coin.

Vera was waiting by the cab stand in front of the library. I scarcely recognized her. She had cut her lovely, blonde hair until it was scarcely longer than a boy's. She wore a plain, white blouse with a simple, black skirt and clumsy workmen's boots.

"Were you followed?"

"Why would I be followed?"

"They are suspicious of students."

"I'm no longer a student. I am a doctor."

"Feh. That makes no difference."

I was taken aback by the severity of her appearance and behavior. She grabbed my hand, and we took off through winding narrow streets, past babushkas huddled under black shawls against the cool breeze blowing off the Gulf of Finland.

The buildings were old, decrepit, and filthy. There were signs of poverty — dirty children playing in the rubbish, disheveled drunks passed out on the streets, and young girls soliciting soldiers.

It was nearly eleven o'clock when we reached a dingy store on a small backstreet overlooking the Fontanka Canal. Vera murmured a password to a sentry and we went through the store, which was stacked, helter-skelter with dusty books, icons, and pieces of jewelry. In the back room, oil lamps illuminated long tables littered with pamphlets and books.

"This is a reading room for workers and peasants," she explained.

I recognized a few medical students and the leader, Golovinsky, whom I had met at Dostoevsky's flat. This was a far more radical group than the students who met in the café. The men had long hair and wore red shirts, baggy, black pants, and worker's boots. The women, like Vera, wore plain, white blouses, black skirts and rough boots. It was as if they were wearing a uniform. In the dim light, Vera appeared to no longer be a soft, sensuous woman but a hard-line revolutionary.

"Who are all these people? What do they call themselves?" I whispered to her.

" 'Narodnaya Volia' or, in English, 'The People's Will.' "

Ivanov attempted, over the din, to introduce me.

Golovinsky shouted him down. "Bah, have you not read your Marx? The peasants need their religious opium."

"Yes, but if we can teach them about the latest scientific discoveries in England, we can …"

"Nyet! All that is worthless. We can wait no longer. It is time to kill the noble class and do away with another tsar."

He spoke passionately and loudly and quickly had the students and workers in the palm of his hand. All eyes were on him. The room went silent. He shook his fist as he spoke. "Comrades. The secret police are treating the death of Count Ignatov as murder and are rounding up Jews, students, and writers. Everyone in this room is a suspect."

The room erupted into furious shouts. "Kill the tsar! Down with tyranny of the so-called nobility! Wipe them out!" Vera translated for me. Even though I didn't understand the Russian words, I felt the passion of his speech.

"Please, silence! Listen to me!" Golovinsky shouted.

The hubbub died out, but there was a muffled scream from outside and the distinctive pop of a pistol shot.

For a moment, there was absolute silence, and then, officers in sky blue uniforms stormed through the bookshop and burst through the door to the reading room. Golovinsky drew a pistol and fired three times.

Blood spurted from the chest of an officer, but more police rushed into the room. I stared straight into the face of a furious officer who slashed at my head with a huge cavalry saber.

Vera grabbed my shirt and dragged me to the floor just as the huge curved blade swished through the air above me and sank into the neck of a surprised, red-shirted worker standing behind me. The saber cleanly severed his head with its little goat's beard. The decapitated head flew through mid-air as the poor fellow's body remained upright for a moment. Blood spurted from his carotid arteries, spraying the room and splattering on my face. For an instant, I wondered if the brain in the severed head understood what had happened.

The saber-wielding policemen drew his sword back for another slash. The next killing blow would have severed my head. That is, until Golovinsky hurled an oil lamp that broke on the door casing. Flames enveloped the secret police officers while two students overturned a table blocking the room against another assault.

The fire spread from the officers to the walls and books, and the room filled with oily, black smoke. I was stunned, but Vera dragged me out the back door in the midst of escaping students.

We fled through darkened streets to a clump of bushes by the canal. There were flashes of gunfire, and red-coated Cossacks raced from the Admiralty down Voznesensky Prospekt towards the flaming building. We were lucky we escaped alive.

"Hold me," Vera said. "Please."

I enveloped her in a crushing embrace. She opened her mouth and we lashed one another with wet tongues. The intensity and aliveness of our momentary lust helped dissolve some of the fear and anxiety. She pulled away and we crept along dim paths, avoiding the streets lit with gas lamps. We headed north until we came to the massive columns of St. Isaac's Cathedral and huddled in the black darkness while the tumult in the streets continued.

"We aren't safe here. Shall we go to your room?" I asked.

She shook her head, wrenched free, and hurried away in the darkness. "Vera, wait. I didn't mean to …"

She didn't look back. I trembled and broke into a cold sweat. My heart thumped wildly. The streets were alive with armed soldiers and mounted police. I huddled in the shadows, too frightened to leave the comforting dark confines of the cathedral.

When, at last, the shouts and gunfire died away, I made for the Nikolaevsky Bridge and, keeping to darkened pathways, reached Professor Sechenov's home. In the grey light of a false dawn, I quietly went up the back stairs and, after a pause, knocked gently on Mr. Tatum's door. I had to confide in a trusted friend. Dr. Bell, for the past several days, was either lost in his own cocaine-induced dreams or was extraordinarily active.

I was still shivering when Mr. Tatum opened the door.

"It is rather early for a social call," he said.

I fell, rather than sat, on a stuffed leather chair, trembling with nervous exhaustion. I uttered a low groan mixed with a sigh. "It appears a bit of restorative is in order," Tatum said.

And aye, he was right. I felt much better after a tot of whiskey.

"So … What happened? What's wrong?" Tatum asked.

"I am in danger and must leave the country," I said.

"Tell me everything."

I related my adventure with the students and the police raid. "The policeman who tried to kill me had a long nose, thin lips, and sandy-colored hair swept back from a high forehead. He will remember me just as clearly. It is not safe for me to walk the streets of St. Petersburg."

"Mr. Doyle, please just listen. They will not harm you."

"No, I must go home immediately."

"Actually, Mr. Doyle, you must stay and help us. Great things are afoot since I delivered the message intended for Lord Asquith to the British ambassador."

"You delivered the message? What about Penelope? I thought she would go to the ambassador."

Tatum ignored my question. "The Government and our Queen are determined to protect the tsar at all costs. In the future, Russia must be a counterweight to the growing power of Germany. There are elements, within and without Russia, who want nothing less than the death of Alexander III. You could be instrumental in keeping him alive."

"That is a matter for the Secret Service and military," I replied. "Not for me."

"It is your duty as a citizen of our realm to continue meeting with the student groups and report everything you learn about the anarchists to me. We particularly must learn the whereabouts of Captain David Campbell, the officer who was tortured in Afghanistan."

"With my Uncle Declan?"

"Yes."

"I don't know the first place to look. Have you contacted Penelope? Where is she? She would certainly know more about Captain Campbell than I."

Mr. Tatum looked away.

"You must know her whereabouts."

"Well, let us just say that Miss Walshingham is a capable young lady and I trust that she needs no help."

"Was she kidnapped?"

Mr. Tatum stroked his chin, and the expression on his face hardened into a scowl. "She went away of her own free will. Now, mind you, Mr. Doyle, the ambassador insists that you keep a detailed record of your activities with the students and Dr. Bell requests your company on student rounds this morning."

"Yes, I keep a diary to record everything."

"Good."

I tried to argue with Tatum, but he would not listen. I gave up, made my way to my room, and slept fitfully for about an hour, haunted by visions of the bloody saber.

At breakfast, Dr. Bell stared at his egg with a bloodshot eye. "Good morning, sir," I said.

His hand shook as he cracked the egg, which splattered over the table. "Damn," he said. Dr. Bell was silent, morose, and hollow-eyed, certainly the results of his cocaine injections. He rose from the table and, with a curt, "Bring the instrument case," took up his hat and went to the waiting carriage. I barely had time to finish my slice of buttered black bread as I ran to catch up.

"We will meet Dr. Gerchakov at the municipal hospital for student rounds," he said, once we were in the carriage. I remembered him, the great bear of a man who had attended the clinics in Edinburgh. As we grew nearer to the hospital, Bell took a small pinch of white powder from a silver snuff box and applied it to his nostril.

Within a few minutes, his spirits lifted and, except for a slight tremor, he seemed to be his old self — or maybe a more frenetic, energetic version of himself.

The city hospital was a sprawling, dark, stone building with long wards filled with the dregs of St. Petersburg. Sick and dying patients were on cots lined against the wall with scarcely any space between. I was accustomed to the astringent smell of carbolic in the Edinburgh Infirmary, but this place smelled of human excrement, pus, and boiled cabbage. Professor Gerchakov met us with two dozen students, including Ivanov and several of the radical students. I searched for Vera but she was not among the students. I felt a pang of remorse. Had the police caught her?

Dr. Bell briskly asked for their names and assigned a patient to each student. This was a standard bedside teaching routine in Edinburgh. These students were not accustomed to our methods, but under Dr. Bell's guidance, they quickly learned to palpate for tumors, auscultate the heart and lungs, and examine the head and neck. When they finished their examinations, Bell, with sparkling eyes and his usual good humor, quizzed each student in turn.

For example, Bell felt the pulse and took in the gasping respirations and blue lips of an elderly man who sat straight up in bed. "Well, Mr. Khartsov, what do you make of this poor fellow?"

"It is a case of pneumonia."

"Excellent, I completely agree."

We went from one patient to another, with Bell questioning each student. He gently pointed out their errors of diagnosis with a smile and sometimes a joke. The Russian students took his criticism with more good nature than his Edinburgh students.

There was a child with a twisted leg as the result of a poorly set fractured femur, several old men with heart failure or pneumonia, and a young woman with bulging eyes and a goiter. Bell was in his element, but the cocaine seemed to have possession of him. He was more agitated than usual but appeared to be in good spirits.

Midway through the ward, we came to a drowsy, middle-aged man with long, unkempt, black hair swept back from his forehead, a short beard, and a long mustache. His head drooped down to his chest, and his purplish-red nose was covered with broken veins. One side of his face was slightly flattened. Both his hands rested on a dirty quilt that covered his legs.

An alert, quiet lad with wide, deeply-set, brown eyes — perhaps ten or twelve years of age and wearing a dirty smock belted at the waist — sat on an old army coat folded into a crude pallet at his bedside. As we approached the bed, he offered a glass of water to the patient's trembling lips; most of the water spilled on the quilt. All the while, the boy never spoke and there was a strange calmness about him.

"Von Diebitsch, what do you make of this fellow?"

Unlike most students who wore dark uniforms with high collars, Von Diebitsch was dressed in a double-breasted jacket, a vest, fawn-colored trousers, and a wide, purple ascot tie. To complete the picture of a foppish nobleman, he had pomaded hair. He smirked and attempted a military bearing. "You will address me as <u>Baron</u> von Diebitsch."

"Well, <u>Baron</u> von Diebitsch, can you give us a diagnosis for this fellow?"

"He is human rubbish — a bum, an alcoholic, and certainly not worth my time."

"Sir, that is a horrible attitude for a budding physician."

Dr. Bell turned to Ivanov. "Ask the little boy about the patient."

Ivanov questioned the boy in Russian. "A week ago, the man was unconscious, on the steps in front of the Mariinsky Theatre. He has barely recovered consciousness."

Dr. Bell, with his hand on his chin, shifted his eyes from the patient's face to his tattered shirt, then fixed on his hands. He examined first one hand, and then the other; Bell's fingers trembled, but his face lit up with one of his 'aha' moments.

"Now, Baron von Diebitsch, look at these hands. Do you still think he is a bum?"

Von Diebitsch adjusted his pince-nez and barely leaned forward. "I see nothing that would lead me to change my opinion."

Bell gave the man a withering glance, and then, his gaze swept over the students. "It is essential to observe every detail of every patient if you expect to make a proper diagnosis."

He lifted the patient's hands from the bed. "Look here. The nails are clean and well-trimmed. The hand is flexible, the skin is soft, and the abductor pollicis brevis that moves the thumb laterally is well-developed. Likewise, in the hypothenar eminence, the flexor digiti minimi and the opponens digiti minimi that control the fifth finger are all hypertrophied. Gentlemen, these are the hands of a musician. I would wager that this man was an accomplished pianist."

The students crowded forward, eager and completely captivated by the professor. He stood back, lit his long curved pipe, and waited a moment before speaking. "Dr. Doyle, if you please, conduct a neurologic examination."

The boy sat as still as a Buddha on the ragged army coat, while I, with reflex hammer, pin, and tuning fork, tested the patient who gave no response to my questions. His left arm and leg were weak, and the reflexes on that side were nearly absent. I then noticed the dilated pupil in his right eye.

"His left side is weak, and the right pupil is dilated as if he had a lesion in his brain," I said.

"Please, make a more specific diagnosis," Bell asked.

"A tumor or a blood clot," I replied.

Bell commenced a minute examination of the man's scalp. He brushed back the long hair and probed with his fingers. He drew himself erect and faced the students, but spoke directly to Von Diebitsch. "As Dr. Doyle mentioned, there is a slight hematoma over his right ear. Gentlemen, this patient has suffered a blow to his head, perhaps when he fell on the steps of the Mariinsky Theatre. He undoubtedly has a blood clot pressing on his brain."

I felt a glow of triumph at making a good diagnosis, but Baron von Diebitsch gave me a look of pure malevolence and bent close to my ear. "You and your damned professor will not publicly ridicule me. I know where you go at night and the filthy company you keep. Watch your step and your mouth, Doyle, or you might find yourself on the wrong end of an Okhrana sword."

My blood turned to ice. How did he know? Was there an informer among his fellow students? I again thought of the officer with the saber. He would surely recognize me again.

In the midst of these black ruminations, Dr. Bell demanded attention. "This man needs an immediate operation. Dr. Gerkachov, can you arrange the operating theater?"

"I am sorry, but I am due at my private clinic within an hour, and no other surgeon is available. So, an operation is quite impossible at this time."

"But this man requires immediate surgery to remove a blood clot on his brain."

"Yes, I agree. And you can demonstrate your technique," Gerkachov replied. "But as I've said, I can't assist."

"I, um, well, let's see …" For the first time, I noticed Dr. Bell was perspiring and had gone slightly pale. He made no reply. There was a coarse tremor in both his hands. I had never seen him hesitate at an opportunity to operate. Surgery was the love of his life. It was the damn cocaine. He must have realized that the drug has affected his surgical skills. This was the jolt he needed to overcome his dependence and quit using the rancid stuff.

"Of course, Dr. Bell and I will be happy to operate," I said, on impulse.

Bell shot me a sharp glance as Gerkachov embraced Dr. Bell with an enthusiastic bear hug. "Capital, capital. I shall send for my anaesthetist. I might be able to watch you open him up and then, regrettably, I must go."

The operating room was dingy and poorly-equipped with enamel pans, bottles of antiseptics, and a stack of greyish towels. Light poured in from an enormous skylight and there were a few gas lamps. Tiers of seats for students rose from the floor to near the ceiling. Eager students placed the nearly-unconscious patient on a white, painted, wooden table in the middle of the room while I soaked the instruments in a solution of carbolic.

The anaesthetist — a bustling, young, bespectacled man — arrived with his bottles of chloroform and a gauze-covered cone. Dr. Bell positioned the patient with his head turned to the left and indicated that I should shave the side of his head with a straight razor. That done, I scrubbed the area with carbolic.

Dr. Bell's forehead glistened with sweat, and his hand shook as he selected a scalpel from the instrument table. He hesitated, and at one point, I thought he might throw down the knife and leave the room.

Instead, with great fortitude, he applied the scalpel to the skin and made a curving incision above and forward of the ear. Not a word was spoken as he turned back the flap of skin, selected a drill, and bored holes in the skull. His head dropped until his chin nearly rested on his chest, and he took several long deep breaths.

When he was steadier, he picked up a chisel and connected the holes. The operation had lasted nearly an hour, since it was not possible to hurry for fear of drilling into the brain. The diagnosis was correct; a purple blood clot bulged against the dura mater, the tough membrane that surrounds the brain.

The students crowded closer to get a better look. Meanwhile, I held my breath for fear of what might come next. A cut in the wrong place could be fatal. With unerring skill, Bell made a perfect incision and swept the clot out with his finger.

It should have been a triumphal moment, but with a choking voice, Bell turned to me. "Doyle, I am not well. Please finish. Excuse me."

Dr. Bell walked away as took his place. I had sutured a bit of skin in the emergency ward, but I had never been responsible for closing a major incision, much less one close to the brain. If the dura mater was not closed, water tight, spinal fluid would leak and eventually become infected. I threaded the finest silk sutures on small needles and set to the job.

This man's life rested in my hands and I was horribly worried that my inexperience would lead to his death, but alas, I had no choice and carried on.

It's not like I didn't know what to do. I did. It was just that I had never done it before, and one false move, one tiny little slip, and I'd surely kill him. So, I tried not to falter.

First, I sutured the dura with closely-placed stitches, then replaced the bone, and finally, closed the skin. If the operation was a success, the patient should show definite signs of re-awakening when the chloroform was stopped.

To my horror, blood oozed from the wound; first, there was one drop at the site of a suture, then more, until there was a steady flow of blood. I feared that I had failed and doomed this man to an unnecessary death.

I pressed as hard as possible, hoping to staunch the flow, but each time I released the pressure, there was more blood. It seemed impossible that a major vessel was pumping blood. It appeared to be a general ooze from the entire incision. I had made no mistakes, had done everything properly. I just couldn't stop the bleeding. Was it me, or did this man suffer from a bleeding disease?

Dr. Bell, reclined on a chair outside the operating room. He was of no help. For the first time since the surgery began, I noticed the ragged little boy sitting in a corner of the operating room, hugging his knees and swaying from side to side.

I gave up my feeble attempts to control the oozing blood and we moved the patient to his bed. The ragged little boy came to him, whispered in his ear, and stroked his face. The bleeding continued, drop by terrible drop, until the bandages and then the bed sheets were soaked with blood.

The patient moved his hands, flexed his fingers, and opened his eyes. These were wonderful signs of recovery. It should have been a triumphal moment, except for the terrible, unrelenting bleeding.

I had an inspiration. "Send for Dr. Pavlov. Tell him we need his blood-clotting plasma!" I shouted. We continued the bedside vigil.

Over the next ten minutes, the pulse, which had been slow and strong, was now growing faster and weaker. I looked in vain for Dr. Bell, but he had left. I needed Pavlov and his plasma, but his laboratory was far away. All seemed lost.

The Baron spoke with an air of triumph. "Bah. He will be dead soon. Look what you've done. I've had enough of you and your arrogant Dr. Bell." He stormed off with most of the students.

He was right and now I was alone — well, except for Ivanov and the silent child. My patient only had a few more moments to live. I had surely killed him.

But then, the little boy, the strangely calm little boy with the deeply set eyes, reached out to the patient. The blood continued to trickle from the bandage, seemingly unabated, while the boy, now with his eyes tightly clenched, took the man's hands.

He stroked them gently and seemed to enter a trance state. There was an intensity which one rarely sees in children and, I will swear, there was an aura of light about his face. The boy muttered a prayer. At that very moment, the trickle of blood stopped. The pulse under my fingers grew stronger and definitely slower.

Somehow, the boy had staunched the flow of blood and saved the man by sheer psychic force. I am a man of science, but I will swear on a bible that something supernatural happened in that moment. The magical little boy used his psychic powers to clot my patient's blood.

I turned to Ivanov. "The boy is a miracle worker."

"Da."

"What is his name?"

"Grigori, Grigori Rasputin," Ivanov replied.

Suddenly, there was a commotion at the end of the ward. Pavlov rushed to the bedside with a syringe filled with a yellow fluid. "Plasma," he said. He plunged the needle into a vein at the patient's elbow and pushed the plunger. "There, now we shall see."
The patient's color and heart rate improved. Pavlov believed that he had saved him, but I knew better. It was the boy. Definitely the boy. If not for the boy, he would've been dead before Pavlov even arrived...

"Thank you, laddie. Thank you... Can you tell me the patient's name?" I asked.

The boy looked up in surprise and said a few words. Even in the Russian, I made out the name. "Modest Petrovich Mussorgsky."

23 August 1881

I was tired and tense with worry today over Dr. Bell and my involvement with the radical students. So, it was a lovely surprise when an old university chum, Dick Ferguson, sent me an invite for dinner. Dicky wasn't in the medical program, but was an engineering student. We played on the same rugby team and had downed many a pint after an afternoon on the field.

It was an easy walk across the bridge over the Neva to his comfortable rooms on the English Embankment. He greeted me warmly and invited me into his library. My old friend wore a finely-tailored tweed suit, a silk tie, and his elegant shoes were polished to a high gloss. When I was seated in a padded chair, with my feet stretched out on an ottoman, Dick poured me a tot of fine single malt whiskey. The aroma of heather made me a bit homesick. Only a few weeks ago, I was excited to get out of Scotland, and now, my heart ached to return.

"Dick, you appear to be prospering in St. Petersburg, while I'm still wondering what to do with my life."

Dick laughed. "It was a pure stroke of good luck. I landed a job with a Glasgow firm that is building an electrical system. Soon, all the aristocrats will have Edison lights in their homes and the street trams will run on electricity."

I told Dick of our adventures on the ship and Dr. Bell's extraordinary powers. I then mentioned the meeting of the students.

"Oh, laddie, stay away from those bastards or you'll wind up rotting away your life in a cell. They are hoodlums and anarchists, intent on killing the tsar and all the nobles," he warned.

"Is it as bad as all that?" I asked.

"Ever since the radicals murdered Alexander II, his son, Alexander III is deathly afraid of assassination. The city is practically under martial law. He has established a new secret police force, the Okhrana. The government is sending students, anarchists, and Jews to prison every day. St. Petersburg has become an unfriendly and dangerous place. But enough of that, let's go to dinner and drink some good Russian vodka."

It was one of those eternal, lovely St. Petersburg nights, so we trotted along the embankment to Nevsky Prospekt and the Grand Hotel Europe. It was nine o'clock in the evening, but a warm sun lit up the street so it felt like a midday stroll. We walked through the grand lobby and into the entrance to the gilded dining room. A uniformed waiter bowed and led us to a table in this most sumptuous of surroundings.

Dicky spoke enough Russian to order beef in sour cream and then salmon and rice with hard boiled eggs, which was followed with a dish of herring layered with grated boiled potatoes, carrots, beets, and onions. I stuffed myself with the luscious dishes and savored every bite. It wasn't until we finished lemon pie and coffee and were sipping brandy that I asked about the tsar. "Maybe I'm naïve, but please tell me. Why do you think so many people hate the tsar?"

Dicky wiped his mouth and cleared his throat. "His father was a liberal who had, in fact, signed documents granting more freedom to the people just before they killed him. Unfortunately, since his death, his son has grown fearful and, as a result, repealed his father's proclamations and keeps the status quo through fear and violence. The new tsar is in virtual seclusion for fear of assassination. He is not a bad sort, from what I hear, but is an autocrat who thinks Russia must be ruled with an iron hand. Aye, the intelligentsia wants democracy, but they won't get it from this tsar."

We talked about politics late into the night when I bid Dicky farewell and made my way back to my room.

3 September 1881

Though I am writing the following entry after the events took place, and my memory may be a tad faulty, I will set down the events to the best of my ability.

I was still thinking about my conversation with Dicky, when, the next morning, just before a lecture, Vera dashed into the hall and, without so much as a "Good morning," took my arm. "Come immediately! We need your help."

Her hair and clothing were more disheveled than usual, and there were deep worry lines around her eyes.

She led me across the university square to a maze of streets that led to a poor residential area on the industrial side of Vasilyevsky Island. She knocked softly on a wooden door until an aged housekeeper let us in to a weed-choked courtyard. Vera crossed to another door, which led to a corridor and to still another door.

I followed her. Golovinsky came out of the shadows with an angry grimace. "Why isn't he blindfolded?" he asked.

"I trust him," Vera said.

He shook his head angrily. "Nyet! You are too soft!" He roughly grabbed my right hand and twisted it behind my back. "Why must I do everything myself?"

"Damn you, fool! Don't break my arm!" I shouted.

"Then don't fight me." He twisted even harder. There was a mad quality to his voice and his eyes radiated the fury of an enraged fanatic. I wilted and made no resistance when he tied a dark rag over my eyes. The door creaked open and he led us outdoors.

I struggled to keep up, but each time I faltered, he yanked my arm. Suddenly, my mind cleared and I remembered Dr. Bell's oft-given advice to use all your senses.

We had made a left turn out of the door and walked on squishy mud. I tried to count the seconds, but lost track after four minutes. We turned left again into another street or alley.

A door opened and there was raucous laughter; a tavern, I thought. I could still hear the tavern when we stopped and Vera tapped softly on a door. By turning my head a bit, I could peek under the mask and had a fleeting glimpse of a narrow alley and an unpainted, wooden building.

Golovinsky pushed me into a room that smelled of cooking and down another flight of stairs. I was nearly overcome by the powerful, acrid odor of burning chemicals. Golovinsky jerked the mask away from my eyes. I was in a laboratory.

The acrid chemical odor was from large flasks of liquids boiling over Bunsen burners. There were benches, retorts, and other chemical apparatus; all tended by two young men with singed eyebrows and an older woman.

Vera led me to an adjoining room where the remains of a loaf of bread, a cut of cold meat, and a bottle of brandy were on a table next to an oil lamp. I first heard their piteous moans, then, when my eyes accommodated to the light, I could see three poor souls huddled on cots with their faces and hands swathed in dirty rags.

"What happened?" I asked.

"There was an explosion," Vera said.

"Gunpowder?"

"No. It was a chemical explosion. Fulminate of mercury."

"Great God, it is a wonder anyone is alive!" I recalled that fulminate of mercury is made by adding mercury to nitric acid and used as a detonator for explosives. If there was more of the stuff, the entire building could go up in smoke.

"What do you want with me?"

"You are a doctor. Take care of these people."

There was no way to run, and this could be another challenge to my budding surgical skills. Golovinsky had settled into a chair, swigged from the bottle of brandy, and gestured with a revolver.

"English Doctor, if you wish to live, save our comrades."

My anger at the abduction was overcome with pity for these poor wretches.

"I will help," Vera said. She set about removing the bandage from the face of a young man with a horrible injury. His skin was seared to a crisp, and a there was a deep gash from his forehead to the corner of his mouth. Shards of glass were embedded in his neck, face, and forehead. Worst of all, a thick fluid dripped from his left eye where a shard of glass had penetrated the cornea.

"This man should be in a hospital. He needs expert care from an ophthalmic surgeon or he will lose both eyes. I can do nothing for him. Maybe Dr. Bell could ..."

"No, we have no choice. You must do it. Make a list of medicines and instruments," Vera said.

"We need everything — morphine, antiseptics, chloroform, bandages, sutures, surgical forceps, and, most of all, a bright light," I said.

Vera sent a pale, sallow youth to fetch the supplies. I rolled up my sleeves and went to work with soap and water to sponge away the worst of the dirt and soot from the burns and deep lacerations. The flesh was blown away from the thumb and index fingers of the man with the horribly injured face.

Both hands of another poor fellow were mangled with exposed bone where there should have been fingers and a thumb. I had been at work on the two men for perhaps twenty minutes, when I became aware of a soft whimpering moan from the furthest, dimmest corner of the room. "Bolli, oh, boll, bolli, oh."

"Bring the lamp," I said.

The moaning, young woman was lying on a pile of rags. Her eyes were closed, her face was deathly pale, and her hair was softly braided in the Polish style. Any man could fall desperately in love with her delicate nose and softly-curving lips. She seemed to offer a bit of peace and sanity in this awful setting. I thought she was untouched by the explosion until I saw the long, tapering shard of glass, like a dagger, protruding from her chest, just beneath the left breast.

I instinctively reached to pull it out but drew back. The glass quivered with each heartbeat. In absolute horror, I realized the point had to be embedded in the heart muscle; its removal would cause an immediate fatal hemorrhage.

"Great God! What is the point of this insanity? Are you totally mad? How can you allow such injuries to occur?"

"You are so British. So foolish. So naïve." Vera had steel in her voice. "A few lives don't matter. Hundreds have already died for the cause. We must destroy the tsar and the nobles to free all of Russia. If hundreds more die, it will be well worth it."

I was a trained doctor but with no surgical experience to help these poor wretches. When the supplies arrived, I set to work doing the best that I could. There was enough morphine, chloroform, and carbolic, but the instruments were old and crude. I gave a double dose of morphine to the poor girl and wished I could do more.

Vera gave chloroform to the men while I cleaned the wounds, removed broken glass, and sutured the deep lacerations with a plain sewing needle and cotton thread.

It took hours to remove the dead tissue and shattered bone from victim's hands and to preserve bits of fingers for a serviceable hand. Meanwhile, the poor girl with the lacerated heart gave one last sigh and died while I was at work on the men. At last, I sank into a chair, drained the last of the brandy and, overcome by fatigue and chloroform fumes, passed out.

When I awoke some hours later, Vera was gone, but my foggy mind registered a strange sight. A grey-haired man, with a jeweler's magnifying loop screwed into his right eye, worked at a treadle that turned a small, circular saw.

Incredibly, he held an egg cradled in his hand. There was a gently whirring sound as he held the egg against the saw, cut away the top, drained its contents into a bowl, and took up a second egg.

He raised his head and shouted at the door. "Comin sie hier, bitte!"

Suddenly, the two young men with seared eyelashes and Golovinsky, carrying a beaker of thick greenish liquid, stepped on tip-toe into the room.

"The nitro is ready," one of them said.

I shrank back away from the madness while Golovinsky, with great care, poured the liquid nitroglycerin into an open egg, which was nestled in a small, straw-filled basket. He deliberately placed the beaker on the table and then, with infinite care, replaced the sawed-off bit of eggshell and sealed it with melted candle wax.

"There, that will be a nice treat for the tsar," he said.

One of my patients, the fellow with mangled hands, raised himself. "We did our job. Now, how will you do yours?" he asked, through clenched teeth.

"It will not be difficult. The tsar pretends to be a man of the people. He prepares his own breakfast, coffee, black bread, and boiled egg. He is in for a deadly surprise."

"Yes, but how will you deliver it?"

"The English woman will do it."

"When?"

"Tomorrow morning."

Who was the 'English woman'? Had they recruited Penelope? My thoughts whirled, but it became clear; she had been devoted to my uncle and David Campbell. Both men had been captured, tortured, and left to die by the Russians in Afghanistan. She had every reason to hate the tsar, but would she turn against England and the Queen?

If she succeeded and it became known that an English woman was responsible for the death of the tsar, there would be an international catastrophe or a great world war. I had to stop her. I had to escape.

Golovinsky left the room with the egg, which was carefully packed in straw. In the distance, I heard his heavy tread on the stairway and, then, only an occasional murmur and the clink of glassware next door. Surely those people had orders to prevent me from leaving.

I knew I couldn't idly wait. I had to create an opportunity to escape.

My only weapon was a small pen knife, but most anarchists carried knives or a pistol. I went to the dead girl who I thought might have a weapon. She was already cold and stiff with early rigor mortis. I went through her clothing, pocket by pocket. At first, I found nothing. Then, I felt a hard lump — a holster strapped on the outside of her thigh held a small, nickel-plated revolver loaded with five brass cartridges.

I blew out the oil lamp and, with infinite care, opened the door into the laboratory. Golovinsky had spoken in German, and many of our medical textbooks were in German, so I had a decent proficiency in the language. With great bravado, I waved the pistol and shouted in German. "Don't move! Hold your hands up!"

"Nein!" growled a large, blonde fellow as he balled a fist. He backed down at the sight of the pistol for a moment, then, with a deep, low growl, hurled himself across the room. I stepped aside and accidentally bumped against a bench covered with flasks and burners.

"Watch out, you idiot! That's nitroglycerine!" the second man screamed.

The bench tilted, and a thick, green liquid in an open flask sloshed with a small wave against the glass. The big man gasped and froze. I gently took up the flask and, again, spoke in German. "If you move, I will blow us to kingdom come. Into the other room — both of you. Now."

They gave up and, with great care, went to the next room. There was only a flimsy lock on the door. I gently placed the flask of nitroglycerine on the floor against the door. "Open the door and the nitro explodes. Don't follow me," I said.

A few moments later, I was on the dark and empty street. I turned to the left but remembered that, on returning, the direction should be the opposite of the way we came. My impulse was to run, but I walked at a normal pace to avoid attracting attention. There were a few drunks in the tavern, but the streets were empty.

I recognized the muddy street and soon came to the Neva River. The English Church was on the other side. I ducked in the shadows as a squad of police cantered across the bridge headed in the direction of Professor Sechenov's house. Were they searching for me? Going home might be risky, so I turned away and kept to the river bank in the other direction.

Dicky Ferguson's rooms were only a short distance across the river. I slipped from shadow to shadow and finally reached his quarters. My old friend listened to my tale of woe. He pulled a long, unhappy face. "Go straight to the police, Doyle."

"No, no, they'll surely put me in prison, and if the English woman is Penelope, it's curtains for her. Think what a black eye that would be for England. I must stop her. Please, my friend, you must help. Send for Mr. Tatum, our valet, at once."

Ferguson saw my point as much to protect the Crown as me. "The tsar is at the Gatchina Palace, nearly forty miles away. There is no time."

"We must try," I said.

"My chaise is fast, but I don't know," he said.

"We have no choice." By the time Tatum arrived, I had cleaned most of the blood and soot from my clothing and, after a cup of tea, felt much better. It was, however, nearly midnight. There was little time, but Ferguson had called out his driver, and with two fresh horses, we were on our way in his light, two-wheeled chaise.

Mr. Tatum gave the driver a handful of coins. "There will be more if we reach the palace before dawn."

The driver took up the challenge and applied the whip with good will. The horses strained at their traces, and off we went at a gallop towards the palace.

There was light in the east when the parapets of Gatchina palace came into view. The horses were flagging, and we were within a mile or so from the moat that surrounded the parade ground when the right-hand horse threw a shoe.

I was all for going ahead, alone on the one horse, but Mr. Tatum sighed. "Sorry, it's already within a few minutes of six-thirty." He had scarcely finished speaking when a terrific explosion shook the earth. Smoke and debris rose in a great cloud.

"We had best get away as quickly as possible," he said.

We had no sooner turned back, with the one horse in the traces and the other limping behind, when a troop of red-coated Cossacks raced by, standing in their stirrups, lances at the ready. Within a few minutes, a dozen blue-uniformed police drew up and surrounded our open chaise.

They would have shot us on the spot had not Mr. Tatum showed his papers to an officer and explained that we were merely eccentric Englishmen out for an early morning sightseeing trip. All seemed well until they found the revolver in my coat pocket. I had forgotten the weapon. It was damn foolish of me. The officers manacled my hands and threw me onto a wagon with other prisoners.

115

Two hours later, I was in Fontanka 16, headquarters for the secret police, which was overflowing with suspects who pushed against the officers and screamed their innocence. At first, the genial interrogator accepted my excuse for having the revolver for self-protection against the anarchists. It was all just a big misunderstanding . . .

I was surely in the clear, especially when Tatum arrived with the British consul, an affable fellow with nicotine-stained hands. They persuaded the police to set me free and remove my manacles.

As we left the secret police's headquarters, there was a shout. "Don't let him go! That man is a student anarchist!" It was the sandy-haired, saber-swinging policeman. The game was up. They pulled me away from Tatum and shackled my hands. Soldiers with bayonets jabbed and pushed me into a black carriage with dazed students and workers.

As the carriage bounced down the street, crowds of people shouted and danced with joy.

"What are they saying?" I asked a fellow student.

"The tsar lives! God saved the tsar!" The student slumped against my shoulder and sobbed. "The stupid people of St. Petersburg are filled with joy that their beloved tsar still lives."

The carriage jostled over cobblestones until it arrived at the Yoannovsky gate of a gloomy and dark fortress. "Where are we?" I asked.

"The St. Peter and Paul Prison," the student said. "No one has ever escaped from this rotten place."

(Though my hand is shaking as I write, and I dread revisiting the horror of this last week, I know it is important to put it in writing. I shall, therefore, try my best to recount it and then forget as much about it as I can, if that is at all possible. I was not allowed pen or paper during my incarceration inside the St. Peter and Paul Prison, hence the gap in dates of this diary. My memory is still clouded by lack of sleep and I still feel the mental turmoil of being inside such a hell-hole, almost as if I were still there.)

When we arrived at the prison, soldiers with fixed bayonets herded the twenty or so of us out of the carriages, across an open courtyard, and down stone steps to a subterranean cell furnished with piles of moldy straw and a bucket overflowing with excrement. There was barely room to stand, let alone sit or lie down. The terrible odor added to our general misery and sense of hopelessness.

Once the soldiers left, the prisoners traded stories about their capture by the secret police. My fellow sufferers were mostly social activists whom the authorities had rounded up on the basis of reports by spies. It was a mixed group. There were students, Jews, and workers, as well as posh, upper-class men and women who had expressed sympathy for the dissidents or antipathy to the tsar.

There were many rumors milling about, but the only certainty was that the tsar had escaped an assassination. After less than an hour of confinement, the cell door clanged open. Two guards seized a victim at random, a boy of scarcely twenty years, for interrogation. The *thwack* of truncheons against flesh, the *crack* of a broken bone, and the howls and screams of the victim commenced immediately and went on for half an hour or more.

The same guards dragged him back, threw him into the cell, and selected another suspect. This went on for most of the afternoon. Two prisoners did not return. The rest were bleeding from their nose and mouth and suffered excruciating pain from dislocated fingers or broken bones. Each time the guards returned, every prisoner was frightened that they would be next. We suffered from fear of being picked, as well as the guilt of not being picked and remaining uninjured.

As a physician, there was little I could do but offer sympathy and soothing words. The police became more and more enraged and cruel when they learned nothing from us suspected regicides. I was at the side of one poor soul, attempting to straighten his broken arm, when a man knelt at my side. "It's no use, Doctor, we are all doomed," he said, in English.

"They cannot be so confounded inhumane. Why does the tsar allow the police to mistreat his subjects so?" I asked.

"It is the tragedy of Russia. In this terrible prison, Peter the Great strangled his own son, and Catherine buried her enemies alive. The best you can hope for is sudden death; the alternative is to slowly die by torture or to lose your mind in a lonely cell."

He spit as he spoke and glared at me with piggish eyes. "A guard called my name. I steeled myself for torture and resolved to reveal nothing of my involvement with the student group or the bomb makers. Two officers led me to a small, plain room on the ground floor where a civilian, or at least an officer in plain clothes, offered a glass of tea. I lifted the glass with trembling hands, and as I drank, the officer began to speak. "The British ambassador spoke with Prince Vladimir and demanded your immediate release."

My heart leaped with joy and I put down my tea.

"Thank you. Thank you."

"Not so fast, Dr. Doyle..." Instead of removing my manacles, he folded his hands and smiled. "We would normally comply with the wishes of the Prince. However, since the case involves a plot against the tsar, it would be unwise to let you go without further investigation."

"And so how long might that take? A few more hours?"

"Maybe... But maybe days... Months... or even years."

"That is completely unjust!" I shouted. "I have done nothing to deserve a long prison term!"

"Dr. Doyle, you're in serious trouble. We have more than enough evidence to hang you, but since we, like you British, are a civilized people, we will not keep you in the usual pigsty, but will place you in a more — shall we say, pleasant — cell."

Two guards marched me, still in manacles, across an open courtyard to a sort of reception room where a fat, old man in the uniform of a general sat behind a desk. He examined the ambassador's note and roared with laughter. His French was terrible, but I understood enough. "Comfortable quarters? Ha!"

A foreigner, an Englishman, like the scum filling our cells." He leered at a non-commissioned officer. "Find a place for the Englishman where he will be comfortable until he hangs with the rest."

The bastard was still roaring with laughter when a detachment of soldiers took me through an iron gate further into the fortress to a damp room. I waited while a silent guard entered my name into a large book and ordered me to remove my clothing.

They commanded me to dress in their prison garb, an ankle-length flannel gown, wool stockings, and high, felt shoes. There was no sound as we tramped through a long, cold corridor through another locked and guarded gate to a small courtyard. I looked at the angel at the top of the cathedral and wondered if this would be my last breath of fresh air and my last sight of an open blue sky.

The Trubetskoy Bastion was a long, low building with individual cells that faced an open, gloomy corridor. The heavy door to the cell on the very end of the building had only a peephole and a small portal for the passage of food. The guards removed my chains and thrust me into a narrow cell. The heavy door clanged shut. My heart sank.

The room was dark; not a single ray of sunshine came through the small, barred window. When my eyes finally adjusted to the gloom, I made out a small, moldy threadbare carpet, a paper-thin cot, and bare damp walls.

Then, my heart stood still and my limbs grew weak. I had never believed in ghosts, but the apparition that I saw rising out from the shadows — from behind a small writing desk in the far corner of the cell — could not be real. It was a horrific, ethereal monster, a supernatural being. Or was my overactive mind hallucinating?

I blinked and looked again. The apparition was still there — small, white-haired, and hunched. A threadbare garment, a sort of caftan, hung about the creature's shoulders and dragged on the floor. The apparition's features were almost obscured by a flowing beard and long, tangled, curly, white hair. The rheumy eyes were vacant, dark, deep-set globes. The wide nose and thick lips might have reflected facial aspects of an African ancestor. It moved forward, with its arm and skeletal fingers outstretched. I heard the *swish, swish* of felt boots on the floor and nearly screamed. I realized the apparition was human, and in horror, I retreated until my back pressed against the heavy door.

"Natalya, ma cherie?"

I caught my breath. "No, my name is Doyle," I whispered, responding in French.

119

My first instinct was to strike the creature, but then my good sense took over and I stood stock still. This was a poor human being who must have been imprisoned for years and who certainly deserved pity. I held out my hand. "I am your new cellmate. What is your name?" I asked, in broken French.

"I have no name. I am officially dead — dead to the world, dead with a bullet in my spleen, dead to my dear wife, Natalya. Oh, Natalya, is that you?"

"Please, I am not your Natalya, but I am a trained physician."

"I have waited so long for them to send you." And with that, the old man tottered and fell into my arms. I carried him to the cot, where he lay back, folded his hands over his chest, and gave a great sigh.

"So many years. So many years... I have saved a candle for such an occasion as this. Light it, please."

I groped my way to the desk and found an old-fashioned flint and steel and a candle in a brass holder. After a few strikes, I caught a spark on a bit of charred cloth then blew until the glow was sufficient to light the candle.

I anxiously surveyed my new world; there was no possible escape. The bars in the window were set in a wall several feet thick. Next to the candle holder, on the desk, was a worn bible and a slate with a bit of chalk.

There were no loose bricks, only solid stone walls. I held the candle to a yellowed, cracked calendar on the wall and painstakingly deciphered the date — 10 February 1837. This was beyond comprehension. Why was this poor gent here? Had he truly been imprisoned here for more than forty years?

I listened for some human sound, but the silence was broken only by the old man's raspy breathing, the scurry of rats, and the drip of water. Finally, utterly exhausted, I threw myself onto the threadbare carpet and went soundly to sleep.

I awoke many hours later. Or was it all a dream?

The old man's voice rose and fell in a sort of rhyme that seemed familiar. The words were Russian, but sometimes, he lapsed into French. "Tatyana, Natalya …" he murmured. Once, with great clarity, he shouted the name *Eugene*.

In the morning, the old fellow's eyes were glued shut with thick, yellow pus, and his eyelids were swollen. I led him to the window and, by the light of a single ray of sunshine, saw pustules at the base of his eyelashes. He was in pain and nearly blind.

I didn't have my bag or any medicine. What could I do for him?

My only remedy was to apply a wet compress with a bit of cloth soaked in the weak tea that came with breakfast. I plucked out several infected eyelashes, and over the course of several days, the infection resolved. His eyes cleared, and his gratitude was touching.

During the days, he scratched on the slate and then erased what he had written. I hoped that he could teach me a few phrases in Russian, or explain his nightly recitations, but his mind was too far gone.

The days dragged one after the other with no communication, no outside human sound. The guard passed our two meals of coarse bread with thin soup and took away the slop jar but remained absolutely silent. I paced back and forth, back and forth.

Day by dismal day, I sank into the most dreadful despair, broken by dreams of my mam or of crushing Penelope in my arms, her lips warming mine and bringing my dying body back to life. I knew not how long I was there, but it seemed like an eternity. One especially dreary morning, the guard opened our door.

A nun of the Orthodox faith put a gold coin in his hand. Her shapeless, black garment and a thick veil covered her body from head to foot. She offered the heavy cross that hung on a gold chain to the guard. He knelt, and with great reverence, kissed the cross. "Thank you, little mother," he murmured. The guard took his rifle and left his post.

She motioned for me and the old man to follow. Was it my imagination, or was there a whiff of orange blossoms? Most of her face was covered, but her eyes looked familiar, and the way she swung her hips as she walked was not like any nun I had ever seen. My heart began to race, and for the first time in days, I had a spark of hope that I might live.

121

The nun spoke to the old man in Russian. His features broke into a twisted smile. He nodded. "Ah, an escape. No, I am too old and frail to leave. This is where I shall stay, but I will help you get away. If, in return, you could take this, I shall die in peace." He withdrew from the depths of his old caftan a rolled bit of paper and pressed his greatest treasure into my hand.

"I will guard it with my life. Be well, my friend," I said.

The nun led us across the courtyard towards a side door of the cathedral. My cellmate, the old man, stumbled, and after a few steps, he clutched his chest and cried as if in pain. He collapsed and fell to the ground. The guard ran to his side, put down the rifle, and knelt by the old man.

I wanted to help but the nun pulled my arm. "It is part of the plan. He is acting. We must go."

We hurried and, in an instant, entered the cathedral and then the mausoleum between the tombs of Romanovs.

"Here, quickly, put these over your clothing." She handed me the cassock of an orthodox priest, a bishop's hat, and an enormous pectoral cross.

I pulled the black robe over my prison garb as fast as I could. "Walk, just ahead of me, slowly through the gate. There will be a waiting carriage. The driver will wear a blue coat," she whispered.

At the gate, a guard with rifle and bayonet barred our way. I wanted to run, but, after having seen the first guard kneel before the nun, had the presence of mind to offer the cross to be kissed. The young guard put down his weapon. "Thank you, Your Excellency," he murmured.

The slow march from the cathedral to the carriage seemed to take hours. At every step, I expected a bayonet thrust or a saber slash from one of the lounging soldiers. Suddenly, one of the guards ran towards me. All seemed lost. I was determined to smash his head with the heavy cross and run, but at the last moment he stopped, kneeled, and spoke with great urgency. "Please, Father, my son is sick. If you could give him a blessing?" he asked.

The soldier kneeled. I made the sign of the cross and recited a soft Latin blessing that I had learned as a child. When it was over, I helped him to his feet and he kissed my hand.

A few moments later, I assisted my companion into the carriage and slumped at her side. The driver did, indeed, have a spanking dark blue coat. We crossed the bridge over the Neva at a bare walk, and only then did the driver whip the horses to a gallop and the carriage lurch ahead. We were off.

The nun gave no inkling of her identity, and a scarf muffled the driver's features. I wanted to hug my savior, but she kept her distance and remained silent. When we were well away from the fortress, on a deserted street, she finally spoke. "Remove the cassock, and remember, not a word — not one word to a single soul."

She pulled off her headdress and long, chestnut curls tumbled out. "Penelope, what... How... Who are you?" I asked. She put her finger to her lips. "Don't ask. It is better that you remain ignorant. But it has been great fun," said she. I fell into her arms, happy beyond words to be with her again. She returned my gratitude with a long kiss, full on the lips, and then wiggled out of her black robe. She was, once again, transformed — now a demure young lady in afternoon dress. I was delirious with joy but no less mystified. She was a great actress, but how had she known I was in prison? Why had she come for me? Despite the fact that she had just saved me, the thought still plagued me — whose side was she on?

We took a roundabout route to Professor Sechenov's home, and once there, I went around the back way to the servant's entrance and slipped into my room unseen. I drew a bath and scrubbed away the prison dirt until Mr. Tatum knocked on the door.

I settled into an easy chair and told of my escape. He listened attentively, as if he was hearing this for the first time, but I wondered if he knew more about my adventure than he let on. Had he contacted Penelope through the British Secret Service?

Mr. Tatum rather solemnly recommended that I not leave my room. Thus, for days now, I have remained sequestered — eating, resting, recuperating and working with a Russian dictionary to decipher the tiny writing on the slip of paper from my mysterious cellmate. What follows is the most accurate translation I have been able to come up with.

d'Anthes' bullet ruptured my spleen, but unfortunately for the tsar, I did not die. My doctor, with the aid of brandy and opium, performed surgery and saved my life. The tsar was enraged and announced my death. He then ordered me to prison where I have languished for I know not how many years. Nicholas arranged the scandal, the duel, and claimed my death to have my beautiful Natalya as his own. Once the world knows the truth, I can die in peace.

Pushkin

10 September 1881

The past week has been one of further recuperation, reading, and study shrouded in a constant fear of being arrested. All the while, I have been remiss in making daily entries, so I shall remedy that situation with this update.

I have not left the confines of Sechenov's house. After my bloody horrific stay in the Peter and Paul Prison, I dream of returning home, sitting in my mother's kitchen and eating her blissfully good bangers and mash.

So what do I do all day?

Well, I spend my days in the library surrounded by books. At the end of each day, I do sprints and calisthenics within the walled garden to regain strength after my inactivity in prison.

What has made the past week tolerable is my daily Russian language lesson. I enticed a sweet, little kitchen maid named Marya to visit my room each night. She teaches me peasant Russian and cuddles in a most delightful manner. Her grammar is imperfect, but I am learning enough of the language to get by and she corrects my mistakes with a delicate kiss. I eagerly return each kiss and tend to make a few more mistakes than necessary. I have learned a great many terms of endearment and can carry on a very limited conversation in the Russian language.

In truth, I would be much better off taking Marya as my wife than Penelope, but I am mad about Penelope and my thoughts are of her even when I hold Marya. Would it be wrong to wed my own aunt? Could I even trust her? I know it would disturb many people, but there is something wonderfully compelling about the idea.

My rest was broken when, this morning, Mr. Tatum tapped on my door and announced that Dr. Bell requested my presence. I had scarcely seen him since my return, and as my own troubles faded, I was again worried for his health and deeply distressed about his proclivity for cocaine.

Fortunately, my concerns evaporated. He was erect, attired in a handsome dressing gown, and polishing off an omelet, a large beefsteak, and toast with marmalade. His cheeks were pink and he had gained weight. He leaned back, lit up his large, curved pipe and breathed out a wreath of fragrant smoke.

"Doyle, help yourself to coffee. There is another omelet and enough bacon for a whole battalion."

I thanked him and was soon stuffing my face with delicious vittles. "Sir, you seem to have recovered your usual robust health."

"Aye," Dr. Bell blew a large smoke ring. "I have determined the proper dose of cocaine to avoid unpleasant side effects. It is a capital nerve tonic. A seven percent solution of cocaine is beneficial."

It would be better if he had given up the drug but he seemed to be his old self. I said no more on the subject.

Bell delicately patted his lips with a damask napkin. "If you'd be so kind as to take a moment to refrain from eating so rapidly, I'd like to discuss some matters of great import with you," he said.

I put my fork down on my plate and sat back for a moment. "Aye, sir."

"I'd appreciate it if you could tell me what you've observed over the past few weeks."

"I've seen a great many exciting and awful things."

"No, not what you've seen. Anybody can see, but only a trained eye can observe. What you have you observed, laddie?"

Mr. Tatum bustled in with an overflowing tray of delicious sugary pastries with more eggs and bacon. Between mouthfuls, I related an abbreviated version of my involvement with the bomb makers and my arrest and incarceration. I ended with an announcement about how I am in great danger, and if the police discover my whereabouts, they will surely put me to death.

Bell helped himself to a lemon tart. "Well, Doyle, you are indeed fortunate. The Russian government cannot admit that escape is possible from the fortress. The third section is particularly adamant that you make no public mention of your mysterious cellmate. If this person was truly the famous poet, it will be a great embarrassment to the tsar. In that you are lucky. His government is eager to see that this all gets swept under the rug and has given a solemn assurance that, in return for your silence, your record will be destroyed and you will be granted complete amnesty," he said.

I was overwhelmed by this good news. After my prison ordeal, all I could think about was returning to Edinburgh. "Sir, does that mean that we are now at liberty to return home?"

Tatum squirmed. "Mr. Doyle, please …"

"I am sorry, but I almost died in that prison. I have done enough and should be allowed to go home," said I.

"Aye, I understand." Bell cleared his throat. "We cannot hold you against your will, but I cannot go, and as a favour to me, I was hoping that you may remain with us just a bit longer."

"Haven't you finished your course of lectures and demonstrations?"

"Aye, but the English Church has organized a clinic and a sanitarium for the care of children with tuberculosis. Professor Sechenov is anxious to test my theory that fresh air, good food, and cod liver oil is curative for these poor children. I have also developed a practice among the wealthy foreigners who live on the English Embankment. You can earn a bit more money by assisting me."

"That is a kind offer, sir, but after all I've been through, I've had enough adventure. It is time for me to return home."

"Laddie, we are involved in more than a bit of adventure here."

"Aye, and I have done my share for the Crown." I answered.

"Before you run back to Edinburgh, laddie, have you any notion of the importance of our mission?"

"The lives of many students hang in the balance."

He struck his clenched fist against his open hand. "Nay, hanging in the balance is more than the lives of a few students. We have fallen into a nasty situation that may affect the bloody balance of power in all of Europe."

"Sorry, but I don't see …"

"Doyle, has your head been so deep in medical books that you have no knowledge of world affairs?"

"Are those affairs so important?" I asked.

"The Queen and parliament are concerned because Germany is gaining power and may soon eclipse our empire. There is bad blood between the Kaiser and our Queen. The tsarist government is far from perfect, but Alexander is a friend of England. If an anarchist were to kill the tsar, there would be a power vacuum in Europe. The Germans would run rampant through Europe, and a Russo-German alliance could endanger millions of lives."

"Dr. Bell, surely the Crown has others who are better trained for this work."

"Nay, the British Secret Service has failed to infiltrate the student groups. You have earned credibility and trust with the students by the time you served in prison. Duty calls. Rise to the occasion. Your involvement could be the factor that keeps all of Europe from engaging in a massive war. Are you man enough for this assignment, Doyle?" Dr. Bell extended his hand.

I grasped his hand. "Yes, sir, I will do my best. There will be students at Pavlov's laboratory. I will talk with them."

Dr. Bell went off to the children's tuberculosis clinic, and despite an underlying sense of nervousness, I had a pleasant walk to the laboratory. Pavlov gave no indication that he was aware of my imprisonment and allowed me to perform several experiments under his expert guidance. Despite his insensitivity to human suffering, the man is a genius and far ahead of his time, especially in the field of blood transfusion and the nervous system. Together, with Ivanov, I succeeded in severing all the nerves to the heart in a dog. Much to our amazement, the heart continued a steady beat as if it had an intrinsic regulating mechanism.

I continued the work, and as we were preparing to operate, Dmitri, the animal keeper, brought a fine-looking female spaniel to the operating table. Most of the curs snapped their teeth or barked viciously, but this handsome animal licked my hand and allowed me to fondle her silky ears. She was mostly white, with brown spots and a handsome, brown muzzle. Her bushy tail thumped against the wooden table, and her large, dark eyes melted all my scientific instincts.

"Dmitri, put her back in the cage," I said.

For the first time, a fleeting smile passed over the poor man's face. It was as if something had awakened in his soul. Sometimes he has an air of refinement, quite unlike a peasant. For the next several days, I brought pieces of meat or bread soaked in gravy to my new friend. When I opened the cage, she put her head between her paws and licked my hand, then gently accepted my offering with all the elegance of a queen.

I couldn't think of a good Russian name, but her royal demeanor deserved a regal name that was equal to her dignity. I settled on the diminutive form of Alexandra — Sasha.

"Sasha, Sasha, come." she wagged her tail and delicately took a bit of meat.

I had not been involved with the transfusion experiments, but with nothing else to do that morning, I went to the blood laboratory. Two subjects were strapped on tables. At first, I did not recognize the poor wretch who was selected for transfusion. His beard was matted with old blood clots and his face was a mass of bruises and torn skin. Blood dribbled from each ear and his nose. The secret police had done their work. With a start, I recognized Golovinsky, who had chosen death by medical experiment rather than death by more torture at the hands of the Okhrana.

Ivanov and Dmitri held his hand and each bent close to his lips as if hearing a last confession. Over the hissing and rattling of the snakes in their cage, I could make out little of their conversation. The words made little sense, but I heard, "German" and "American." At my behest, Pavlov gave each subject enough morphine to dull their sensibilities during the gruesome experiment. I actually assisted Pavlov in isolating and canulating the donor's brachial artery and prepared the tubing for a direct blood transfusion.

Dmitri caught one of the giant rattlesnakes with a loop behind the creature's head and, with obvious reluctance, held the snake's body. He brought the terrible head, with its open jaws and exposed fangs, to Golovinsky's arm. The creature struck repeatedly, injecting its deadly venom. Golovinsky convulsed and his clotted wounds again dripped blood. The venom was, indeed, an anticoagulant.

Pavlov quickly placed a tube in a vein at his elbow and started the direct transfusion. Blood flowed from the donor into Golovinsky, but it was too late. With a last cry, his body stiffened and he died. "We could have kept him alive for another day. The damn fool," Pavlov swore.

I was about to leave for lunch, when a wild-eyed young man in a military uniform burst into the laboratory. "Dr. Doyle, there's been a terrible accident. You are wanted at the military hospital."

We climbed into the waiting droshky, and on an impulse, I shouted to Ivanov. "Come quickly, and bring Pavlov's serum."

We were away. The driver, sensing a tragedy and perhaps a large tip, whipped the horse to a frenzy. We dashed away to the other side of the city.

"What happened?" I asked.

"I'm in the Corps of Cadets. We double-loaded the noon gun, an old, bronze six-pounder. It exploded during the changing of the guard," the boy sobbed.

It was a scene from hell. Bodies were strewn about and the floor was slippery with blood. They were young boys with their limbs blown to smithereens and chunks of metal in their chests and bellies.

Dr. Bell was already at work on a head wound, and a half-dozen Russian surgeons were amputating limbs, suturing wounds, and ligating bleeding arteries. Dr. Bell pointed to a fellow on a makeshift table in the corner. "Doyle, make that lad comfortable. He is far gone. We can do nothing to save the poor fellow."

He was a slender boy of perhaps fifteen years with blonde, curly hair and a pale, bloodless face. His right arm was horribly mangled and his uniform was drenched with blood.

He was already lifeless. There was no need for morphine to relieve pain. By force of habit, I felt his wrist. Was there a flicker of a pulse? I put my ear to his chest and heard a distant thump. I resolved to do everything possible. "Orderly, please, over here. I need carbolic, ligatures, a scalpel, and a saw."

I snipped through the bit of skin that held his elbow to the upper arm and found an oozing brachial artery and vein. A single ligature controlled the bleeding. It was necessary to remove the lower humerus with a saw, and then, I stitched the skin over the stump. The entire affair had taken only a few moments, but the boy remained lifeless.

I was afraid that the shock of surgery had carried him off. I pressed my ear against his chest, but aye, there was still that distant thump. Almost as an answer to prayer, Ivanov appeared with a flask of Pavlov's serum.

We injected fifty, then one hundred, cubic centimeters of the fluid into his arm. I felt a weak pulse at his wrist. The boy was still alive. I straightened my aching back and noticed an older man, dressed in a frock coat and dark blue trousers, leaning on a cane, watching my every move.

He was obviously a gentleman and maintained his composure in the midst of chaos. "Will my son live?" he asked in refined French.

"He has a chance now," I said.

The man made a slight bow. "I am Prince Chernovsky. If my son, Konstantine, lives, I will owe you a great debt."

"I will do everything in my power to see that he lives."

"Thank you."

My patient rallied after a coffee enema. Prince Chernovsky insisted on removing the boy to his home. We placed him on the velvet seat in a splendid, gold and white, four-horse carriage. I stayed at the patient's side through the entire journey to his mansion and the boy's bedroom. A dozen liveried servants rushed about, securing pillows, fresh bandages, hot tea, and brandy.

The boy's mother burst into tears and had to be led from the room. At last, the child opened his eyes. It was as if he had returned from the dead. I felt a tremendous sense of accomplishment and slumped in a chair with overwhelming fatigue.

"Doctor, would you like tea or coffee?" a voice asked, a few moments later. The speaker was a rather plain, angular, young woman, dressed in a modest, floral-patterned dress from her neck to the floor. Her hair was tightly pulled back from her forehead into a bun. She was my age, or a little younger, and spoke perfect English.

"Coffee, please."

"I am Konstantine's sister, Agafea, but mother calls me Kitty," she said, with a smile. "And you are a doctor from England?"

"Edinburgh, Scotland actually, although my family is originally from Ireland. My name is Arthur Conan Doyle."

The coffee arrived in a lovely silver service along with an assortment of cakes, biscuits, pâté, and a dollop of caviar. I was let down and had a case of nerves after the operation, and was rather overcome by the richness of the room, the silver tray, and her kindness.

"Our family is grateful to you for saving my brother."

"Aye, but he is still in great danger."

"I will be his nurse. You should go to your home and rest, but tomorrow morning, you must return to care for the antiseptic dressings."

"Excuse me, but how do you know about antiseptic dressings?"

"Must all women be idiots?"

"Sorry. That's not what I meant."

"I trained as a nurse in London and plan to teach in the country. We must educate the peasants if we are ever to have true democracy here."

For all her gentility, anger simmered just beneath her surface, an unspoken resentment of a sort. I said no more, finished the excellent coffee, and wolfed down enough biscuits and cakes to make a substantial supper. Agafea plumped the pillows and spooned broth into the boy's mouth.

"His youth saved him," I said.

She brushed aside a lock of mousy brown hair. "Don't be so modest. Father said you saved his life when everyone else had left him to die," she said.

I was preparing to leave when Prince Chernovsky stepped into the room.

"I want to engage you to care for my boy until he has recovered," he said.

"Of course, I will visit him as often as necessary."

"I will pay you well. What is your fee?"

I had no idea what the charge should be. He could easily pay one thousand pounds, but would he be insulted if I didn't charge for my services? "I am Dr. Bell's assistant and work at his direction. Perhaps you could make a donation to the new sanitarium for children with tuberculosis."

He paused, perplexed at my novel suggestion. "Yes, I will do that." I sensed his embarrassment. "Dr. Doyle, there is to be a ball for the Duke and Duchess of Edinburgh. Agafea has no escort. Would you be so kind as to take her to the party?"

My mind whirled. Agafea was plain-looking and no beauty. I didn't know how to dance nor even how to address the nobility, but I knew it was too good an opportunity to turn down.

"Yes, sir, I would be honored if Agafea is willing."

She blushed and smiled, but I sensed she was not taken with the idea. "Please call me Kitty," she said.

The prince provided his carriage for my ride home. It was late, and as usual, I went around to the servant's entrance. There was a rustling sound and then a low whimper at the door.

It was the dog, Sasha. I petted her silky ears and she licked my face. I took her into the kitchen. She daintily polished off the leftovers from the Sechenov evening meal and followed me up the back stairs. At the side of my bed she laid down, put her head on her paws. I am writing this in my diary under her wistful gaze.

18 September 1881

I haven't written in over a week since I've been waiting for Vera and Ivanov to tell me what really happened with their assassination attempt at the palace. In the meantime, Sasha has captivated Mr. Tatum and the kitchen servants with her doleful eyes and her tail-wagging gratitude for food. The poor dog was semi-starved but quickly filled out on leftover lamb chops and salmon filets.

I have been attending the chemistry lectures, hoping Vera and Ivanov will show up. The police and official St. Petersburg claimed a gas leak caused the palace explosion, but I knew that was not true. Vera and Ivanov finally appeared this morning. We decided to have an early dinner at the Idiot's Café, a low, smoky place overlooking the Moika River and a favourite student haunt.

I arrived early and watched boats plying the river while a couple of scruffy fellows drank tea and played chess. The sun was low, and the buildings around the square cast long shadows. Vera and Ivanov arrived together, dressed in casual student garb rather than the semi-uniform worn by the dissidents prior to the wave of arrests.

I had collected a few fees from some of Dr. Bell's English patients and generously ordered tea with salmon, sour cream, and pickled mushrooms. Vera and Ivanov were subdued and nervously glanced over their shoulders. The chess players picked up the pieces and left.

"What happened at the Gatchina palace?" I asked, rather bluntly, after a bit of small talk.

"Didn't you read the paper? It was a gas explosion," Ivanov answered.

"I don't believe that. I risked my life to help your comrades and spent a miserable time in prison and deserve to know the truth."

They looked at one another with hooded eyes. "The Okhrana raided the apartment and killed everyone on the spot," Vera said.

"What about your injured comrades?"

"Dead."

"And your other comrades?" I asked.

"The police executed the leaders, and most of the members are in prison."

"What caused the explosion?"

"Doyle, we appreciate you help but it is none of your business. For all we know you could turn informer to save your neck," Ivanov said.

"He deserves to know." Vera said.

"He deserves to know nothing."

"What difference does it make? The movement is finished anyway," Vera said.

"Ack, you're right." Ivanov ground his teeth and then his countenance wilted. "Buy me a vodka and I will tell you."

I waived at the waiter and ordered a vodka. He soon brought a bottle and glasses. I poured and Ivanov downed a glass. "Golovinsky delivered the eggs to an English woman."

"Do you know her name?" I asked.

"No. but she had connections with the royal family."

"Golovinsky bound and gagged the babushka who tended the tsar's hens and who usually delivered the eggs. Our friend waited in the woods and watched while the English woman, disguised to look like the babushka, delivered the eggs to the kitchen. She left them in a pan of water on the stove ready for the tsar. Timoshenko, the wood cutter, filled the stove with wood and started a fire. Five minutes later, the eggs exploded."

"Why wasn't the tsar killed?" I asked

"That is the tragedy. Every morning, like clockwork, he usually makes his own breakfast like a common working man. But on this morning, of all mornings, he had a headache and stayed in bed."

"How do you know?"

"Golovinsky told me everything just before the snake bit him," Ivanov said.

In my excitement over saving the boy, Konstantine, I had forgotten the whispered conversation just before Golovinsky died. "Yes, I remember that. What did he say about the Americans and Germans?"

Ivanov's eyes widened and he dropped his glass. Bits of glass and vodka splattered on the floor and, for a moment, we were busy cleaning the mess.

"Well?" I asked, "Will there be more attempts on the tsar's life?"

"There are always plots; we will never stop until he dies."

"Have you heard of an Englishman who has sworn vengeance on the tsar?"

Ivanov was clearly startled, as if I had touched a nerve, but he recovered in an instant. "No, that is foolish talk," he said. "And why are you so interested?"

"I don't want any more deaths."

Vera and Ivanov were too fearful to tell more, but I had learned enough to guess the truth. Was the English woman — Penelope? Was she that involved? Whose side was she on?

I bid them farewell and set off for a short stroll to the Chernovsky mansion. Prince Chernovsky was pale and tired from lack of sleep. Young Konstantine had no fever but was very weak. The skin about the stump was slightly inflamed and a drop of pus oozed from the incision.

"I will remove the infected stitch. Please soak a forceps and scissors in the carbolic solution."

Agafea put down her book and sterilized the instruments.

"You are reading *Origin of the Species* by Darwin," I said.

"Yes, I enjoy reading about science," she answered.

"Instead of the great psychological works of Russian literature?"

"Our authors are dark and often depressing. I suppose it is our chilly northern climate. But, then, I enjoy Poushkine's poetry, so …"

"Poushkine?"

"Yes, you English call him Pushkin," she said.

"Ah yes. The great poet of Russia. Tell me about him."

"Pushkin's great work was *Eugene Onegin*, a tragic love story, but he wrote many other poems. He died after a stupid duel with a Frenchman."

"You say he died?"

136

"Yes." She paused a moment. "Although, there have always been rumors that he survived and was sent to prison or Siberia. There was also talk about Tsar Nicholas' role in his death and how, afterward, he supported Pushkin's wife and children." I thought of my old cellmate and said nothing more on the subject.

When the instruments were well soaked, I removed the stitch in Konstantine's stump and drained a bit of yellow pus.

Agafea saw the pus. "Oh dear, does he have a deep infection?"

"It is nothing, Agafea. He will be fine."

"Call me Kitty. I hate the name Agafea. It sounds like a witch's name."

"Aye, Kitty." She forced a smile and took my hand. She was trying to appear brave, but I could tell she was worried.

"I have never been fond of dances and balls, but my father insists that I go, so I shall … But please, you don't have to escort me if you don't want."

"No. Of course I will go, but I am not especially fond of balls."

"Well, we can wallow in misery together."

She wore a nondescript dress, and her hair was tightly pulled back into a bun at the back of her head. I was not attracted to her and wondered if I had made a mistake in agreeing to what might be an utterly painful experience. "About this ball," I stammered. "Is there anybody else you'd prefer to go with?"

"You shouldn't miss the ball. The empress is giving the party in honor of the Duchess of Edinburgh, the tsar's sister."

"Still …"

"It is a masked ball. You will see true Russian excess. There is nothing like this in England and might be your only chance to witness our decadence first hand." She squeezed my arm and gave me a cold kiss on the cheek.

Despite Marya's best efforts to brush and iron my once-elegant, black dress suit, it was shabby in comparison with the Russian's colorful uniforms. Sasha perked up her ears at the tap on my door. There was a twinkle in Dr. Bell's eyes when he placed a bulky package on the table.

"Open it. We can't have you attending a royal ball with a princess looking like a common tramp."

The package contained a Scottish evening suit. "Oh my!" I exclaimed. The trousers were made of fine wool in the black and dark green Black Watch tartan pattern, and the light grey Barathea jacket with silver buttons had the Edinburgh Medical School crest. Its dark red, light red, and yellow colors stood for liver, blood, and pus. A white waistcoat completed the outfit.

"It is quite grand," I spluttered. "Thank you."

"Put it on," Dr. Bell said.

I pulled on the shirt and stepped into the trousers while Mr. Tatum fussed with the studs. He held out the waistcoat and then the jacket. It all fit perfectly.

"I almost forgot. It is a masked ball," I said. "What should I do?"

"Here, go as a Scottish highwayman." Dr. Bell unfolded a large tartan handkerchief.

A while later, I was sitting in a spindly chair in the Chernovsky's grand reception hall waiting for Kitty. After an hour, I paced about, pausing to look at a vase, painting, and gilded ornaments while the footman watched as if I were a potential thief. With nothing better to do, I visited Konstantine. He was pale and his breathing was shallow. His mother was crying. The wound was slightly red and swollen, but it was not that bad and required no further treatment. I reassured his tearful mother and returned to the foyer.

There was a rustle at the head of the marble staircase. It was Agafea, wearing a sparkly, small tiara in hair that fell to her shoulders in soft waves, and a cream-colored ball gown that revealed her shoulders and just a hint of bosom. When she reached the foot of the stairs, I had the presence of mind to bow and take her hand. "Miss Kitty, you look quite lovely tonight," I said.

"You are too kind, Arthur."

She smiled and her dark blue eyes twinkled with humor. Her mother trailed along behind, wringing her pudgy hands. "Please Kitty. I beg you not to go."

"Mother, stop it! Father wants me to go and I need to show my face."

"If Konstantine was feeling better, I'd go with you, but we should both stay here with him."

"I am going to the ball, Mother."

"Oh dear, what will people say? All the respectable ladies in attendance will have a chaperone."

"Mother, please. I am of age. Besides it makes no difference what people say." We went off in the great family carriage. Nevsky Prospekt was jammed with carriages, armed guards, soldiers with fixed bayonets, and mounted officers. The guards who stopped us at the great columns of the palace were satisfied with Agafea's curt answers, but it was well after ten before we crossed the parade ground and reached the entrance of the Anichkov Palace.

We ascended the great staircase lined with white-wigged footmen dressed in splendid black satin and gold velvet costumes. The entire expanse of galleries, ballrooms, and the great hall were lit with hundreds of candles. I felt like a true pauper in the midst of this Russian splendor.

A mazurka was in progress when we entered the great hall. Wild dancers stamped to the right and then the left, whirled in a circle, and then formed a grand chain. There were officers of the Royal Guard in white and green uniforms, Hussars, aides to the royal family, diplomats and government officials, all with gold braid and glittering medals. Even the waiters and servants wore bright red and blue uniforms that outshone my Scottish attire. A seventy-piece orchestra filled the air with waltzes, the polonaise, and folk dance tunes.

I indicated a particularly resplendent captain in a gaudy green and gold uniform. "Who is that?" I whispered.

"A fool in the Seminofsky Regiment." Kitty replied. She adjusted her silvery mask and led me to a quiet corner. "You are quiet. Are you enjoying this ostentatious display?" she asked.

"I cannot but help contrast this opulence with the charity hospital. The money spent on champagne alone would feed the poor of St. Petersburg for a week." I said.

"I agree. I am a liberal and a terrible disappointment for father."

A waiter offered tiny, delicious pies and crystal glasses with vodka. Despite our liberal instincts and good intentions, we couldn't refuse. We wandered among the throng, sipping and nibbling while observing Russian high society.

"Come. We must pay our respects to the duke and duchess," she said.

We drifted with the revelers through the red and gold rooms to the concert hall where the English duke with his Russian duchess held forth. The duke scowled, as if he wished he was on the deck of a ship in the Royal Navy, but brightened when he noticed my Scottish outfit. "The University of Edinburgh. Ah yes, a fine school," he said. I glowed with pride.

I mumbled a reply and then, out of the corner of my eye, caught sight of a masked woman with orange blossoms in her long, chestnut hair dancing with none other than the be-medaled German Count. Could it be Penelope?

I took Kitty by the waist and madly whirled her through the dancers, bumping into couples and drawing hard looks in my attempt to reach the couple. I saw her once more, on the arm of Count Carl von Wittenberg before she disappeared in the crowd. "Who is that woman?" I asked Kitty.

"I believe she is Miss Walshingham, a lady-in-waiting to the Duchess of Edinburgh."

The mystery deepened. If it was indeed Penelope in the entourage of the Duchess and living under the same roof as the tsar, he was in great danger. It explained the 'English woman' who delivered eggs to the kitchen.

"I am tired, please. Let us leave." Kitty said.

We took a carriage back to the Chernovsky mansion. Instead of a darkened, sleeping mansion, every light was on. Servants ran to and fro with packets of pills, bottles with colored liquids, and a bowl of steaming soup.

"What is wrong?" Kitty demanded.

"The young prince has taken a turn for the worse," the old footman said.

We ran to his bedchambers. Prince Chernovsky' face was as dark as thunder. He was about to strike me with his fist but held back when Konstantine cried out. His poor wife sobbed uncontrollably and wrung a handkerchief. A maid applied cold clothes to the boy's hands and face while he nestled on silken pillows in a canopied, four-poster bed. At first glance, he appeared to be more frightened than ill.

An elderly, bearded doctor, introduced as the surgeon to Prince Chernovsky's regiment, sat at the bedside. "In cases of this nature, it is sometimes necessary to amputate the arm at a higher level," he said.

Great God! I thought. *Have I committed a terrible error? Was the bone infected?* The boy had fever but also a runny nose, and he sneezed. There were swollen lumps in his neck but no further discharge of pus from the amputation stump. The old surgeon was already sending for his surgical kit when I remembered a child in the infirmary with similar symptoms.

"Kitty, wait! Please hold a lamp to his face." She brought a gilded oil lamp to the bedside.

"Konstantine, open your mouth." I gave the order in French. The boy understood and opened wide. There were spots inside his cheeks. I gave a great sigh of relief. "Ah yes, these red spots are typical of measles."

"Dear God, another complication," the Prince said.

"The boy is suffering from a common case of the measles. There is no need for an amputation. Tomorrow, he will have a rash all over his body, and within a week, he will be fine."

The old doctor looked at the strawberry spots inside the boy's mouth and pulled his beard. "He is correct; Konstantine has measles. I am sorry, sir, for not checking his throat," he said.

The Prince pumped my hand, and his wife embraced me with a tearful hug.

"We are again in your debt."

As I prepared to leave, the Prince pressed an envelope into my hand.

"My dear Dr. Doyle, take this."

"That is not necessary."

"These are ballet tickets. Please use my box at the theater. There is plenty of room for your friends and, as a favour, take Agafea. The poor girl is worn out from looking after Konstantine. Please, take them. You have done so much for us."

It was near dawn when I finally crawled into bed, which was already warmed by Marya, my dear scullery maid and comforting friend. She was drowsy, but delightful, and more than made up for Agafea's cold peck on the cheek. Marya giggled when I gently squeezed her bottom and whispered a Russian phrase of love in her ear. Of course, I said a few words incorrectly so she would kiss me again and again …

19 September 1881

Prince Chernovsky's box at the Imperial Bolshoi Kamenny Theater was in the second tier to the right of the great stage. We had a glorious view of the boards and the gilded rows of box seats. Before the ballet began, we watched the milling crowds of people finding their way to the gold and blue chairs on the first floor. These preliminaries were as entertaining as the performance.

Kitty pointed to a box on the first tier, just below us and opposite. It was similar to ours, but roomier and more luxurious. "That is the Imperial Box, but the tsar doesn't like opera and rarely attends," she said.

The orchestra tuned up and then blasted away for the opening act while the gigantic blue and gold curtains swung back to reveal the cast. The performance was the ballet, *Tsar Kandavi* or *Le Roi Candaule*. It was terribly confusing, and I was never exactly sure about what was transpiring onstage. It seemed that Tsar Kandavi seized power, and then, King Gyges went to live with the shepherds; after that, I became hopelessly lost.

Very quickly, Mr. Tatum went to sleep, but Dr. Bell followed the performance with attention and apparent enthusiasm. Once I lost track of what was happening onstage, my eyes and mind inevitably wandered to a strikingly beautiful girl in the dim shadows of the Imperial Box. A large, bearded gentleman stood in the shadows with his hand on her bare shoulder. I nudged Kitty. "May I borrow your opera glasses? I think the tsar might be here tonight."

I focused the glasses and pretended to watch the stage but really fixed mostly on the girl's bare shoulders, rather striking bosom, and lovely features. As I admired the girl, the tall, portly man kissed her lips. I passed the glasses back to Kitty. "Is that the tsar?"

This was definitely turning out to be more interesting than the ballet. "I can't be certain, but he does not appear to be the tsar," she said, after several minutes of study.

"Then who is it?"

"I would wager that it's the Grand Duke Vladimir, the tsar's brother."

I tried paying attention to the ballet, but the amorous scene in the Imperial Box was much more interesting.

"It's my turn. The glasses, please." I said.

Dr. Bell scolded me with his eyes for the slight commotion.

"Sorry," I whispered and took the glasses from Kitty.

Things heated up during the "Pas de Venus". The nubile, young girl in the box climbed on the duke's lap and was deep in the old boy's beard.

"How scandalous. The grand duke is a notorious playboy and drunkard. The opera company regularly supplies him with girls, but I never dreamed that they would carry on so... so blatantly," whispered Kitty. Her eyes were glued to the Imperial Box.

Scandalous or not, I enjoyed the passionate scene, which was more interesting than the ballet. Suddenly, the girl slid off the duke's lap and collapsed. The duke adjusted his trousers and made a fast exit.

The girl lay motionless on the floor of the box, but the audience, intent on the performance, paid no attention. Of all those hundreds of people, I alone had witnessed the scene.

"Dr. Bell, a girl in the Imperial Box is sick or injured."

"The authorities need to be informed," said Kitty. She spoke rather imperiously to an usher who, in turn, found a military officer who led us, pell-mell, past guards to the Imperial Box. The girl was dead on the floor with a smear of dark blood and a neat, small hole in the back of her head. "This is a case for the police. As witnesses, you all must remain here until the police arrive," said the officer.

"What exactly happened?" Dr. Bell asked.

I told him everything. "I am certain it was the grand duke, but he does resemble the tsar," Kitty added.

Dr. Bell gazed at the stage, lit his pipe, and breathed out a cloud of smoke. "The dancers in this ballet are quite beautiful, are they not?" he remarked.

"Yes, lovely creatures. But sir, shouldn't we be searching for a killer?" I asked.

"Think before taking action," he said.

The police were not Okhrana thugs, but a polite, uniformed policeman and a pleasant, smooth-faced, blonde man of about forty who introduced himself as Inspector Marti Koivisto. As we shook hands, I thought the slim, pale inspector appeared more like a scholar than a police officer. He kept our little group in the wings of the Imperial Box, out of the view of the audience while he questioned the security guards. They shrugged and pointed to us. Kitty introduced herself as Agafea and explained who we were, with emphasis on Dr. Bell, the distinguished university lecturer.

"Dr. Joseph Bell of Edinburgh?" the inspector asked, in heavily accented English.

Dr. Bell bowed slightly. "Yes."

"I have read your articles on scientific crime detection and spent a week in London, observing Scotland Yard. You are far ahead of us in criminal investigation procedures. Tell me, what do you make of this young woman's demise?"

"You are most kind, but my associate, Dr. Doyle should first tell what he observed," Dr. Bell said. "He had a much better view of the incident."

"Inspector, could this be an assassination attempt on the tsar?" I asked.

"I am only concerned with this murder. It is best to make no mention of the royal family," Inspector Koivisto replied. My brief description of the man and woman and her sudden collapse lasted only as long as scene three in the third act. The audience was still oblivious to our little drama.

Inspector Koivisto listened carefully and made no comment. He motioned for us to enter the box. "Dr. Bell, your opinion, please?" he asked, after a minute inspection of the scene.

Dr. Bell motioned with his pipe. "Dr. Doyle, will you be so kind as to place the young woman in the position you noted immediately prior to her collapse?"

With the aid of the uniformed policeman, we turned the young lady over, noting a bruise on her right nipple, and then placed her in a sitting position, facing the back of the chair. "Hold her head in the exact position as you remember," Dr. Bell said, when her head flopped to one side.

"I don't see how this will ..."

Dr. Bell interrupted the inspector rather impatiently. "Please, Inspector, if you will, indulge me."

I had the uniformed policeman hold her arms around the back of the rather high upholstered chair, as if she was embracing a lover, while I held her head as if she was in the act of kissing lips slightly above her level. The smudge of blood and the hole in her skull was centered at the top of her head. Dr. Bell sighted from the hole up and across the great theater.

"We must probe the wound, but unfortunately, I don't have my instruments."

"Sir, would a lead pencil suffice?" I asked.

"An admirable suggestion."

My almost-new lead pencil fit nicely into the small skull defect. Dr. Bell slowly advanced the pencil deep into the skull, withdrew it once, and then again. "I must follow the exact tract of the bullet if we are to find the killer," he said.

"A bullet? Come now, it would be impossible to fire a rifle without a single person hearing the shot," Inspector Koivisto said.

"I will explain in a moment. Ah, here, Inspector, push the pencil ever-so-slightly."

The inspector held the pencil delicately between his thumb and index finger, closed his eyes, and pushed the pencil, millimeter by millimeter, until the tip was approximately four centimeters inside the girl's head.

His eyes lit up. "Yes, the probe touched a hard object within the brain."

"It is a bullet lodged in her brain. An autopsy will provide proof of my observation." Dr. Bell said.

"Why are you so certain?"

"Elementary, my dear Inspector. Trust me, you will find a bullet of approximately .30 calibre lodged in the woman's brain. Now, Doyle, this is most important; hold the head in the exact position," Dr. Bell said. He dropped to his knees, as sighted along the pencil, and pointed to the top tier of boxes. "Based upon this angle, the assailant had to be there, in the last row, between the two entrance doors. Inspector, see for yourself."

"Yes, but..." Inspector Koivisto positioned himself and sighted along the pencil. "I still don't understand how it could have been a gunshot. There was no noise and no smell of gunpowder."

"If you followed all the latest scientific advancements, Inspector, you'd know that an inventor at the Krupp works in Germany has developed a powerful gun that operates on compressed air. It fires a conical lead bullet and makes almost no sound. I suggest we have a look at the upper tier directly opposite to discover the shooter."

Inspector Koivisto gave instructions to the uniformed officer to discreetly remove the body through the wings to the morgue for an autopsy, while we made our way through back corridors to the opposite galleries.

During the entire proceedings, which to a layperson must have seemed gruesome in the extreme, Agafea had maintained her composure and appeared to be intently interested. Even when I placed the pencil deep in the dead girl's head, she did not flinch.

"Would you prefer to go home, Miss Kitty?" I asked.

"Why?" she tossed her head. "Just because I am a woman? Besides, you may require an interpreter."

There were only a few scattered spectators in the upper gallery where the presumed assailant had fired the fatal shot. Dr. Bell moved back and forth until we had a clear view of the Imperial Box. "The assassin fired the fatal bullet from this vacant seat. He probably aimed at the girl's companion but, in the dim light, hit the girl instead."

Inspector Koivisto sniffed the air. "There is no odor of gun smoke."

"Believe me, Inspector, the assailant used a powerful air rifle." Dr. Bell said.

The light was so dim we could hardly make out the individual chairs. Dr. Bell, on hands and knees, inspected the aisle from one entrance door to the next. "Doyle, please light a match."

I struck a lucifer and held it, while he, as intent as bloodhound, minutely inspected the carpet and sniffed beneath each chair.

In the meantime, Inspector Koivisto discretely questioned the nearest spectators. No one had heard or seen anything unusual. I was beginning to doubt Dr. Bell's theory, when the match burned down and scorched my fingers.

I struck a new match and, in the flare, noted a sparkle as if from a metallic object beneath the chair. "There, sir. What is that?" I cried.

Dr. Bell took up a small circlet of paper with a bit of gold leaf that had sparkled in my match light. On the outside was the letter 'H'. "It's a discarded cigar band." Dr. Bell said. He held the band to his nose and inhaled deeply. "Latakia. Yes, I am positive the cigar was made with tobacco from Latakia. Those who appreciate tobacco consider Latakia to be the world's finest."

Koivisto shook his head. "I am sorry, Dr. Bell, but anyone could have left a cigar band."

"This is not just any cigar band, Inspector. This is from a Hirschsprung cigar, made in Denmark, and favoured by wealthy Germans. This brand is not available in Russia and far too expensive for most people," Dr. Bell replied.

"I am sorry, but there is so little evidence," Koivisto said.

"The evidence is there, Inspector, it is just up to one to extract its meaning. The owner of the Hirschsprung Cigar Company is a distinguished physician with strong ties to Germany. Discrete enquiries at the German Embassy will prove that I am correct."

"We shall see about that." Inspector Koivisto placed the cigar band in an envelope. "I will arrange the autopsy for ten tomorrow morning. Will you join me, Dr. Bell?"

"Doyle and I will be there, with pleasure."

We all departed and I walked Kitty home. In the Chernovsky drawing room, she rewarded me with a cold peck on my cheek. There were no cabs. During my long walk home, I turned over in my mind the recent assassination attempts. Had the killer expected the tsar, or were there plots to kill the entire royal family? Once again, my thoughts turned to Penelope — was she involved?

I was disappointed to find only Sasha in my room. Marya, the little tramp, must have found more pleasant company. I have passed the time by rubbing Sasha's belly and reading a medical text, but I can no longer keep my eyes open.

20 September 1881

The pathologist had already made the usual Y-shaped incision from neck to pubes and the girl's viscera were in a messy pile on the table. Inspector Koivisto seemed about to regurgitate his breakfast, even though the odor of rotting human flesh and excrement was no worse than usual. As a medical student, I had learned to cope with noxious odors in the dead house with copious amounts of cologne, cheap tobacco, and breathing through my mouth.

"Ockk, dere is nozzing in the chest or belly," The pathologist said to us, in his heavy accent.

He made an incision from one temple to another around the back of the head and yanked the scalp forward over her face. Then, with a saw, he removed the top of her skull. The bullet was embedded deep in the pulpy mess that was her mid-brain. She had died instantly. The lead was dented where it had first struck the skull, was hollow at the base, and measured three tenths of an inch in diameter — exactly .30 calibre.

Dr. Bell was, as usual, correct. It was hard to tell if Koivisto was angry or impressed. His lips were compressed in a grim line. "Inspector, find the owner of a .30 calibre air rifle who smokes Hirschsprung cigars and you have your killer," Dr. Bell said.

"Come, let us go. I will be sick if we stay here any longer," Inspector Koivisto said.

We went to lunch at a small café. We finished bowls of Solyanka, a spicy soup with pickled cucumbers. While we waited for a platter of pickled mushrooms, cured fish, and deviled eggs, Koivisto leaned back in his chair. "We have a spy in the German Embassy," he said.

"Is it ethical to spy on a foreign government?" I interrupted.

"Ethical or not, it is a must. There is so much tension between us and the Germans. You see, over the past year, Grand Duke Vladimir has instituted a government policy to force Germans in the provinces to speak only Russian. They are resisting, and Duke Vladimir is as unpopular as the tsar. My spy reports that a

Count von Wittenberg, the new naval attaché, is quite vocal about his disdain for Vladimir."

"And the count regularly smoked Hirschsprung cigars, yes?" Dr. Bell asked.

"Yes, and the count did not return to his quarters last night."

The inspector toyed with a bit of deviled egg. "You are very astute and deserve to know more. I have a source in the palace who keeps us informed so we can better protect the family. The tsar and the empress planned to attend last night's performance but, at the last minute, changed plans. The grand duke arranged a little tryst and attended in their place."

The inspector offered to pay the bill, but Dr. Bell waved him away. "It is our greatest pleasure to be of assistance and service to the Crown."

"What do you make of it?" I asked Dr. Bell, as we left.

Bell tossed a ruble to a street beggar before he answered. "I suspect the real target was the tsar. The cigar band could have been planted to lead us astray, but there are indications of German involvement. There are many German professors at the university. Are they inciting the students?"

I had to think about that. We were nearing the river before I replied. "The students don't need an outside influence to kill the tsar. The Germans, however, may supply money and advice to aid in the job."

22 September 1881

Yesterday and today have been, well, quite difficult, and I did not get a chance to write in this journal last night.

Yesterday, I was dreaming of going home to Auld Reekie when, at breakfast, Mr. Tatum, rather more forcefully than necessary, took me away to the British Embassy. I was tired and hungry and did not enjoy the ride, even though the carriage was drawn by four splendid, matching black horses.

At the embassy, an armed guard passed us on to an undersecretary and thence to the inner sanctum of Sir John Ecclestone, her Majesty's Ambassador to the Russian court. Sir John, for all his sixty years, was a handsome man and a flinty, hardened veteran of many a diplomatic war. He offered no refreshment and didn't waste time with small talk, but bore into me with his stern, grey eyes. "Mr. Doyle, Her Majesty, the Queen, is disturbed by the recent attempts on the life of Tsar Alexander III, and rightly so."

I stood rigidly at attention, wondered what was coming, and dared return his penetrating gaze.

"Mr. Tatum has made you privy to the Queen's request that we do everything possible to prevent his assassination. Is that not correct?

"Yes, sir," I replied.

"Then, why does the Russian Secret Service claim you were involved with an assassination plot?"

"I was actually attempting to STOP the plot."

"You are an embarrassment to the Crown, Mr. Doyle."

"Sir, I came here to assist Dr. Bell, but now, I would actually prefer to be home in Edinburgh!" I was about to make a more impudent reply but Mr. Tatum pinched my arm. "Mr. Tatum and I did our best to warn the tsar, but the police took me in custody and I spent several bloody miserable days in prison on false charges. I have done more than my fair share for the Crown, sir," I choked out.

The ambassador made the smallest hint of a smile as if he was laying a clever trap. "Yes, that is in your favour, and as a result, you are well positioned to be of further service to the Queen."

"I would be honored to help, sir, but I must decline."

"And why is that, Mr. Doyle?"

"I am sympathetic with the plight of the Russian people."

"Your sympathies are of no concern to me. You will do your duty or face the consequences."

"Consequences?"

"Your father could find himself incarcerated for his debts. His brother, your uncle, is a known supporter of the Irish cause. He may find himself under lock and key, and you may be tarred with the same brush. It could be difficult to practice your profession with such a stigma attached to your name."

I had never been threatened in such a way before. I gulped, thought for a moment, and then chose my words carefully. "I understand the global ramifications if the tsar and his government are brought down, but, with all due respect, who is to govern Russia is a matter for the Russian people and of little consequence to the British Empire."

"You are quite naïve, Mr. Doyle." Sir John beckoned us to a map of Europe and the Middle East on a large, well-polished rosewood table. "The Franco-Prussian War upset the balance of European power. Germany has the upper hand — not only in Europe, but in the Ottoman Empire. The Germans have financed and engineered railroads from Istanbul to Damascus and Baghdad that threaten our lines of communication from Egypt to India through the Suez Canal. The death of another tsar will lead to chaos in Russia. Germany will dominate Europe, the Middle East, and Russia all the way to the Urals."

"What is Germany's motive?"

"The age of coal and steam is over." He tapped his finger on the map and traced a line from Baghdad to the Black Sea. "The future is oil, Mr. Doyle, oil. If Russia falls into chaos, Germany will control the world's greatest oilfields. In a few years, the world will run on oil. A strong tsar is necessary to hold Russia together and to be Britain's ally against Germany."

153

"All that is well and good, sir, but what do you want of me?" I asked.

"Nothing more than what you've already done. Continue your involvement with the student anarchists and keep your eyes open for the British officer, David Campbell, who intends to kill the tsar.

The ambassador clipped the end of a cigar and sniffed its aroma. "You have had some involvement with Miss Walshingham, a clever woman who has made herself indispensable with the Duchess of Edinburgh," he said, rather offhand. The ambassador lit a lucifer and thoughtfully rotated his cigar in the flame until it glowed. "That clever lady is an enigma. Where do her sympathies lie?" *Aha*, I thought. *This must be the real reason for my summons to the Ambassador.* "I am sure she is a loyal British subject," I said. I hoped the ambassador did not detect the lack of certainty in my words.

Sir John waved us away with a curt dismissal. "My secretary will fill you in with the details."

Adrian, the secretary, spoke in a condescending, plumy, upper-class English voice. His large, red nose showed the effects of an affectionate relationship with the bottle. I hated him on the spot, especially when he compelled us to take an oath of allegiance to the Queen.

He then handed me a small document. "This will identify you as an agent of the British government. It may be of some use if the Okhrana stops you again." Next, Adrian's well-manicured hand pushed a small box across the desk containing a two-inch, .40 calibre derringer pistol and twenty brass cartridges. His voice turned cold. "Conceal this on your person. You are to kill, if necessary, to protect the tsar and his relationship with the crown. Miss Walshingham and her deceased husband's associates may be enemies of England. Kill them, as well, but only if necessary."

I abruptly left Mr. Tatum at the embassy, went straight home, found Sasha lazing in the kitchen, and set off at a near-trot with the dog running at my side. We left the large homes and bypassed the factories. The whole time, my mind was in a whirl; I could not possibly kill Penelope. Would that make me a traitor? I desperately yearned to return to Edinburgh, remove myself from all this deadly international intrigue, and get on with the practice of medicine.

The exercise cleared my head, and it was good to get away from the stench and noise of the city. After a few miles, we came upon summer houses with green gardens. Sasha's comic antics soothed my troubled soul. She gaily chased rabbits, and when her eyes fastened on a bird, she pointed with her nose and delicately raised her front paw.

After a long, invigorating walk, we came to the dockyards, rested on the embankment, and watched ships coming and going in the harbor. There were many Russian navy vessels and ships with every European flag in the anchorage. It is getting to be fall and a cold wind whipped a chop in the water. I shivered, found shelter in a cheap tavern, and made a hearty workman's lunch of beer, black bread, and soup.

Sasha, with a grateful wag of her tail, finished the scraps, while the jovial proprietor explained how business had picked up with the gathering of the Baltic fleet for the tsar's review. It seemed as if all of St. Petersburg was anxious to see the tsar come out of his self-enforced isolation to review the fleet.

I dawdled in the long, northern evening and didn't arrive home until late. Marya fluttered over Sasha. "They are waiting for you, Arthur. You must hurry to Dr. Bell's room," she whispered.

I sniffed the fragrant blue smoke from Dr. Bell's great, curved Meerschaum even before I arrived at his room. It meant he was deep in thought or troubled by a new case. Professor Sechenov paced the room in a state of high agitation, but Dr. Bell at his desk, sorted surgical instruments and peered at the labels of medicine bottles. "One cannot predict whether these cases require an operation or will be amenable to medicines," he said.

Sechenov wrung his hands. "We must hurry. Countess Tolstaya's message indicated great urgency and it is a long way to Tsarskoye Selo. The royal carriage is waiting and we must go."

I was tired from the long walk, but sensed another adventure.

"Ah, Doyle, lad. We must leave at once. Take the instrument case and let us be on our way. Professor Sechenov will explain everything," said Bell, as he packed the last bottle.

The gold gilt carriage with red wheels drawn by four shiny, white horses was indeed a royal means of travel. The driver and his assistant, in green and gold uniforms, could have passed as generals in the army.

The assistant leaped down from his high perch and handed us in to the spacious interior with soft velvet seats. There was room to stretch out and sleep, but Professor Sechenov aroused my curiosity. "Professor Sechenov, you mentioned Countess Tolstaya. Is there any chance we will meet her husband, Count Tolstoy, the great writer?" I asked.

"Bah, I think not. The man has become a socialist reformer. Many think he is mad, especially when he speaks of anarchy. The fool is totally out of favour, but his wife, the countess, is not. She is a lady-in-waiting to the empress, Maria Feodorovna."

"What is the medical problem?"

"The empress was enjoying the gardens at Tsarskoye Selo when she became ill with terrible abdominal pain. I fear it may be an inflammation of the appendix, the American disease. Her physician thinks it is a medical problem," Professor Sechenov said.

"Who is the physician?" Dr. Bell asked.

"It is quite awkward. He is a German specialist and physician to Princess Yurievskaya.

"Who is this princess?" Dr. Bell asked.

Professor Sechenov pursed his lips. "It is a sorry episode in the lives of the royal family. When the wife of Alexander II became ill, he took a commoner, a woman named Dolgorukov as his mistress. After his wife died, he married the woman, but instead of making her his empress, he gave her the title, Princess Yurievskaya. She is jealous of the Empress Maria for taking her place in the royal household."

"Where is the tsar?" Dr. Bell asked.

"Somewhere in the wilderness with his friends, hunting bears." The lengthening Russian night was upon us, when, beneath a misty full moon, we rolled into the courtyard at the gates of

Catherine the Great's palace. Servants with lanterns led us through gilded corridors to the bedroom of Empress Maria Feodorovna.

In the light of a single candle, I could appreciate magnificent gilt chairs, carved tables, velvet wall hangings, brocade curtains, and, in the middle of the room, our patient was covered by rumpled quilts in a great four-poster, canopied bed. Except for the sound of raspy breathing and her occasional moan or a low scream, the room was deathly silent. A servant girl with trembling fingers first rubbed the empress's hands and then applied a compress of cold water to her face.

Professor Sechenov was clearly in awe of his surroundings. "C-countess Sophia Tolstaya, may I p-p-present Professor Joseph Bell," he stammered.

The countess Tolstaya, a middle-aged woman with a tired, lined face, was dressed in severe, black, mourning clothes in respect for the assassinated Alexander II. She wracked with sobs and held a tear-soaked handkerchief to her face. She said nothing, but nodded briefly to Dr. Bell.

The other person in the sick room was a handsomely-dressed gentleman wearing a monocle attached to a long, red ribbon who hovered at the bedside holding a large syringe. He clicked his heels and made a little bow. "Boris Meyer, Doctor of Medicine, University of Berlin and senior physician to Princess Yurievskaya. I am about to administer a stimulant." I remembered Vera saying that the Russian elite preferred German or French doctors to Russian physicians.

Dr. Bell approached the bed, pushing the German aside. "More light, please."

The servant girl rushed to ignite gas lamps, and in their bright glare, I could see the pale, sweaty face of the empress. She was beautiful, with large, round eyes that were dimmed with pain and fever.

The German, Dr. Meyer, lowered the syringe and he sadly shook his head. "The empress is in extremis. You have made a needless trip. If this injection doesn't restore her to health, she is doomed."

Dr. Bell ignored the man and took up her wrist. "It is too fast to count," he said. The German was a thickset fellow with big shoulders, a pointed beard, and wooly eyebrows. He carefully placed the syringe on a table and stepped between Bell and the patient. "I say, there is no need for your examination. This is my case."

Bell ignored the man and pulled away the quilts.

Meyer attempted to restrain him and there ensued a pushing match. "Listen, you damn English pest, leave her alone!"

Nothing angered Bell more than to be called English. He was Scottish to the bone. I barely saw his short punch, but Meyer staggered back. His face reddened. "Gott damn you!" he bellowed.

He came back at Dr. Bell, but with an old trick learned on the rugby field, I caught his foot with my ankle and tripped him up before he could reach Bell.

Meyer fell, sprawling on a bright blue carpet, blood spurting from his nose. The Countess Tolstaya and Professor Sechenov huddled in a corner, aghast at the display of professional temperament. "I will get the guard!" Meyer shouted.

"Good riddance to you, sir. Doyle, lock the door and we will go to work," Dr. Bell said. I turned the lock. Bell first held a candle to her eyes. Then, with his ear to her chest, he listened to the heart and lungs and finally palpated her abdomen. "What is this?" He pointed to a purple swelling on her left arm. "Countess, please tell me exactly the sequence of events that led to her illness."

In that moment, the empress clutched her abdomen with both hands and a long, drawn out scream came from her blue lips. Then, her head drew back and her limbs went rigid. Her back arched, and her legs and arms beat an angry, painful rhythm against the bed. At last, in the mere flicker of a candle, the convulsion ended, her eyes opened in terror, and her breathing just stopped. All her muscles were in spasm.

"Crivvens! Doyle, give her ether — NOW! We must break the spasm or she will die!"

I could not imagine giving ether, a drug known to depress respirations, to a patient who was not breathing. Bell pulled the bottle of ether from his medicine case.

"Sir, she isn't breathing. Ether will surely bring her end sooner," I said.

"Damn you! Just start the ether!"

With shaking hands, I poured a few drops of the pungent anaesthetic on a folded handkerchief held over her face. For a horribly bloody-long moment, all seemed lost.

But then, after what must have been thirty seconds, she made a choking noise deep in her throat and took in a short, strangled breath. I took away the ether.

"Michty me!" Bell shouted. "Keep giving the ether!"

She took another short breath and her spasms eased. Her neck relaxed and her arms went limp, but she continued to breathe.

I touched her forehead. "Sir, her skin is hot, as if she were on fire."

Bell ran the back of his hand over her face. "Sechenov, Madam Tolstaya, please, we need ice. Get ice and cold water."

The maid flew out of the room, followed by the countess. It seemed like forever, but in what must have really only been five minutes, they returned, accompanied by two sleepy young men, each carrying two buckets of ice. They left their cold burdens and, with terror in their eyes, departed in haste.

"Lock the door again," Bell said. He then stripped the quilts and bedding away from the empress.

"No, you mustn't expose the empress!" Countess Tolstaya shouted.

"Cover her with sheets soaked in ice water," Bell said.

Outside, Dr. Meyer demanded entrance and guards pounded on the door. The noise aroused the entire palace, but we refused to unlock the door.

Through the uproar, we heard shouting. "The empress is dead! They murdered the empress! Oh, God save us. Where is the tsar? Call the tsar!"

"Och!" Bell removed the Webley revolver from the instrument case and handed it to the professor. "Sechenov, shoot anyone who comes through that door. We must not be disturbed."

The whole mad ordeal continued until the grey light of a false dawn seeped through the windows. As tiny fingers of light poked into the room, the empress's fever came down and the spasms grew less frequent.

I gradually reduced the dose of ether as her breathing became deep and regular. Dr. Bell sat at the bedside and timed her pulse with his folding gold watch. "Her heartbeat is down to one hundred."

Dr. Bell put away his watch and, after examining the swollen purple bruise, turned to Countess Tolstaya. "Countess, now please tell us the exact sequence of events."

The countess, who had been violently sobbing wiped away her tears. "We were in the English garden, admiring the flowers and having tea, when Princess Yurievskaya sent her maid with a gift for the empress, which was wrapped in beautiful red silk..." She took a deep breath and continued. "The note said the princess wished to make amends and be friends with the empress." Countess Tolstaya was again wracked with violent sobs.

"Please, go on," Dr. Bell said.

She collected herself and continued to speak. "We returned to this room to open the present. There, on the table... The crumpled silk wrapper lay next to five beautifully-carved matryoshka dolls, each smaller than the next so they nestled inside one another. The dolls represented traditional peasant girls, except for the smallest, a baby."

"Interesting," Dr. Bell said.

"Princess Yurievskaya had them specially carved. The empress removed the dolls, one by one. She was almost childlike with her delight, but after removing the last doll, she cried out with pain and clutched her wrist. I thought she had a minor sprain, but almost immediately, she complained of pain in her stomach and went to bed."

"And then?" Bell asked.

"I sent for Professor Sechenov, and later, Princess Yurievskaya kindly sent her personal physician. He was about to administer an injection when you arrived. He left the syringe on the dresser."

"Ah, ha..." Professor Bell inspected each of the dolls and, with a certain amount of theatrical flair, removed the remains of a brown insect from inside the last and smallest doll. "There is our culprit."

He held up the tiny, brown object. "The remains of a male of the species, *Latrodectus Theridiidae*, better known as the Black Widow Spider. The female devoured her mate and then bit the empress on the wrist."

"Are you certain?" Professor Sechenov asked.

"Aye. See here." He pointed to the empress's wrist. "A small punctuate wound in the middle of the purple swelling. Severe abdominal pain and muscle spasms are typical symptoms. The question remains, how did the spider get into the dolls?"

The empress opened her eyes and gazed about the room. "The noise, please stop the terrible racket," she whispered.

"ENOUGH!" The countess flew to the door. "The empress lives. Do not disturb her. She needs peace and quiet."

The shouting subsided, but Dr. Meyer continued to demand entrance. The countess admonished him and he skulked away.

"It would be difficult for a spider to enter the smallest doll. Could it have been placed there on purpose?" Professor Sechenov asked.

"I believe so... And there is more." Dr. Bell closely examined the syringe with its contents that Dr. Meyer intended to administer to the empress. "I suggest you analyze the contents of this syringe for strychnine."

"Strychnine?" Professor Sechenov asked.

"Strychnine causes the exact same symptoms as the bite of the Black Widow Spider. The venom causes muscle spasm, a high fever, and death by asphyxia. Meyer may have intended to poison the empress, and if there was suspicion, he would have produced the spider and claimed the death was accidental. Perhaps it is just as well that the spider bit her before he had a chance to give the poison."

The door flew open. A captain of the guards entered with a drawn saber and Meyer at his side. "Arrest these men!" Dr. Meyer shouted.

In an instant, Dr. Bell snatched up the syringe and placed the needle against Dr. Meyer's arm. The German doctor's face contorted. "No, please… Not that, please!"

"Confess, or I will inject the contents. It is strychnine, is it not?"

Meyer blubbered, broke down, and under Dr. Bell's prodding with the needle, admitted he had planned the empress's death. The guards took him away. The unknowing servants continued to clamor for our deaths, but thanks to Madame Tolstaya, we hurried away unmolested.

This evening, I was enjoying a bit of Dr. Bell's single malt whiskey while Professor Sechenov soundly beat Dr. Bell at chess. "Dr. Bell, congratulations, you were entirely correct about the empress and the strychnine. I must say, I am impressed," Sechenov said, as if to make amends.

The Professor bowed, and just the tiniest hint of a smile crossed his lips.

Mr. Tatum looked up from a two week old *London Times*. "Where have you gentlemen been?"

"Oh, out and about," I answered, cheekily.

"Well, when you were out and about, I gleaned some interesting information through a friend. I have been told that The Russian Secret Service brought in a German physician for the attempted murder of the empress."

"Really?" I smiled at Dr. Bell who did not return the smile.

"Yes, and during the interrogation, a very agitated Princess Yurievskaya arrived and accused the poor man of attempting to murder both her and the empress. She insisted on immediate punishment by burning his tongue with a red hot poker. The doctor died almost instantly."

Dr. Bell leaned back, extended his long legs, folded his hands over his chest and muttered to himself. "Was he acting alone, or was he part of a more sinister plot to destroy the royal family?"

"My concern exactly," Mr. Tatum said.

Dr. Bell puffed his pipe for a moment. "There may be three factions interested in killing the tsar — the student anarchists, perhaps the Germans, and we still haven't found the English officer, Campbell."

"The Okhrana has effectively destroyed the student groups. What is Penelope up to? Is she working with the German or is she still loyal to the Queen?" I asked, both out of curiosity and hoping I might get some inside information which I could use to ultimately win her affections.

"Mr. Doyle, that little problem may be in your hands," Mr. Tatum said.

Dr. Bell blew a perfect smoke ring. "In the meantime, Doyle, don't neglect your medical education. You have a woeful lack of knowledge concerning common poisons."

Bell had not lost his knack for making me feel inferior, but with twinkly eyes, he tossed a well-thumbed volume of Lucifer's *Common Poisons* onto my lap. "Study this with care if you have any interest in forensic medicine."

23 September 1881

During the night, a cold, white mist settled over St. Petersburg. This morning, when I went out, eerie spires and steeples loomed above the fog only to vanish seconds later. On the streets, heads and shoulders of ghostly people appeared above the mist, then mysteriously dissolved. Except for the muffled ringing of a church bell, the streets were silent.

It was disorienting and I had a queer sensation of foreboding. Perhaps it was the growing cold; I had brought clothes for the summer, thinking we were only going to stay for a few weeks. If I knew that we would be here this long, I would have brought my heavy tweeds. As it was, I pulled the collar of my jacket tighter and found my way through silent streets to Pavlov's laboratory.

The secret police had rounded up all their suspects, and during the past few days, there were too few victims to continue the blood coagulation experiments. Further work would depend on another purge or pogrom.

Pavlov remained convinced that a substance in the plasma portion of blood influenced clotting and that he would eventually cure the royal bleeding disease. He concentrated more than ever on conditioned reflexes and brain function.

Dmitri has taken a special interest in the snakes and, to Pavlov's great joy, taught them to search for food at his whistle. This has supported Pavlov's hypothesis that even the primitive brain can respond to secondary stimuli.

Unfortunately, poor Dmitri has become absent-minded. On several occasions, he forgot to clean the animal cages and, more than once, left the cage doors open.

When I arrived, Dmitri sat at his crude table, rocking back and forth, holding his head in his hands. I was sure he said, "Pain, the terrible pain …" in English, but then I was probably mistaken. At my questioning, he knocked his head with a fist and merely shrugged his shoulders, like any poor peasant.

I assisted Pavlov in an intricate operation to stimulate the vagus nerve within the skull, but we had hardly opened the animal's head when he died. That ended the operation.

On the way out, I pointed to my head and, with signs, asked Dmitri if he felt better. Dmitri's face was an ashen mask, without expression. He rocked back and forth and didn't respond. I assumed he simply wanted to be left alone.

Ferguson had invited me to lunch at the Hotel Europa, and since the fog had lifted, I decided on a leisurely walk along the Embankment. Immediately outside the laboratory, a poorly dressed, but pretty, girl stepped in my way and timidly held out a scrap of paper. I tried to brush her off, thinking she was a beggar or a prostitute. The girl shivered, either from cold or from fright. "Please a message for you, sir," she said. I barely grasped her meaning, but took the paper. It was a hurried, penciled scrawl on a cheap bit of foolscap paper. "Tonight, Pen —"

"Who gave this to you, and where?" I asked.

The girl barely whispered. "La Maison de Beaux Rêves."

Before I could question her further, she ran down the street and turned into an alley. I followed, but she was fleet-footed and I lost sight of her. After another minute, not knowing in which direction to run, I stopped, out of breath, and examined the slip of paper. It must be a message from Penelope but what and where was La Maison de Beaux Rêves?

Ferguson was at the bar, but a waiter whisked us to a table near the window. Dick was eager to tell me about his latest sport, a thirty-foot sailing yacht. I didn't have such interesting news and waited to talk until we had finished the main course and were spooning up a chocolate pudding and sipping a nice Madeira.

"Dick, what is La Maison de Beaux Rêves?"

"Oh, Doyle, that is no place for a nice Edinburgh lad. The House of Beautiful Dreams was once a fine hotel but is now a notorious gentleman's club. The worst dregs of the Russian officer corps and dissolute noblemen engage in the vilest sort of vice there. When they are finished with a girl, her body often ends up in the river."

"Is it open to non-members?"

"Absolutely not! The members pay a big initiation fee for the privilege of keeping rooms for their women and to have a private place to gamble and drink. They allow guests, but the place is heavily guarded and there is a password. I am shocked that you would even consider going there, my friend." Dick said.

Dick paid the bill and clapped me on the back. "If you want a woman, there are plenty of actresses and dancers in St. Petersburg. You don't have to go to the Beaux Rêves. Come with me. You will have more fun sailing. There is to be a regatta when the tsar reviews the fleet."

"I am just curious. Where is this den?"

Dick lit up a cigar and puffed, thoughtfully, before speaking. "Don't even think of going there; more than one visitor has lost his life in a drunken brawl or a duel. These Russians are unpredictable."

"I wouldn't but it's, just, well, I have an old friend who …"

"Ahhh yes, an old friend… Well, if your *old friend* really must know, it is the yellow building in Suavaroskaya Place next to the Embankment."

I was totally confused. Penelope had brushed me off and disappeared. Why should I care about her? But was she in the clutches of evil and in desperate need of my help?

By the time I arrived at my quarters and took Sasha for a walk, I was resolved to ignore the message and mind my own business. I mentioned the incident to Mr. Tatum who snatched the slip of paper from my hand and held it to the light, searching for a hidden message.

There was nothing more. He became serious. "This could be a genuine plea. If so, she had only seconds to write, meaning she is in danger. On the other hand, it could be an attempt to lure you into a trap."

"Either way, Mr. Tatum, I don't see how anything dealing with Penelope is really any of my business," I said, though it really wasn't the truth.

"If this involves a threat to the tsar, it is our business, yours as much as mine. Penelope is either onto something or else she is part of another plot. I must investigate; don't do anything until I return." Mr. Tatum clapped on his hat, immediately dashed away, and hailed a droshky.

Sasha put her head on her paws and whined while I paced the floor. I simply wanted to return home, start a medical practice, and do a bit of writing.

I wrestled with my thoughts. *Penelope doesn't care about me, so why should I care about her?* But then, I couldn't forget those brief, but passionate, kisses. Perhaps I might have a chance with the girl. I brooded over the single word 'tonight' that indicated urgency and suggested danger. But whose side is she on? She did save me when I was in prison . . . *If she is in trouble*, I thought, *I should save her . . .*

The idea of visiting a gentleman's club aroused my interest. I had heard of the 'hells' of London, where young rakes gambled and indulged in every vice. In Edinburgh, the most sinful evenings were student club haggis dinners, an academic lecture, and a debate about some obscure issue. At the end of the evening, a half-dozen of us or so would get tipsy with a bottle of port.

A very grim-faced Mr. Tatum returned shortly after seven o'clock, just as Dr. Bell and I sat down to a light supper. He removed his coat and accepted a cup of tea with a boiled egg.

"Mr. Doyle, Penelope has been secluded in the palace with the entourage of the Duchess of Edinburgh. Our agents have observed her leaving at night to visit various suspicious groups and the German Embassy. We don't know if she contacted her husband's colleague and is working to kill the tsar or if she's still on our side."

"I am interested in Penelope, but is she really our affair?"

"Aye." Dr. Bell lit up his pipe. "There is a great deal at stake. We must see this affair to the bitter end."

Mr. Tatum pulled his ear and made a sad face. "Penelope is very resourceful, but she may be over her head with a Count Lopukhof, an especially handsome man from an Ulan regiment. The army is heavily influenced by the German military and many officers are bitter about the tsar's reforms. They may well be plotting another assassination. This Count is a ruthless killer, known for beating soldiers without mercy. His colonel seconded him to the

Palace Guard, ostensibly as punishment, but perhaps to place him close to the tsar. Penelope and the count have disappeared. He may have taken her against her will, or she may be working with him. The count frequents the Maison de Beaux Rêves."

"If this is so important, why not send a trained agent who could do a better job?" I asked.

"This is a delicate situation; it would not do for a British agent to kill this Lopukhof. If you goad the man into making the first move, then succeed in killing him, it will appear to be a simple crime of passion."

I put my head in my hands. Mr. Tatum's argument made sense, but I wasn't a killer. On the other hand, I was intrigued by the prospect of seeing the Maison de Beaux Rêves. Furthermore, I couldn't let Dr. Bell down.

"What do you suggest?" I asked.

"You will gain entrance to the club, dressed as a debonair young dandy in your evening suit. The Maison de Beaux Rêves is heavily guarded by off-duty secret police officers, but you will not be going in blind. One of my informers told me the password, 'Sevastopol.' "

"How does he know it is correct?"

"He learned it from a drunken friend and assured me it is valid. Even better, he also knows the location of the valve that shuts off the gas to the entire building."

"What good is that?" I asked.

"If you get into serious trouble, fire a single pistol shot. At the signal, he will shut the gas valve and the lights will go out. In the darkness, you will have a better chance to escape. Early in the evening, women will mainly be on the first floor on the lookout for customers, and most of the regular members will be upstairs in the gambling den with their own mistresses. That is where I expect you will find Penelope, but remember, this Lopukhof is an expert swordsman and has killed men in duels," Mr. Tatum said.

I carefully fastened the studs, polished my shoes to a high shine, and smoothed the wrinkles from my dinner jacket.

"You will attract less attention if you are disheveled and drunk. Rinse your mouth with brandy and put a few drops on your collar, but drink no alcohol after you arrive. Keep your wits about you," Mr. Tatum said.

"He should look a bit older. A light powdering of flour in the hair will do the trick. You had best take the Webley," Dr. Bell said.

Unfortunately, I could not conceal the big pistol and would have to rely on the little derringer. Even then, it made a bulge in my coat. We decided on the waistcoat pocket where it would appear to be a pocket watch.

"Now, laddie, one more thing. You must stagger a bit to appear as if you are drunk." Dr. Bell said. "Please, give it a go for us."

I wobbled across the room in my best imitation of a drunken gait. Dr. Bell watched closely. "No, no, no. That won't do. Think what a drunk really looks like. Practice a wide-based gait, like a patient with tertiary syphilis." That was the clue I needed, since I had studied many patients with syphilis of brain.

"Now, pronounce Se-VAST-o-pol like a Russian," Mr. Tatum said.

Dr. Bell gave me a brotherly clap on the shoulder and took one hundred rubles from his wallet. "Doyle, stealth and deception tend to be superior to brute force, but there are also times when this may be helpful." He then handed me his cane. "Be careful."

The driver had apparently taken many a customer to the Beaux Rêves, for he made a knowing leer when he held out his hand for a tip. Once on the street, I wobbled on a wide gait, feeling my way over the cobblestones with the cane. The red door was flanked by two grim, uniformed guards who barred the entrance with crossed sabers. I mumbled the magic word, "Se-VAST-o-pol." With no change of expression, the guards opened the door to a warm, darkened room filled with semi-naked men and women.

The light was low, the windows were hung with crimson velvet drapes, and the furniture was covered with red damask. There were several large, stone fireplaces with roaring fires. Gas lights, shaded with red glass, cast a scarlet glow over the room, and huge mirrors reflected wildly gyrating women and men. A hairy man with a naked girl on either arm splashed in a giant pool. With a roar of delight, he turned his face to a stream of foaming yellow liquid that spurted from the mouth of a woman's statue in the middle of the fountain. Marble cherubs gaily pissed streams of foam over the cavorting women.

The hairy man caught a mouthful and sprayed his companions who laughed with apparent glee. To my utter amazement, the fountain was filled with champagne. Beyond the pool, a dusky Nubian, wearing only giant gold earrings, swayed to an African rhythm sawed out by a trio of women with strange, stringed instruments.

I leaned on my cane and stared, dumbfounded, at exotic blondes, brunettes, tall girls, short girls, and several with oriental features who twisted their hips to the music. Others reclined on lush, upholstered divans. A woman exuding a musky scent appeared out of the reddish gloom and took my arm. "What is your preference?" she whispered.

I slurred my words. "A glass of champagne."

She breathed into my ear. "We have three enchanting ladies experienced in the arts of love, from Paris — or would you care for a fresh, young virgin?"

I mumbled in French and accepted a glass of the bubbly, but remembered Mr. Tatum's words of caution. I spilled the drink which added to my appearance of a bumbling drunk.

Meanwhile, I lurched on my cane, seemingly in search of a companion for the night. I could hardly tear my eyes away from the myriad varieties of voluptuous women, with breasts bared to the fondling of men. I had never dreamed that such a place existed. I tried to remove all lustful thoughts from my head and remember my mission; it was not easy…

Even though it was early, many of the officers were in the last stages of intoxication and reeled about, from one woman to another. The main sport appeared to be ripping off their clothing and dragging women into the pool. I sank onto a plush divan with a doll-like oriental girl who spoke neither Russian nor French. Without a word, she sat on my lap and immediately began to loosen my trousers, but I brushed her off and looked over her shoulder.

At first, in the reddish glow, all the women looked alike, but I gradually distinguished the blondes from the brunettes, the slender from the plump, and the exotic from the plain. None of them resembled Penelope, even if she was disguised. From Mr. Tatum's description, I recognized the curving staircase that led to the second floor gambling den.

I gave the oriental, doll-like girl a friendly squeeze and wobbled up the grand marble steps to yet another double door, flanked by two guards. Once again, my mumbled "Se-VAST-o-pol" did the trick.

Despite clouds of tobacco smoke, the vast room glittered beneath brilliant gas lamps in great chandeliers. I was arrested by the sight of a mural, *CRIMEA*, depicting the Russian flag waving over valorous Russian cannons blasting away at English soldiers. One wall was filled with paintings of nude women and another showed a mounted Cossack driving a lance into a great, bleeding stag.

Men in full dress uniforms or evening clothes, and women in the latest Paris fashions, surrounded green baize tables with roulette wheels or games of baccarat. The scene was beyond my wildest imagination. Scantily-clad women went about carrying trays with glasses of champagne or stronger drink. Aside from the loser's sighs, or the occasional happy shout of a winner, the room was relatively quiet.

I nearly lost my balance on the step that led down to the room, but my misstep surely gave credence to my assumed drunkenness. I hobbled to the nearest table where officers and painted women were assembling about a roulette wheel and numbered squares. I bumped into a short, troll-like fellow with a penciled mustache standing next to the wheel.

"Will the gentleman place a bet?" he asked.

I was at a loss, but wordlessly took Dr. Bell's one hundred ruble note from my wallet. The fellow whisked it out of my hand and, with a disdainful grimace, gave me one blue chip.

The others piled chips on numbered squares, seemingly at random. Since my mother's birthday fell on the seventh day of July, the seventh month, I placed my single chip on the red seven.

The croupier, the same fellow who snatched my one hundred rubles, spun the wheel and sent a small, white ball on a tilted track in the opposite direction. The wheel spun and spun, then slowed. After an eternity of waiting, the ball dropped into a red pocket, number seven.

The croupier raked in stacks of red, white, and blue chips from the other players, then, disdainfully, pushed a pile of blue chips to me. I counted twenty-seven, worth the incredible sum of two thousand seven hundred rubles, more money than I had seen in months. "The money, please," I mumbled in my drunken voice, despite my urge to continue.

"No, no, it is not done. You must not stop," the other players muttered.

"It is customary for the winner to continue play," the croupier said, his face an angry mask.

I rapped the table with my cane. "Je veux mon argent," I said, with great emphasis on each word. The croupier and players were silent.

I pushed the stack of chips toward the croupier who, with a show of anger, tossed ruble notes fluttering down the table. I counted each one, stuffed them in my pocket and, with a nod, hobbled on.

I went a few steps, leaned heavily on the cane, and caught midst the acrid tobacco smoke a faint familiar scent. I sniffed again, but there was nothing. I went in the direction of a buffet table at the end of the room.

There it was, again, unmistakably, a whiff of orange blossoms — but there was no sign of Penelope. I hoped to sharpen my wits and accepted a cup of coffee from a sweet young waitress. All the while, people were muttering in French, "That drunk young man took his winnings" and "That damn cad's no gentleman."

I tensed when a heavily-muscled man with black, mutton-chop, side whiskers rose from a baccarat table, threw down his cards, and bared his teeth at me with an angry scowl.

I gave my best imitation of a silly, drunken smirk, went on sipping my coffee, and paid him no attention. A moment later, his scowl changed to a wicked smile, as if he had found a new toy. It was then I noticed his arm locked around a woman's neck. Was it a fond embrace or was she a prisoner?

Her face was heavily rouged, and her mouth was a red slash, like any common harlot. I squinted over my cup at that brute of a man. His dark blue, double-breasted jacket and skin-tight, blue breeches with a red stripe tucked into black, knee-high boots, gave every indication that he was a cavalry man. A gold, hilted dress sword hanging from his belt added to my sense of alarm.

"Who is that man?" I whispered to the nearest waitress.

"Count Lopukhof," she replied.

It was then that I saw wilted orange blossoms in the woman's tight ringlets. Penelope? My heart skipped a beat. Was there warning in her eyes or was she daring me to action?

The count's wicked smile in an instant turned to a mean grimace. "Your name, sir?" he asked.

"Conan Doyle."

"A damn Englishman?"

"Scotch-Irish, actually."

He roared with laughter. "Oh, dearie, where is your quaint little plaid skirt?"

I threw my coffee dregs in his face. Lopukhof tensed, and in a flash, he released Penelope, drew his sword, and slashed the air only inches from my face. There were scattered cheers and a shout of "Down with the English!"

I released the sword blade from Dr. Bell's cane and made a clumsy attempt to parry his thrusts. It was no use. He flicked the razor-sharp steel back and forth, from one side to another, slicing through one arm of my dinner jacket, then the other.

With a look of wicked joy, he made a long slash down one trouser leg but did not draw a drop of blood. He showed off his expert swordsmanship and total mastery over me, his hapless victim. The crowd stamped their feet and roared their approval at this new sport.

I side-stepped, dodged backward, and stabbed at his chest with the cane-sword, but there was no escape from that slashing blade. He lunged forward with a wicked grin while swinging the cruel steel blade hither and thither.

Then, apparently tired of sport, he smashed the flat of his sword just above my ear. I saw stars and fell on one knee. Another blow struck the other side of my head and I went, almost insensible, flat on my back.

The roaring in my ears subsided, while the bloodthirsty crowd noisily urged him to finish the job. Through blurred eyes, I watched the sword deliberately approach until the tip broke the skin of my throat.

Before he could give the final, killing thrust, a slender officer — in a resplendent white and gold uniform with a visored, black cap drawn down over his eyes — stepped over my prone body.

He thrust a slender rapier into the count's bulging crotch and then slashed with the tip of the blade until there was a gaping, bloody hole. The count bawled with pain, and blood streamed down his leg.

He roared and turned on his new assailant with bare hands. My savior adroitly side-stepped and drew the tip of his rapier across the count's face, leaving a scratch on his nose.

I came to my senses, fumbled in a side coat pocket for the pistol, and found the derringer in my waistcoat. The count was going back for another bare-handed attack when I drew the pistol to aid the gentleman who had saved my life.

My poorly-aimed bullet nicked the count's left ear, but he was unfazed. The onlookers howled for blood. It looked like my savior was going to be slaughtered by the count and then, surely, I would be next.

And then, just as the count was about to execute a killing blow, the gas lights dimmed and sizzled out.

I was lost in a strange room filled with hostile enemies and black as a tropical night. It was then that I heard a familiar voice behind me whispering in my ear. "Come with me."

Was I dreaming, or was it the voice of — Agafea? I was stunned.

How did she come to be in this place?

I was confused but didn't argue as hands dragged me on wobbly legs through the darkened room. We bumped against bodies, rammed tables, and reached a stairwell, where, I realized, there were two sets of hands pulling me along. We didn't stop until we reached a room on the third floor.

The small, slender soldier who was my savior lit a candle, and without the hat, I realized that he, or should I say she, was indeed — Agafea!

I couldn't believe it. What was she doing here, and why was she dressed like an officer? I practically burst into tears because I was grateful for her assistance.

And then I recognized, beneath her heavy rouge and paint, the pert, upturned nose of the second woman. My dear Penelope suddenly threw her arms around me and planted a smeary kiss on my lips. She pulled away and, with her hands on her hips, glowered at me. "What took you so long?" she asked.

"No, the question should be, why are you here and why is Agafea dressed like an officer?" I asked.

Agafea smiled. "The ladies here find my uniform very attractive."

I stared, speechless, and then averted my gaze.

Agafea shook her head. "I thought you would have guessed by now. I prefer girls to boys. In this place, I can satisfy my desires and the women keep my secret. I am much kinder than the men."

I turned scarlet. "It is unnatural," I mumbled.

"Ah, yes, I should've expected as much from you, Scottish Calvinist. From the day I was born, my father desperately wanted a son to take his place in the regiment. As a child, I learned to become that boy he never had. It was not hard since I never played with dolls or liked dresses but loved to dress as a boy. Father let me take fencing lessons instead of sewing and taught me to shoot. So, now, I have certain propensities and I don't intend to change," Agafea said.

There was no time to learn more because, as we spoke, the shouts and disorder downstairs increased to a tumultuous, angry roar. Before Penelope wiped the paint from her face, feet pounded up the stairs and fists rapped on doors.

"Open up! Who is in there?"

"The two of you, in the bed, cover up. Quick!" Agafea whispered, as she removed her uniform, flung it over the back of a chair, and literally dove into the bed. The door was still ajar.

"Shouldn't we lock the door?" I asked.

"They will be less suspicious of an open door," Agafea said.

Three men, holding candles and pistols, shoved their way into the room.

"Can't you see we have a customer?" Agafea said, in French, with a low, seductive voice.

The officers saw the uniform flung aside on the floor and me in bed with two women. Penelope planted her painted face on mine and Agafea made violent motions beneath the blankets. To all appearances, we were in the midst of an orgy of love-making. It worked; the men backed out of the room with a curt apology, but left the door open. If it wasn't such a tense encounter, it would probably have been the most exciting moment of my life. I had never enjoyed the focused attentions of two women at the same time and it was heavenly to be in their arms and have their warm bodies so close, even though I knew Agafea would have preferred to be alone with Penelope.

We continued our charade until the men were gone and it was safe to leave. Despite fearing for our lives, I savored being enveloped in the warmth of Penelope's arms until, with a bit of wriggling, Agafea crawled next to Penelope and shared a squeeze and giggles. I was left alone on the cold side of the bed. My head ached from the count's blow, but I got out of bed, shut and locked the door, and surveyed the room. There was an oversized bed, a mirror on the ceiling, a table, chairs, and a closet filled with an assortment of clothing. My suit was in shreds, but I still had the sword cane and one bullet left in the derringer.

Penelope rolled away from Agafea. "How do we get out of here?" she asked.

"We wait until they are asleep from alcohol or opium. There is a secret passage to the street and I have bribed the guards," Agafea said.

When the commotion died down, Agafea dressed in her uniform, put her hair up in a tight bun, and pulled the cap's visor down over her eyes. The transformation was remarkable.

"Now, we need a shawl for Penelope and a long woman's cape for Dr. Doyle." Agafea laughed. "They will think I am an officer leaving with two women. And here, you will need this candle."

I put the candle, matches, and the derringer in a pocket and hid the cane beneath the long, dark cape. We clasped hands. Agafea led the way along a pitch-black corridor to a hidden door, down one flight of creaky stairs, then another, to a locked door. She produced a key and opened the door onto a dark alley. I took Penelope's hand and commenced to run, but tripped and went flying, head over heels. My cape fell away.

"Halt!" A match flickered; a bullseye lantern flared and lit up the alley. My slashed trousers and dinner jacket were the giveaway. Two uniformed men with bayoneted muskets blocked our escape route.

Penelope opened her shawl, revealing a nearly-bare bosom, and cooed seductively. "Boys, you must be lonesome out here all by yourself while the officers party. Come, let's have a good time."

While the two young soldiers admired Penelope, I rolled over, found the derringer and, with a lucky shot, put out the bullseye light.

We were off and running, with bullets zinging over our heads. The guards raised the cry while we ducked in and out of alleys. Within minutes, there was the clatter of hooves, and random gunshots popped in our direction.

We had not gotten far enough away; all seemed lost. We would be shot or captured in the next few moments. "Follow me. NOW!" Agafea said softly, but with urgency.

And then, with what seemed insane recklessness, she led us across the open Palace Square just as a troop of horses came down Nevsky Prospekt and cantered beneath the Triumphal Arch.

We put on another burst of speed and zigzagged across the open square. We were surely lost, but Agafea ran into shadows between two large buildings and led the way to a small, hidden, side door. She twisted a key in a well-oiled lock, opened the heavy door, and dragged us down uneven stone steps into what could have been in a tomb.

Water dripped in the distance. I felt my way along a cold, damp, stone wall while carefully placing my feet on stone steps leading down into a dark, cavernous room. There were loud rustlings, and something small brushed against my leg. Penelope uttered a strangled scream. "Rats!"

"It is nothing. Be quiet and light the candle," Agafea said.

I fumbled for the matches and struck a light. In the still air, the candle burned with a tall flame revealing a room with stone walls and immense pillars that went on endlessly in the gloom. Everywhere I looked, cats lounged on stacks of wooden crates. A large orange tom flicked his tail and regarded us with suspicious, orange eyes until he leaped down and rubbed against Agafea's leg.

She stooped and petted the cat. "Strays from all over the city find shelter in the cellars beneath the Hermitage and volunteers give them food. Every week, I bring all the scraps from our kitchen and look after the sick animals," she said.

"Why are they tolerated here?" I asked.

"They control the rats and mice that would destroy the paintings. There is no time to lose. Follow me." She led us up flight of stairs to a splendid room with an arched ceiling and giant columns. The walls were hung with paintings. Even I could recognize the work of old masters.

"This is part of Catherine the Great's collection." Agafea said. She hurried us through galleries, into another hall filled with Egyptian mummies and statues of ancient kings and queens, and then through the Greek and Roman gallery. I was getting a private tour of the Hermitage, so magnificent it was almost easy to forget that we were in danger. However, Agafea hurried us along until we came out a back way onto the bank of the Neva River.

She extinguished the candle and, in the dark, led us down a bank to the water's edge where mist drifted in from the sea.

Agafea felt in the dark. "We are in luck, the skiff is still here."

"What are we to do?" Penelope asked.

178

"Take the skiff and drift with the current on this side until you reach the English Church. Then, and only then, go to the other side. You will be safe if you do exactly as I say. I will leave you now. Good luck."

I helped Penelope into the little boat, cast off, and, as Agafea said, the current carried us, hidden in the mist, until the homes along the English Embankment and then the church loomed above.

I rowed hard to cross the current until our skiff touched the muddy bank of Vasilevsky Island. We stood on the muddy shore for a time, listening to the burbling of little eddies on the Neva.

I could hear her soft breathing, but Penelope was an indistinct shadow in the dark, wispy fog. She shivered and pulled the shawl tighter. A fish jumped. A sea bird squawked and rose on urgent flapping wings. If only I had wings, I would fly away with Penelope. Dawn was not far away.

I pulled the skiff to higher ground. "Penelope, why were you with that man, in that place?"

"The count is a real man, not a damn silly boy."

"Then why did you send a message for help?"

"It is part of the game, a great game that you and that doctor are in — one that is way over your heads."

She beat on my chest with her fists and burst into tears. I was confused. Why did she cry? I hated seeing her distress. Was I in love with this strange girl? I dried her tears with my torn sleeve.

"But, Penelope, we are under orders from the Queen."

"Oh, who cares about that wretched woman? What has she done but persecute your people and make war?"

"Are you a traitor?" I asked.

"A traitor? What is a traitor? Words, words, you will never understand. It is time for a new Europe and we must embrace new words and thoughts!"

She clutched my lapels and spoke with a new urgency. "You must choose sides." She melted into my arms and I feverishly sought her lips. I wasn't sure what she meant, but at that moment, I would have done anything she asked. "Penelope, dear …"

I leaned in to kiss her and she pulled away. In an instant, without another word, she was gone. I was stunned. Every time, just

179

as we were getting closer, she would run away. Where did she go? Half an hour later, I crept into Dr. Sechenov's garden, removed my muddy shoes, and slipped up the back stairs to my room. Mr. Tatum, in a tattered dressing gown, sat in my leather covered chair with his feet on a leather ottoman. The room was lit by the stump of a single candle.

Sasha sleepily rose and licked my hand. I sat on the bed, took off my slashed suit, and carefully stuffed the ruble notes I had won inside a book. Mr. Tatum regarded me through lowered lids, as if he was half asleep, but his voice was crisp. "Tell me every detail of your encounter with Count Lopukhov."

I couldn't lie, but I didn't provide every detail of my singular adventure. I mentioned a 'young officer' who came to my rescue, without giving away Agafea's secret, and said only that I had spoken with Penelope for a few minutes. He looked at me with those hooded eyes for a long time.

I suspected he knew I was not telling everything. Perhaps, the person who shut off the gas had already reported to him.

"Mr. Doyle, I thank you, and the Crown thanks you. Sir, you have put yourself in great danger for service to the Queen." He rose and clapped me on the back. "If it was up to me, I would give you a medal for bravery."

24 September 1881

This morning, when I put one foot on the floor, the room whirled and, all of a sudden, I went down. I was still dizzy with a pounding headache when Marya arrived with the morning tea.

She immediately fetched Dr. Bell, who listened to my story. "Arthur, my boy, you should get a medal for your work. Unfortunately, you have a bit of a concussion. Cold compresses and a day's rest will set you right," he said, after a bit of poking and prodding.

Marya arranged pillows so I could have tea in bed. The dear girl ran to the kitchen and returned with towels soaked in cold water which she applied to my poor head. Within an hour, when Dr. Bell returned, I felt much better.

"Arthur, the American ambassador sent an urgent message requesting my assistance. Since you are in good hands, I will be away most of the day," he said.

"Is it a medical problem?" I asked.

"An American citizen is dead."

"Is it anyone we know?"

"The Texan who brought the snakes to Pavlov."

"Cowboy Bill?"

"I believe that is what he was called. Aye," Dr. Bell replied.

"I am coming with you," I said.

"No, you must rest."

While we were on the ship, Cowboy Bill was the picture of good health. I could not believe he was dead. "I insist on going with you," I said.

"Hmm, well, maybe some fresh air will be good for you. If you insist on going, fetch the instrument case and follow me," he said.

I was up and dressed when the ambassador, a middle-aged fellow named John Foster, arrived in a troika, a light carriage drawn by three horses. Poor Sasha was outside and, to my embarrassment, leaped into the carriage and settled herself at my feet. Mr. Foster was a typical Yankee with a top hat, bow tie, a black frock coat, and the most amazing long, flowing, white side whiskers.

"My, oh my! That's a good looking dog. Reminds me of my Rover."

"What kind of dog was Rover?" I asked.

"He was a good bird dog, probably with some Pointer and Beagle. When I was a boy, we hunted together on our farm back in Indiana," the ambassador said.

I was relieved that he did not object to Sasha and was mystified that an ambassador could have such a humble beginning on a farm out in the wilderness. His low background made mine look almost aristocratic. "Sir, if you grew up in the country on a farm, how did you end up being an ambassador?"

"Well, that's the beauty of America, boy. Anybody can become anything they want if they are willing to work hard enough for it. Yes, I grew up on a farm, but I didn't stay there. You see, I walked for many miles to hear Abraham Lincoln talk at one of his great debates with Stephen Douglass and that changed my life. Lincoln inspired me to go east to study and get a college degree. Then, I got into politics and became Secretary of the Navy under Grant," he said. "Anybody who is willing to work as hard as me might be able to do the same."

"Aye. May I ask … There was a navy man on our ship, an engineer, named Gritz, claimed he built electric boats," I said.

Mr. Foster squinted and looked away. "Never heard of the fellow," he snapped.

He was abrupt and said no more; I settled back and scratched Sasha's ears. The driver whipped up the three matched, grey horses to a fast pace. I knew little about horses, but Dr. Bell became excited. "What breed are these horses?"

"Orlov Trotters, came out of an Arabian stallion years ago. There is nothing like them; when hitched to a troika, the center animal trots while the two on the side canter," the ambassador said.

We were flying along. "How can I help with this business?" Dr. Bell asked, once we left the city streets.

"I love horse racing and, you see, this fellow, Cowboy Bill, had a remarkable way with horses. He was clever, too. Learned the language well enough to get a job training race horses for a Colonel Shirapov." the ambassador said.

182

"How did he die?" Dr. Bell asked.

"They say he took his own life. But I knew Cowboy Bill and I just don't believe he was the type of man to commit suicide."

"Yes, I can look into it for you."

"I have to tell you, I don't trust these damn Russian officers. They don't do a damned thing but drink and gamble. I want someone who speaks English to look into this matter and you are well known for your ingenious detective work. I am grateful that you have agreed to accompany me today."

The rains had settled the dust, so the drive through the country was pleasant. The leaves were turning yellow, and the birch trees were already dropping leaves. Within an hour, we reached a regimental summer camp with a race track, stables, and officer's quarters. We paused to watch grooms exercise horses, and then, the ambassador directed our driver to Captain Shirapov's stables.

A half-dozen somber grooms and trainers idled under a tree with wide, spread limbs in front of the stable. Inspector Koivisto of the St. Petersburg police met us at the stable door with a wide smile and an extended hand. He shook hands with the professor. "Welcome, Dr. Bell. It's good to see you, but why are you here? The cowboy's death is a clear case of suicide."

"I would be interested in your findings, especially, since we have come a long way," Dr. Bell said.

"The man clearly killed himself with his own pistol."

The ambassador puffed out his cheeks and spoke in a loud voice and in poor French. "The dead man was a citizen of the United States. And as a representative of the U.S.A., I demand a full investigation. If you don't cooperate, I will go the tsar himself."

"Well..." Inspector Koivisto scowled and jutted out his chin in a fit of anger, but his demeanor quickly changed. "Fine! Out of respect for Dr. Bell, I will allow him to view the scene. But I am certain he will merely confirm my conclusions."

Sasha scampered at our heels as we entered the long, low shed with stalls where a half-dozen horses fed on hay and oats. A small double door led to the trainer's room. The stables were clean, with the pleasant smell of hay and horse. The room where Cowboy Bill had lived was comfortable though spartan. Cowboy Bill, dressed in a blue shirt and tan trousers, leaned back on a chair with his legs folded beneath. He looked almost jaunty with a red scarf at his neck, but his dim, sightless eyes were glazed.

"This is exactly how we found him," Inspector Koivisto said. "I opened his shirt to inspect the wound, but touched nothing else. He does need to be buried or shipped back to the United States at once."

Dr. Bell, chin in hand, surveyed the room. There was one window, a small, black, iron stove, and a neat, made-up bunk. The body faced a table with a nearly empty bottle of brandy and one glass. It appeared as if Cowboy Bill had been drinking alone. A pair of high, cowhide boots stood next to the door. The floor was spotless. Nothing was disturbed and there was no blood. In a way, the death scene was serene; too serene.

"May I see the wound, please?" Dr. Bell asked.

Inspector Koivisto casually pointed. "Here is a hole in his shirt over the entrance wound on the right side of his chest. There is no exit."

Dr. Bell went to his knees next to the body and gazed, intently, at the small bullet hole just beneath the breast on the right side. He gently palpated the surrounding skin and, after a moment, deliberately moved his index finger medially towards the breast bone. "Hmm, strange. There is very little blood."

"Yes, I commented on that in my report and concluded that he was dead before he had a chance to bleed."

"Where was the weapon?" Dr. Bell asked.

"In his right hand with his finger on the trigger." Koivisto replied.

"May I see the weapon?"

The inspector removed the revolver from a leather bag and passed it to Dr. Bell. It was an old-fashioned pocket pistol that had seen hard use but was clean and well-oiled. The wooden handle was scratched, and the brown finish on the barrel was worn down to bare metal. The barrel was marked, 'Patented 1855, Samuel Colt.'

Dr. Bell removed the cylinder and examined the chambers. "Inspector Koivisto, will you permit me to fire a shot?"

184

"Sir, I don't see the point. I must be leaving here soon; this isn't my only case, you know." the inspector said.

"Please, in the interest of truth, allow me just one shot. It will require but a few seconds."

"Very well."

"Dr. Doyle, kindly place a wad of paper just to the right of that hole in the wall."

I had not noticed the rat hole, perhaps two inches or less in diameter in the far wall, right at floor level. I tore a page from my notebook, wadded the paper into a small ball, and placed it as directed.

Dr. Bell took careful aim and pulled the trigger. There was a soft *bang* and a puff of smoke. The wad of paper 'jumped,' with a bullet hole left in dead center. Behind the paper, a small lead ball was about half-embedded in the wood.

"There! Your evidence! This was not a suicide."

The inspector balked. "What? I don't see how you can say that after firing one shot."

"It is basic ballistics. The ball is only .31 calibre. The powder charge was sufficient to kill a rat, but it would hardly scratch a man. Cowboy Bill could not have killed himself with this pea-shooter of a pistol."

Not a word was spoken while Dr. Bell spent a great deal of time filling and tamping his curved pipe with Cavendish. When it suited him, he lit up and puffed a cloud of fragrant, blue smoke.

The inspector coughed. "This is preposterous. Of course he died by his own hand. There could have been a heavier load in the chamber. There is certainly no other cause of death."

"Hmmm." Dr. Bell put down his pipe and minutely scrutinized the body. "Dr. Doyle, maybe you can shed some light on this case. If you will, tell us what you observe and your conclusions."

Why did he always have to treat me like a school boy, especially when I was not feeling up to par? I walked about the room glancing here and there.

I idly noted a plate, fork, and spoon, with another glass on a shelf. A dish towel hung from a nail next to the sink. To stall for

185

time, I took another look at the body. Damn, why hadn't I noticed it before? There was bleeding in his eyes. "Sir, there are sub-conjunctival hemorrhages in both eyes."

The tiniest hint of a smile appeared and disappeared on Dr. Bell's lips. "Ah yes. How could I have missed it? So sloppy of me. Thank you, Dr. Doyle." He then looked around the room. "Gentlemen, Cowboy Bill was dead before he received his gunshot wound. This is murder and should be treated as such," Dr. Bell said.

"Bah. Preposterous! How can you say that without demonstrating any other cause of death?" Koivisto responded.

"Dr. Doyle, kindly remove that red scarf from his neck."

The red scarf, what the Americans call a bandanna, was tightly knotted in back and folded in a triangle in the front of his neck. The knot was so tight that I had to pry it apart with a surgical probe. There was a slight bruise over Cowboy Bill's windpipe but nothing else.

Dr. Bell pointed at the bruise with his pipe. "Hemorrhages in the eyes indicate compression of the jugular veins causing severe intracranial pressure."

"They could've been caused by sand or dirt that got in his eyes while he was working with the horses."

"No, Inspector. An assassin garroted Cowboy Bill with his own scarf."

"I am sorry to say this, Dr. Bell, but that's impossible. That bruise is nothing. I say he died by his own hand."

"I most respectfully disagree, sir. He died by the slow compression of his jugular veins and the carotid arteries with his own scarf. It had to be a slow, painful death by strangulation. The knot was pulled tight when a stick or other instrument twisted the scarf about his neck." Dr. Bell said.

"But how can you prove it was murder?" asked Mr. Foster.

"Mr. Foster, since the deceased is an American, I need your permission to prove my point with one simple skin incision."

"Well, I don't know. This is highly irregular," the ambassador said. "We don't know if he has family and if they would approve of such a thing."

"Even if I can prove that he was murdered?" Dr. Bell asked.

Mr. Foster dithered, pursed his lips, and pulled at his side whiskers. "Is it absolutely necessary?"

"Yes, with one small incision I will prove that a bullet did not cause his death."

"Very well, Doctor."

"Doyle, a probe and a scalpel, please."

I placed the instruments on the table while Dr. Bell rolled up his sleeves and removed Cowboy Bill's shirt. No one spoke while Dr. Bell deliberately inserted the steel probe into the wound. The probe slid along the top of the fifth rib for a distance of four inches and obviously did not penetrate the chest cavity.

With a quick slash, he laid open the skin and demonstrated the round, lead ball buried in muscle tissue. There was no bleeding and it had not struck a vital organ.

Dr. Bell plucked out the harmless ball. "This bit of lead did not cause his death. The assailant first killed Cowboy Bill then fired the shot to make it look like suicide," he said.

The ambassador turned white, covered his mouth, and ran from the room. "Inspector, you must search for an exceptionally powerful man. The murderer was probably a soldier trained in the killing arts," Dr. Bell said.

"Da." Inspector Koivisto wrote in his notebook. "I stand corrected, Dr. Bell. It does appear to be murder, but still ..." he said, rather sullenly.

"If you need more proof, Inspector, here it is." Dr. Bell rinsed the instruments and his hands at the sink and picked up the dish towel. He inhaled deeply and glanced up at the empty glass on the shelf. "If you look closely, you will note that both the towel and the empty glass have traces of brandy. Another person drank with the victim and then rinsed the glass in hopes of misleading us to think that Cowboy Bill drank alone."

Damn, I had missed another clue. In the hope of redeeming myself, I again examined the corpse. I saw nothing new, though idly wondered why the left hand was open but the right was tightly clenched. The fingers were rigid even more than one would expect with rigor mortis.

I did not want to touch that cold, dead hand but forced down sour bile and pulled on his middle finger with all my strength. It broke with a sickening snap as I pried it open. At first glance, there was only a handful of horse feed inside his fist, but on closer inspection, I could see that a coarse brown powder was mixed in with the oats.

"What is this brown substance?" I asked.

"Ah, Doyle, you might amount to something, after all." Dr. Bell said, as he rolled the brown powder between his fingers. He smelled it, placed a small amount on his tongue, and poured the remainder into a glass jar. "It is quite bitter and appears to be some type of ground root that has been mixed with the oats."

Sasha came dashing into the room, her bushy tail sweeping back and forth. She immediately laid back her ears and, with her nose in the air, circled the corpse on stiff legs. She sniffed the dead body and, with surprising tenderness, licked the outstretched left hand.

At that moment, a carriage drawn by a fine pair of chestnut bays dashed into the little, grassy yard in front of the stable.

The driver, a white-haired but heavily-muscled man in the uniform of a Cossack sergeant, dropped the reigns and slowly stepped down. The fellow, with a hard, weathered face of an old campaigner, opened the carriage door and carefully assisted an army officer with a colonel's epaulettes and gold braid out of the carriage.

The colonel, nearly as old as his servant, stumbled, but the servant caught his arm and spoke gently to him. "Batya, take care. Please take care," he said.

"Batya means father, a term of endearment for a good commander. His driver was an old *denshchik*, or as the English say, a 'valet' or 'personal servant,' " Inspector Koivisto whispered.

The colonel tucked his chin into his chest and stood very erect, facing the crowd as if he were reviewing troops. He had the air of a man accustomed to command. Unlike many high ranking officers, he was clean shaven, except for a long salt and pepper mustache.

We came to attention and Koivisto saluted. "Good day, Colonel Shirapov," he said.

The colonel turned and gallantly assisted a strikingly handsome woman down from the carriage. She was an inch or two taller than the colonel and clung to his arm with a possessive air while holding a bright red parasol. She was at least twenty years his junior, dressed in the latest Parisian style and adorned with rings, bracelets, and a diamond necklace.

"Where is the American?" she asked. "I want to see Mercury."

"I am sorry. The American is dead." Inspector Koivisto said.

"Oh, that is too bad. He was so good with Mercury." She shook her head. "Still, I'd like to see my horse. Would someone please bring out Mercury? I am looking forward to seeing my husband ride him in the steeplechase tomorrow."

Colonel Shirapov said nothing, but he tensed and one eye twitched. We waited at the open stable door while a groom went to fetch the horse. The groom hesitated, was about to say something, but unlatched the gate. Mercury, a great, black stallion, laid back his ears, feebly kicked, and attempted to rear.

"I can't." The groom backed away. "The horse is too dangerous. Only the American could handle him. I will not," he said.

"That horse is sick," exclaimed Mr. Foster.

Colonel Shirapov walked a few steps. "He is just high strung… If you have finished your investigation, please leave my property," he said, in a low voice.

"He was perfectly gentle when Cowboy Bill worked with him," Mr. Foster said.

"I am a doctor. Please let me see him." Dr. Bell edged his way closer to the stall and peered intently at the stallion. "His nose is congested and there is sweat on his hindquarters. He does indeed appear to be ill and he should not be ridden."

"No!" The old Cossack growled. "Obey my colonel! That is an order. Prepare the horse."

And so they did. There was nothing else to do; we trudged away to the troika while Inspector Koivisto arranged for the body to be delivered to the American Embassy.

I whistled for Sasha. I called again and, in defiance of the colonel, returned to the stable. The poor dog was lying on a pile of hay, frothing at her mouth. Her eyes were closed and her head lay on her paws. She barely moved when I picked her up and carried her to the troika. What had happened to her? I felt bloody awful.

I petted her tangled fur and talked to her as if she were a baby. She didn't respond, and mucous bubbled from her nose. I was convinced she was dying, but she feebly raised her head when Dr. Bell looked into her eyes and applied his stethoscope to her chest.

He sighed and sat back with his legs outstretched, silent and deep in thought. What did he think happened to poor Sasha? What was wrong with her?

Dr. Bell said nothing and seemed unconcerned about my obvious distress. I hated him at that moment, but then I realized that maybe he had larger issues than the health of one poor dog on his mind. Had cocaine hardened him to all suffering?

It was my fault. I should not have brought poor Sasha on this trip. If I had left her at home, she would be fine now. What had she gotten into here that had made her so sick? I felt so horrible about saving her from the lab only then to lead her to her death here …

I stroked her silky ears and begged her forgiveness. She made a low *woof* and licked my hand. It was as if she sensed my distress and, even though she was ill, wanted to comfort me. I carried her to the troika and we set off for home.

The ambassador talked about horses most of the way home. "Mercury is a great horse, but hard to handle. Cowboy Bill claimed he could talk to horses like an Indian. Within three weeks, he had Mercury eating out of his hand, and damn, was that horse ever so quick. You've never seen such a fast horse, especially when Cowboy Bill took the reins. Now, that young woman expects Colonel Shirapov to ride him and win the steeplechase, but the colonel can't handle Mercury the way that Bill did. If you ask me, the whole thing is going to end badly."

We arrived home in the late afternoon. I carried Sasha to my room and gave her a bowl of water. She took a bit but gagged, spit, and went to sleep.

I prayed that she would feel better and stayed by her side for the next few hours, petting her as she slept. When she awoke at nine p.m. or so, much to my relief, she stood on shaky legs and walked about the room. I was overjoyed. Later this evening, she lapped up a bowl of soup, breathed normally, and thumped her tail just like her old self.

I went to tell Dr. Bell the good news and found him pacing the room with excited, glittering eyes. Blue, fragrant smoke hung over the room like a mist. "Ah, Doyle, that is wonderful news! Pour a dram for yourself and sit with me for a moment."

Ah, so he did care after all. I cupped the glass of whiskey in my hands and inhaled the peaty smell of prime Scottish single malt while Dr. Bell paced the length of the room and back. He stabbed the air with his pipe. "Well, there is still one piece of missing information, but by tomorrow afternoon, we will see the case solved," he said.

"But sir, all we know is the method of the murder. We have no motive, let alone a culprit."

"Au contraire, my lad. It is perfectly clear, and you and your canine friend helped us find the missing clue."

What was he talking about? How was he always one step ahead of me or, for that matter, everybody else? "I don't understand, sir."

"You will soon, laddie. You will soon. Now, go and get some rest. I have work to do. Goodnight."

Reluctantly, I went off to bed and was drifting off to sleep, when Sasha pounced on the bed and licked my face. I cuddled with her and soon we were both floating off into dreamland.

25 September 1881

I slept like a dead man until the grey light of early dawn. My head felt better, so I dressed and took Sasha for a short run before breakfast. Sasha frolicked and barked at a carriage that came to a halt on the side street by Professor Sechenov's garden.

The driver, as well as the passengers, wore peasant's garb — dark trousers tucked into high boots, long shirts belted at the waist, sheepskin vests, and wooly astrakhan hats. It took a moment to recognize Mr. Foster, the ambassador, who held the reins, and Mr. Tatum. Dr. Bell was heavily disguised with a sort of Muslim scarf about his face.

"Ho there, Doyle, my lad. We are perfectly famished from a hard night's work. Would you like to join us for breakfast?" Dr. Bell asked.

An hour later, we tucked into ham, omelets, a heap of dark bread, smoked salmon, succulent lamb chops, and gallons of sweet Turkish coffee.

I knew better than to enquire about their mysterious nighttime adventure until Dr. Bell lit his pipe, sighed, leaned back, and blew a perfect smoke ring. "Doyle, read this paragraph." He tossed a book in my lap. It was *Oriental Herbal Remedies*.

I read the paragraph, "*Rauwolfia Serpentina* or Indian Snakeroot: The dried root, an ancient remedy, is an effective tranquilizer in cases of insanity. An overdose may cause collapse and even death. When accidently ingested by horses or cattle, there is nasal congestion, sweating, lethargy, and, occasionally, death."

"How did you know about this drug?" I asked.

"Aye, 'tis a doctor's job to know about the properties of all of God's herbs."

"Your knowledge is encyclopedic, sir."

"Books help refresh it, Doyle ..."

"Do tell all, sir."

"Well, your friend, Cowboy Bill, had gained the trust of Mercury, but the horse would not tolerate another rider. The murderer is afraid to let the colonel ride in the race and attempted to poison Mercury with the powdered root of *Rauwolfia Serpentina*. I knew this for certain when Sasha had identical symptoms after licking a small amount of the residue from Cowboy Bill's hand."

"Aye, I figured something along those lines when she got sick, but still . . ."

"I would wager that Bill was killed when he confronted the murderer with the evidence."

"Do you have proof?"

"The proof is in this little bag of feed from Mercury's stall."

"But how did you get it?"

"We just paid a little visit to the stables last night. While Mr. Tatum entertained the grooms with vodka, Mr. Foster and I removed the feed from Mercury's stall."

"But, he is a vicious animal."

"Mr. Foster knows a trick or two from his days as a farmer. There isn't a horse in the world that can resist peppermint candy."

"We not only removed all the adulterated feed, but left new clean oats, hay, and two buckets of water. Mercury will be as good as new by this afternoon."

Mr. Tatum chuckled. "I bet one hundred rubles on Mercury. The grooms were happy to give me ten to one odds."

"We still don't know who murdered Cowboy Bill," I said.

"We will soon. Now, off to the races. Dress in your best day suit and a top hat."

Mr. Foster met us with his fine carriage and greeted us with twinkly eyes. "Ah fellows, it is a grand day. Inspector Koivisto is my guest."

The inspector drew himself into a corner of the carriage and barely nodded to Dr. Bell. "Frankly, I don't understand what a horse race has to do with murder," he said.

Dr. Bell chuckled. "You will see, Inspector. All in good time. All in good time."

The circular track wound through birch and spruce trees. Steep slopes, fences, piles of logs, and small streams were obstacles to test the jumping skill of each horse and rider. Grooms decked out in silk shirts, tight breeches, and high boots exercised horses, while a throng of spectators with telescopes and opera glasses crowded the open fields that surrounded the track.

The race was a highlight of Russian social events. Even the Tsar was drawn out of seclusion. He, with his splendid entourage, was seated in an enclosure near the starting line. His body guards and company of soldiers were scattered among the crowd of ladies in bright gowns and large flowery sun hats, men in uniforms, and civilian officials with medals, top hats, and walking sticks. The gay crowd moved to and from tables set with champagne and edibles. It was utterly decadent and, at the same time, grand and fantastic.

I took a glass of bubbly and a helping of caviar while listening to whispered rumors. Mercury, the favoured horse, was nowhere to be seen. "The grooms are afraid of him," one anxious fellow said.

The crowd cheered as the first horse, a fine-looking, chestnut mare ridden by a guard's captain and led by a groom, came to the starting line. More horses, riders, and grooms followed until only Mercury was missing.

The crowd became quiet. Then it cheered when Mercury, ridden by the colonel in jodhpurs and high glossy boots and led by the old Cossack sergeant, came onto the track. The horse was stiff-legged and his ears were twitching.

Colonel Shirapov sat rigidly in the saddle and held the reigns with both hands. The horse balked just short of the starting line. The colonel raised his whip, but the old man whispered in the horse's ear. Mercury settled and pranced to the very outside position. Mercury was nervous and dashed across the starting line. The colonel turned him back to the line, and after two attempts, the umpire shouted. "Away!"

Mercury balked and was last to start. Then, with a shake of his great head, he shot down the track. Colonel Shirapov's face was set in a rigid mask. I was struck with the thought that he was bloody terrified.

Mercury gracefully leaped over the first obstacle and gained two lengths on the nearest horse. He sailed over a pile of logs and went into the lead.

The crowd cheered when he went high in the air over a small stream to land on a steep precipice. The colonel bent forward, with both arms around the horse's neck. Mercury was now well in the lead, his forelegs reaching out with every stride and his strong hindquarters driving him onward.

The crowd screamed and surged toward the finish line.

Looking like a black demon, Mercury came into the homestretch a half-dozen lengths ahead of the nearest horse. He pounded toward the finish but hesitated, tossed his head, and triumphantly crossed the line.

The crowd's loud cheers quickly turned to stunned silence as the horse abruptly put out his forelegs and kicked up his hind legs.

The old colonel shot over the horse's head and landed on his back. Mercury, with a deadly gleam in his eyes, reared up and came down with both forefeet on the colonel's chest. The hooves crushed the colonel's ribs with a sickening crack. Geysers of blood shot in the air with each heartbeat then subsided into a red pool on the track.

The old Cossack was there in an instant, kneeling at the colonel's side. With all the tenderness usually seen in a mother with a sick child, the old man lifted the bloody corpse in his arms while tears rolled down his cheeks.

"Oh dear lord, what have I done? What have I done?" Dr. Bell sighed.

I will never forget the image of the weeping, devastated old man who stood in the sun before the silent crowd, refusing to give up the crumpled body to the doctors.

Dr. Bell pointed. "Inspector, there is your man."

I elbowed my way through the crowd with a grim-faced Inspector Koivisto. Just as we arrived at the track, a giant of a man came through the silent crowd. He spoke a word to the old *denshchik* but took the colonel's body in his own arms to the tsar's enclosure.

"My God, the colonel must have been a favourite of the tsar himself," Koivisto said.

The old man stood stock still, his arms outstretched and tears rolling down his face. Koivisto and I led him away to a quiet spot where, between heaving sobs, he talked. Later, Koivisto interpreted for me.

"I was a good *denshchik* and cared for him like my own son for nearly forty years. He was done with racing until he married that damn woman. She gave him that wicked horse and expected him to ride like a young captain. I tried to stop it, but the American found out. So I had to kill him." He held out his strong, gnarled, scarred hands. "I thought it was the only way to protect the colonel."

It was a slow, sad walk back to the carriage. During the journey home, Dr. Bell huddled in the corner of the carriage, his arms folded tightly over his chest. He didn't say a word, but stared into the distance.

Ambassador Foster was garrulous after imbibing more than his share of champagne, while Mr. Tatum, under the guise of polite conversation, drew him out. "Oh yes, we have Alaska. Next, we take Siberia and the Pacific Ocean is ours. The United States Navy, by God, we are building a navy that will show the world we can fight," the ambassador bragged.

"Do you have any special ships?" Mr. Tatum asked.

Mr. Foster belched and patted his stomach. "That is a secret, my man." He leaned forward and put his mouth to Mr. Tatum's ear. "But I can tell you, the future is not floating on the surface of the ocean, but beneath it."

30 September 1881

Dr. Bell has not left his room all week and has taken only small morsels of food since the race. He blames himself for the colonel's death and, aside from regular injections of cocaine, remains slumped in a chair staring into the distance.

I have taken on most of the work at the children's tuberculosis clinic. There is a little girl there with straw-colored hair — five years old at the most — who is at the point of death. Without a doubt, her entire left chest is filled with pus. An operation is indicated, but I dare not attempt such a capital procedure.

So, this morning I went to his room and begged him to help. "Please, Dr. Bell, you must operate."

"I cannot." He waved me away. "Doyle, you have seen these operations. It is nothing. You can do it. Just incise the skin, remove a bit of the seventh rib, and probe through the pleura until you encounter pus and drain it."

"But I can't …"

"Aye, you can, lad. And you must. There is no one else to do it."

So, I will try tomorrow.

I only pray that I do not do further harm to that poor, suffering little girl.

1 October 1881

Early this morning, with Ivanov administering a few drops of chloroform, I did the operation exactly as Dr. Bell directed. There was a great gush of green pus and, by noon, Katrinka — for that is her name — took some food for the first time in days.

I am elated, literally walking on air, at this small success. Not only that — but the arm stump of young Konstantine has also healed.

I bubbled over with excitement this afternoon when I reported the result to Dr. Bell. A smile flickered over his lips. "Good, good, Doyle. You have been a bit off-color, lately. This is exactly what you needed."

It is most amazing. His eyes were clear, and there wasn't the slightest tremor when he knotted a silk cravat that matched his fine, grey, tweed suit.

"It is a fine day. Let us walk to the clinic," he said.

He set a fast pace and, in high spirits, twirled his new walking stick with a bright silver knob. Once he stopped and eyed a small, round stone, took a stance, swung the cane like a golf club, and sent the stone flying down the road.

"Dr. Nikolay Pirogov will visit the clinic this afternoon. Do you know of his work?" he asked.

I had to dredge through a distant anatomy lesson and finally came up with an answer. "There is Pirogov's aponeurosis over the biceps muscle. An amputation through the heel of the foot is named for him, is it not?"

He sighted along the cane at a duck rising off the Neva. "Yes, good memory. Pirogov is known for surgical work during the Crimean war and is a first-class scientist. Sadly, he is no longer active in surgery."

At the clinic, we donned clean, white aprons and carefully washed our hands between each patient. I glowed with happiness as Dr. Bell examined my little patient and said I had done well.

Professor Pirogov arrived just as we commenced a most difficult operation on a ten-year-old boy with infected nodes in his neck. I studied the famous man, hoping for inspiration. He was not the imposing great surgeon I had expected, but was stooped, walked with a limp, and was nearly bald. He sat on a high stool with his chin resting on one hand while Dr. Bell gently dissected nerves and arteries in the neck away from tubercular lymph nodes. Sweat trickled down my brow when he inserted the last stitch and I stopped the chloroform anaesthetic.

"Well done, sir. Well done." Pirogov said.

Dr. Bell rinsed his hands. "Thank you," he muttered.

Pirogov pulled at his well-clipped beard. "I must put to you a most difficult situation. The tsar's son, Grand Duke George Alexandrovitch has tuberculosis of the glands, not unlike this lad. The tsar requested my opinion about surgery but I am no longer operating. Dr. Bell, would you be good enough to see the boy?"

His fatigue dropped away, and he straightened his stooped shoulders. "There are many capable Russian surgeons, aye?" Dr. Bell asked.

"They are all afraid of the consequences if the boy should die."

"Ah, now that is a challenge I'll accept. I shall be happy to see young George tomorrow morning."

And so, in the morning, we will journey to the tsar's Palace. I dread to think what will happen to Dr. Bell if the surgery fails and the boy dies. But Dr. Bell seems confident in his surgical skills, so I hope all goes well … Certainly, if anyone can save the boy, it is Dr. Bell.

2 October 1881

After breakfast, we were in the royal coach with the gilded Romanov crest, galloping off to the Gatchina palace some twenty miles south of St. Petersburg.

Once we arrived, a silent, rather cowed, young aide-de-camp led us to the tsar's study. The royal family's quarters were not what I had expected, but were simple and plainly furnished.

Alexander III, Emperor of Russia and King of Poland, is a mighty figure — tall, solid, with a long, reddish-brown beard and a high forehead. He was not covered with medals, as I had expected, but wore a simple military jacket with no decorations. The tsar sat on a plain chair in front of a desk covered with documents.

Professor Pirogov stepped forward, bowed, and introduced us. The tsar spoke in French and Dr. Bell replied in French. The tsar went to the point. "Dr. Bell, can you cure my son?"

"I can operate, but only God can cure your son," Dr. Bell replied.

The tsar's heavily-lidded eyes showed a flicker of respect. "True," he said, and beckoned to his aide-de-camp. "Fetch my son George."

The tsar went back to his papers while we waited. A rather plain-looking governess carried the sickly, pale boy in her arms. He was an attractive little fellow dressed in a blue sailor suit but was stick thin and rather lethargic for an eight-year-old.

"Remove his shirt please," Dr. Bell, rather unceremoniously asked.

The flustered governess looked to the tsar, who nodded. Dr. Bell said not a word, but examined the boy's neck, then listened to his chest, and prodded the abdomen.

"Dr. Pirogov, do you agree these lumps are infected tuberculous nodes?"

The old surgeon clasped his hands in thought. "I do agree and have advised an operation."

"It should be done. Make your arrangements," the tsar said, and held out his arms for the boy, who eagerly went into his embrace. The tsar fondly stroked little George's hair and murmured into his ear before handing him back to the governess and returning to his work.

I could've been mistaken, but there was a bit of moisture on the tsar's cheeks after the boy left. There and then, no matter what I had heard about him, I concluded that Tsar Alexander was not a bad man, and I resolved to do my best to protect him.

Dr. Bell, with Pirogov and an elderly footman, selected a bright, airy room immediately across a corridor from the tsar's private quarters for an operating theater. Dr. Bell wasted no time but scheduled the operation for the next day.

So, now we shall see Dr. Bell in action. I would never want to have to perform surgery under such pressure, but he seems to relish the challenge.

We shall see…

3 October 1881

Professor Sechenov, Pirogov, and three of Russian's foremost surgeons observed our meticulous antiseptic preparations. The poor governess had tears in her eyes when we placed the small, quivering grand duke on the solid oak table.

I whispered to the boy and dripped ether on gauze over his face. He bravely coughed just once, inhaled deeply, and went under the anaesthetic. Dr. Bell made an incision from the angle of his jaw downward, spilled a few drops of royal blood, and dissected the infected nodes from the nerves and vessels in the neck. We could hear the tsar's heavy tread in the corridor all through the operation, which lasted over one hour.

There was one particularly ticklish moment after Dr. Bell nicked the external jugular vein with his scalpel. He pressed the bleeding vessel with one finger and adroitly applied a stitch with one hand. There was a collective sigh of relief when he removed the last infected node.

The boy awoke from the anaesthetic but vomited and vomited until there was nothing left in his stomach. Dr. Bell and I maintained the vigil throughout the afternoon and evening. The tsar, with his face set in a rigid mask, held his son in his arms and paced the floor when the poor child whimpered with pain.

After midnight, the tsar retired to his quarters just across the hall, but he returned within half an hour.

"Bah, how can I sleep when my son is near death?"

"Your Majesty, you must rest, for tomorrow may be another trying day. Dr. Doyle will stay with him through the night. Here is a sleeping draught."

The tsar downed an extravagant dose of laudanum with one gulp and returned to his quarters. A little after midnight, the governess coaxed little George into taking a few sips of milk, and at last, he settled into a light sleep, breathed quietly, and had a strong pulse.

For all my determination to remain alert, I, too, dozed off...

4 October 1881

In the wee hours of the morning, I was awakened by a strange thumping sound. George was resting easily, and the governess was lightly snoring. Had I dreamed, or was there, again, the sound of a dull *thump* in the corridor?

Perhaps, the tsar was returning to see his son, but then the sound was gone. I went to the door and listened, but there was nothing…

Then, I heard something which sounded like a faint rattle. Was it the wind stirring a tree branch? An animal scratching in the garden? I listened for a long minute. There it was again, a faint rattle.

I took the single candle from its holder and gently opened the door into the corridor. There, immediately at the entrance to the tsar's bedroom, his personal guard was unconscious on the floor with a gash on his forehead. At first, I thought he must have fallen and cracked his skull, but he was a healthy young guardsman and there was no smell of liquor. Someone had attacked him.

Before I examined him, there it was again — a faint rattle from within the tsar's bedroom. The scene in Pavlov's laboratory, with snakes sinking their deadly fangs into the poor old caretaker, rose like a dread scene from hell in my mind.

I had no weapon, was in stocking feet, but sensed there was a rattlesnake in the tsar's bedroom.

The candle flame flickered from the slight draft as I opened the door into the tsar's small, plain chamber. Was it a hallucination? No.

Why was a uniformed British officer in the tsar's bedroom?

A single oil lamp in a far corner cast a flickering, yellow light over a garish scene. I guttered my candle with two fingers and moved further into the room. The figure in the uniform of a British officer set a large basket on the floor and, with the tip of his boot, lifted the top. The rattling increased, then there was hissing and, finally, the scrape of scales on the basket. I watched, as if in a hypnotic trance, while a reptilian head as large as my fist rose from the basket.

203

In the dim light, there was no mistaking the flat head and dull, venomous eyes of a gigantic Texas rattlesnake.

As if responding to a charmer's melody, the snake rose from the basket, its head swaying back and forth. The entire seven-foot reptile coiled, uncoiled and, in a nightmarish moment, was suddenly at full length on the wooden floor.

It was only then that I saw the massive bulk of the tsar resting, fully clothed, on the top of an oversized soldier's cot in the far corner of the room.

Unfortunately, I was too far away to stop the venomous creature and no match for a deadly rattler. The tsar was out cold from the laudanum, on his back, with one arm hanging almost to the floor.

With a sibilant hiss, the snake raised its head as if sampling the air, hunting for food. I should have cried out, aroused the palace, but there was no time and the tsar was still deep under the influence of the laudanum. The snake, as if sensing the helplessness of its prey, raised its head and flicked its tongue.

I huddled with my back to the wall, in the shadows, as the officer picked up the basket and slowly backed away.

I waited, then threw an arm around his neck with a stranglehold. He struggled. I administered a short chop to the back of his head. He wilted in my arms.

With his head thrown back, I stared at his face. My God, it was Dmitri, the caretaker from Pavlov's laboratory. Why was he dressed as a British officer?

Could this man be David Campbell, the British officer who had sworn vengeance on the tsar? Aye, my mind was in a whirl.

Ivanov had deliberately placed him in Pavlov's laboratory. I had not been mistaken when I heard him muttering in English. Penelope must be behind this diabolic plot. Who else could have helped him gain access to the tsar's quarters?

There was no time for idle thoughts. The great, horrid snake made the sibilant rattle, his warning of an impending strike. The creature was within a foot of the tsar's dangling arm. It seemed helpless, but I had to save the tsar.

Ah, the whistle, the whistle Dmitri used to call the snakes for food. At first, I couldn't produce a sound from my parched, pursed lips, but I finally managed a feeble, high-pitched tone. The snake did not respond. It was again coiled, its great head moving back and forth, on the scent for food. I whistled again and, slowly, the head turned. Was it my imagination, or were those dull eyes searching for new prey?

It was an utterly terrifying moment. I whistled again. The snake turned and, with one coil after another, silently moved in my direction. The snake's primitive brain had followed a dim Pavlovian instinct to find food in the direction of the whistle. I had saved the tsar. For now…

Unfortunately, it appeared as if I was now the chosen food source. I pushed the unconscious officer, Dmitri — or was it David — into the corridor. I retreated, completely terrified and without a notion of how to save myself from the snake that kept slithering faster and faster towards me.

For a moment, I thought of slamming the door, leaving the snake and the tsar alone. But then, I thought of the tsar holding his son just as any loving father and backed further into the hall.

I stumbled backward onto the felled guard. He groaned and rolled over. There, beneath his body was a rifle with a fixed bayonet.

The snake was now halfway out the door and into the corridor when I, with trembling hands and not a moment to lose, took up the guard's rifle and commenced a terrible dance with the poisonous beast. We parried, back and forth, now thrusting, now retreating. The whole time, I fixed my focus on those awful fangs.

The rifle was a short cavalry carbine, so even with the bayonet, my reach was not even as long as that terrible, thrusting body.

In short, I had only made the reptile angry.

The snake had ignored the two unconscious men; the eyes in that flat, deadly head were only for me. I whistled and retreated down the hall where the only light came from a single candle in a wall holder. Any further and I would be in total darkness. The guard groaned and, for just a moment, the snake turned aside.

I thrust the bayonet behind the creature's head but missed the vital spinal cord. He struck with lightning speed and barely missed my leg. With one more thrust, I drove the tip of the blade through the body and impaled the writhing snake to the wooden floor.

It was still alive, writhing and striking out but unable to slither forward or back. Yet, the open mouth and deadly fangs were as dangerous as ever.

The snake struggled, but the bayonet did not give. I had a moment's reprieve. I removed the light dress sword from the guard's scabbard and, in one fell swoop, I severed the snake's head from the body.

Now, what to do with the mess? A dead snake, an injured guard, and a sick English officer. The tsar, even after a heavy dose of laudanum, would rise at first light and the palace would come awake. I wrapped the snake's body in bedclothes soiled by our patient's vomiting.

Later, I convinced the governess the bundle was infectious and must be burned. A dash of medicinal brandy on the face of the unconscious guard provided an explanation for his dereliction of duty.

That left a very sick, dazed English officer who I had known as Dmitri but was almost certainly the missing officer, David Campbell. His trousers were not so different from a Russian officer. Perhaps, without his jacket and British insignia, he might pass as a palace guard. I dragged his limp body into a corner of the sick room and covered him with a quilt.

Little George opened one sleepy eye and said just one word. "L'eau."

I held his head while he sipped from a cup of water. The governess awoke immediately and took charge of the boy. It then occurred to me that the poor guard would be shot for neglecting his duties. Out of sympathy, I roused the poor man, put a bit of sticking plaster on his wound, propped him up, and replaced the carbine into his limp hand. If needed, I could claim the brandy was a wound disinfectant.

All in all, it was not a bad night's work.

Nothing was amiss, when, at the crack of dawn, the tsar tramped into the room on heavy feet and swept little George into his massive arms.

An hour later, Dr. Bell arrived, as fresh as ever, and after examining George, allowed the boy to go with his governess to his own room. We were alone with nothing to do but to pack our instruments and leave.

"Sir, we have a problem," I said.

"Oh come now. It is a fine morning and our patient is recovering nicely," he said.

"I believe I have discovered the English officer. He is there, under a quilt."

I carried the poor man to the oak table. He was light as a feather and clearly suffering from a chronic illness.

"He is very near death," Dr. Bell said.

I related what I knew of Dmitri's headaches, confusion, and loss of memory. Dr. Bell commenced his usual sleuth-like examination, noted the scars on both hands, more scars on his torso indicating old bullet wounds, and the emaciation. "Ah, Doyle, he is certainly the British officer. What do you make of this?" He had pulled down the lower lip to expose a blue-black line on the lower gum, just beneath the teeth.

I recalled an old patient, a lead miner, in the insane asylum. "Burton's line!" I cried. "Lead poisoning."

"Very good, Doyle. Excellent. Sadly, his brain is affected and he is near the last stages of the illness. If his kidney's fail, he is a dead man."

"But why?" I asked.

"The wounds, Doyle. Think about it. From the looks of these old bullet holes, he has one and possibly two lead balls within his body." Bell set about, with his long, sensitive fingers, to palpate every inch of the man's torso. His index finger came to rest high in the officer's armpit. "It is here, lodged in the subscapularis muscle. We must remove it."

"Shall we take him to a hospital?"

"There is no time to lose, and there is no better operating room in all of Russia than right here. Quick — carbolic and open the instrument case."

It made sense. The sooner the lead ball was removed, the better his chances. The royal family and the entire household was either with little George or at breakfast. We had the room to ourselves for at least an hour.

Bell kept his finger on the place where he had located the bullet while I splashed carbolic on his hands over the patient's chest. He needed only a probe, the sharp curved scalpel, and a rat-toothed forceps to remove the bullet, a .65 calibre musket ball.

Our patient uttered a sigh but scarcely moved during the brief operation. "Now, fetch that young aide-de-camp; demand a carriage and four fast horses."

We told the young man that our patient was a visiting physician who had swooned at the sight of the great tsar. He understood completely and helped us carry the English officer to the carriage.

"We could have used Mr. Tatum," I said. "Where is he?"

A look of exasperation — or was it worry — passed over the professor's face. "I am sorry to say that he never appeared this morning. It does not bode well for him."

Indeed, there was no Mr. Tatum at our quarters either. During the rest of the day, I forced tea, broth, and water into our patient with the intent of washing the lead from his system.

He roused a bit by late afternoon, but by then, and even late into the evening, Mr. Tatum was still missing.

5 October 1881

This morning, David Campbell came around when Sasha licked his face. An inscription on an antique gold watch in his trousers pocket proved he truly is the lost English officer. Bloodletting has gone out of fashion these days, but Dr. Bell decided to take a pint of his blood to reduce the amount of lead in his body.

It did seem to help. He can now walk a few steps and no longer holds his head in pain. Marya has taken over his nursing care, and when she takes breaks, we have resumed our delightful language lessons.

There is still no sign of Mr. Tatum. It would seem something awful has happened to him. I visited the embassy, spoke with the ambassador's secretary, and made enquiries at the Hotel Europa. No one has heard from him.

Just before dinner, the footman ushered Inspector Koivisto with two uniformed policemen into Dr. Bell's sitting room.

"I regret to be here under these circumstances," the inspector said.

"Is it about Mr. Tatum?" I asked.

"Yes, very likely. You must come and identify the body."

The police cab, drawn by two aged hacks, took us to the waterfront near the western end of Vasilyesky Island. We alighted and, led by the inspector, walked to the very end of a wooden wharf where two officers and several sailors in high boots and thick sweaters stood by a canvas-covered corpse.

"We don't have all day. Remove the canvas," Koivisto brusquely said.

Without ceremony, a young policeman pulled the rough canvas aside. The body was bloated from immersion in the sea, and part of the face had been gnawed away by fish. I instantly turned away and did my best not to vomit. Dr. Bell remained stolid and studied the corpse.

Most of the corpse was intact and it was indeed our valet, or rather, our friend, the British secret agent we knew as Mr. Tatum. I had become very fond of Tatum with his quiet good humor and common sense.

I refused to look at the dismal body and choked back a sob. This whole trip was just a bloody awful mess and I yearned to go back home and try to forget it all. I just prayed that Tatum's life, and the lives of the others who had died, were given for the sake of a lasting peace in Europe and not in vain!

Dr. Bell, in his usual professional manner, knelt and continued to inspect the remains. "Where was he found?" he asked.

"A fisherman discovered his body, tangled in old cables, immediately beneath this wharf."

"When?" Dr. Bell asked.

"Just before noon," Koivisto said.

Dr. Bell consulted a small, black notebook, turned several pages, and marked the place with his finger. "I last saw Mr. Tatum on the morning of October the first. He was at the embassy during the mid-afternoon and did not show up on the morning of the second as was his usual habit. He disappeared sometime during the early evening or night of the first."

He again consulted his notebook. "There was a full moon that night which would have produced an exceptionally high tide early on the morning of the second. During the late evening, up to perhaps two a.m., there would have been a strong incoming current."

One of the onlookers spoke up in Russian and said something that sounded like he agreed with Dr. Bell about the strong tide currents over the past several days.

"Tell me, please, what is the direction of the incoming current at the end of the wharf?" Dr. Bell asked.

The fisherman pointed. "Go to the end of that dock and see for yourself."

He was indeed correct; flotsam and bits of seaweed drifted our way from the end of a dock where two vessels were moored side by side, perhaps a half a mile away.

Dr. Bell snapped open his watch and intently observed the floating debris for a full five minutes until Inspector Koivisto impatiently broke the silence. "Come, come. It is getting late. We shall deliver the body to the morgue for an autopsy in the morning. We shall be happy to deliver you to your rooms."

"Nay." Dr. Bell waved him away. "We shall remain for a while. Come, Doyle, let us walk. This clean, fresh, sea air will clear our minds."

It was a classic example of Dr. Bell's perfectly innocuous statements that were loaded with foreboding and gravity. I was not surprised when we set off at a good pace along the sea wall towards the dock with the two moored ships.

The nearest vessel was a screw-propelled warship of the latest design with forward and aft turrets, each with powerful cannons. German colors flew from her stern.

The dock extended five hundred feet from the embankment, and the second ship was partly hidden from view. She appeared to be an older cargo vessel with both sails and steam. A peculiar, tattered ensign fluttered in the dying breeze from her aft mast.

I made out a black cross with a circle containing the figure of an eagle in the center and an anchor in the lower left hand corner. "Ah, it is the ensign of the German commercial fleet," Dr. Bell exclaimed.

Two blank-faced guards stamped back and forth from one side of the wharf to the other, blocking our way to the pair of ships.

"We are visiting friends," Dr. Bell said.

The guard halted and held his rifle squarely in front of his chest. "Verboten."

"Why?" I responded in German.

"Eintritt untersagt," the second guard replied, in a most unpleasant, surly manner.

"Seems like we are forbidden," I muttered to Bell. He nodded, and I realized that he spoke better German than me and I should let him do the talking. I was all for barging past the guards, but Dr. Bell thought otherwise. "They are up to no good. It is best we leave now," he muttered, in English.

We strolled, chatting in French, appearing to be aimless sightseers, but we were fully alert and surreptitiously observed the German ships. The sun was nearly at the horizon, casting long shadows, but we made out crewmen scurrying about the two ships and more rifle-toting guards. "There must be a way to get close to those vessels," Dr. Bell said.

"I shall nip around and see my friend with the sailing yawl," I said.

Later, that evening, I called on good old Dicky Ferguson. We shared a bottle and a bit of cheese. He said he would be more than happy to take us for a sail tomorrow. So, we have a plan and now need a good night's rest.

I cannot not know for sure, but I have a feeling that the fate of the tsar — and all of Europe, for that matter — rests with our little sea journey on the morrow.

6 October 1881

"We must not be recognized," Dr. Bell said. The professor had secured a natty yachting outfit; cap, blazer, ascot, and white, duck trousers. When we met at a rickety dock on the Neva, Dicky Ferguson provided me with a black, wool cap and fisherman's garb. This meant that I had to haul on sails, lift the boom, and bail the bilge like a common hired hand.

Within minutes, my once well-manicured physician's hands were covered with sticky tar. When we entered the bay, the yawl heeled over in a brisk breeze and skipped along over a light chop. We tacked out over clear water and, with quick changes of sails, tacked and dodged between the anchored ships.

"Now, turn back to the German ships!" Dr. Bell shouted.

Dicky brought the tiller around and the yawl spun on her keel, while I desperately hauled in the main sail and pushed it to the other side. The jib sail came over with considerable flapping, and we went off on a course for the moored Germans.

Dr. Bell, to all appearances, looked the part of a casual nautical observer, training his long, brass telescope first on one ship and then another.

"Did you know," Ferguson shouted, "The entire Russian fleet is in port for the tsar's review? There . . ." he pointed. "Carr and McPherson, our countrymen, built those three cruisers, the *Ozight, Rasboynik* and the *Opritchnik* here in St. Petersburg." They were older, three-masted ships with iron hulls and steam engines, mounting Hotchkiss guns on either side.

We were hull down, flying past a great, Russian, armored cruiser, close enough to make out an officer with three golden eagles on his epaulets. "That's the admiral!" Dicky shouted. "On Sunday, the tsar will review the whole fleet from his flagship, the *Nakhimov*." She was a grand four-stacker with a sleek iron hull. There were more ships, gunboats from France and Sweden, and a late model cruiser from Germany.

"Our fleet arrives tomorrow with Her Majesty's yacht, the *Victoria and Albert*, just in time for the festivities on Sunday." Dicky said.

We swept down on the German ships, tacked, and came about. Dr. Bell crouched low behind the coaming, with his telescope trained on the Germans. "Can you stop for a better look?" he asked.

Dicky immediately flung over the tiller. "Doyle, let go the main halyard!" he yelled.

Without knowing one rope from another, I let go of the main sheet. The boom went out and the sail shivered. "No, no, you fool! The main halyard."

I finally got the idea, un-cleated the right rope, and the main sail came crashing down the mast into a tangled heap. Our boat wallowed on the waves while Dicky and I ran about like maniacs to set things right.

Meanwhile, Dr. Bell, hidden among folds of the heavy canvas sail, trained his telescope on the German cargo ship. "Doyle, focus on the space between the two ships."

I took the brass instrument and managed a close look at a most peculiar structure. Low in the water, almost invisible, was a black object supporting a wooden platform that appeared to be a landing stage between the two ships. "There is a semi-submerged vessel beneath the wood platform," I said. "It seems to be similar to what I saw in the hull of the ship that we came here on."

"Did you note the black pipes extending up from the mystery ship?" Dr. Bell asked.

We set the sails again and rolled down wind back to our dock on the Neva. While we tied up, a grizzled old fellow shouted out to us. "Be you English?" he asked.

"Scottish!" Dicky shouted.

"Close enough. An Englishman rented my skiff and hasn't returned. I need my skiff," he said.

Dicky translated for us. "Ask him what the Englishman looked like," Dr. Bell said.

The description was close enough. Tatum had rented the skiff. We could not help the man further, but assured him that, soon enough, he would be compensated.

As a thanks to Dicky, Dr. Bell offered dinner and drinks at the Hotel Europa. I had a quick change of clothing and enjoyed enough fine food and drink to be a bit tipsy on return to our quarters.

I left Dr. Bell at the door to his sitting room but turned when he spoke. "Come, Doyle, we have a guest," he said.

Colonel Sir Cameron Beachy-Edwards, pale, slender, and as impressive as ever, sat bolt upright on a straight chair, with both hands folded over the knob of an elegant, ebony walking stick. "Where is Sergeant James O'Grady?" he asked, without so much as a greeting.

"Unfortunately, the sergeant is dead." Dr. Bell said.

The colonel hunched forward and leaned heavily on his cane. For a moment, he lost his aplomb, but recovered his British stiff upper lip. "No! What was the cause of death?"

"Apparently, he drowned." Bell said.

"I find that hard to believe. James O'Grady or, as you called him, Tatum, was a strong swimmer." the colonel said.

"The Russian police have arranged an autopsy for tomorrow morning," I said.

"This presents us with a most troublesome situation. The sergeant was looking after security for Her Majesty's yacht, which arrives tomorrow. His dispatches suggested trouble from either the anarchists or the Germans. He was so concerned, I rushed from Paris by rail across all of Europe. We must be especially vigilant because Edward, Prince of Wales, is aboard the yacht. If there is an attack on the tsar while he reviews the fleet, the Prince would also be in danger." Sir Cameron said.

"O'Grady's body was in the harbor not far from two rather suspicious German ships. Perhaps he died during an investigation" Dr. Bell replied.

"Indeed. Why do you suspect the German ships?" the colonel asked.

"A cargo ship is moored next to a well-armed German naval vessel and something, perhaps another boat, is hidden between the two."

"In one of his dispatches, O'Grady said the American ambassador let slip something about a submersible vessel. It is hardly possible that the Americans would have a submarine boat in these waters."

When Colonel Beachy-Edwards paused, Dr. Bell spoke. "And we thought you should know. The lost English officer, David Campbell, is here with us."

Colonel Beachy-Edwards brightened. "Indeed, I wish to speak with him."

"He is suffering from severe lead poisoning as a result of an old bullet wound. His illness explains his rather strange behavior since he left Afghanistan," Dr. Bell said.

"Poor Campbell was actually quite brave in the war," The colonel said.

We had placed David Campbell in Mr. Tatum's room. He was attired in Tatum's tattered dressing gown, and when we walked in, Marya was spooning gruel into his mouth. Beachy-Edwards took his hand, and for a moment, Campbell's eyes lit with recognition. "Ah, ah, colonel," he mumbled. He did indeed show signs of improvement, but then, as quickly as his lucidity had appeared, it slid away...

The colonel, yawning and claiming exhaustion from his arduous train journey, insisted on sleeping on a spare narrow cot in the sitting room.

7 October 1881

Over breakfast, the colonel complained about overcooked eggs and that we didn't have proper marmalade. By the time we were able to scrounge up enough marmalade to satisfy his rarified tastes, we were late for the autopsy.

The pathologist had already made the long, Y-shaped incision from chest to lower abdomen. The organs were disintegrating from bacterial action, but the stench didn't faze the colonel. He had seen death at first hand on many fields of battle. He looked at the gnawed face for several minutes, squinting, from one angle to another. "Indeed, it is O'Grady," he said.

"Ah, what have we here?' Dr. Bell exclaimed. Blood clots and free blood oozed from the open peritoneal cavity. "Doyle, five pounds says this blood is from a ruptured spleen. You may have the honor of proving my point or winning my money."

I accepted his challenge and, with some reluctance, removed my jacket, rolled up my sleeve, and thrust a hand up to my elbow into the rotting mess of intestine. The soft, spongy spleen, in the left upper quadrant of the abdomen, was ruptured into three pieces. Dr. Bell was correct, as usual.

"Mr. Tatum suffered a traumatic rupture of the spleen. The loss of blood explains his inability to swim, or else he was dead before he entered the water. He either fell from a height or an assailant gave him a terrific blow to the abdomen," Dr. Bell said.

"O'Grady was expert with knife, gun, or fists and was agile as a cat. I can't believe he fell or was defeated by a single opponent," the colonel said.

"I agree. This was most certainly murder," Dr. Bell said, and added, "Let us repair to more comfortable surroundings." So, we returned to our quarters.

While Marya served tea in the sitting room, the colonel withdrew a sheaf of papers from his leather dispatch case. He fixed me with his piercing grey eyes. "Mr. Doyle, you provided Sergeant O'Grady with detailed accounts of your activities on the *Servia*, but I am unclear with regard to your discovery of an unconscious American engineer and your encounters with Miss Walshingham," he said. He drained his cup of tea and scowled. "I demand a full explanation."

"Sir, I fully expected Miss Walshingham, or rather, Mrs. Foley, would make a report to you and there was no need for me to …" I said.

"Young man, Miss Walshingham suffers from hysteria. Her father sent her to school in Zurich, where she fell in with radical Russian students. The Secret Service recruited her because she is a brilliant linguist, even knowing she had a tendency towards emotional and other psychological disturbances. She can assume any role or personality and, indeed, serves admirably as lady-in-waiting to the Duchess of Edinburgh. She had an affair with Captain Foley and planned to accompany him to Russia —"

"Excuse me, you said an affair. I was under the impression that they were married?"

"No. They never married."

I was speechless. Penelope had lied and led me on? Why would she claim to be married to my uncle if it wasn't true? Nothing about that women made sense.

"Speak up, Mr. Doyle. Explain your encounters with Miss Walshingham "

I could not lie to the colonel or to Dr. Bell, but I chose my words carefully to protect Penelope. "In truth, it was a chance meeting, but we indulged in a romantic tryst in the hold of the ship. An intruder, brandishing a gun, interrupted our bit of romance. I thought he was the murderer and struck a blow that rendered him unconscious."

"Could you identify the cargo?"

"No, there were three large wooden crates and, ah, yes, I remember, they were labeled 'Brooklyn Naval Yard.' "

"Crates that were unloaded in Kiel?" the colonel asked.

"Yes, sir. I observed cranes remove them from the ship."

The colonel studied his papers and sighed deeply. "I hope you were careful in your dealings with that woman. She is involved with the anarchist students, the German naval attaché, and rebellious Russian officers. She is the link connecting several plots on the tsar."

"But, sir, she saved my life by extricating me from prison and, well, say what you will, but isn't it also possible that she is working to keep the tsar alive?" I asked.

The colonel heaved a great sigh. "I wish I could believe that."

Dr. Bell, with eyes closed and hands folded over his chest, had listened to our conversation. "None of this explains the death of Mr. Tatum, or rather, Sergeant O'Grady. I suspect the Germans were responsible."

"Sergeant O'Grady assumed, wrongly, as it turned out, that Count von Wittenberg murdered Lord Asquith. He searched of the count's cabin and found diagrams that correspond to the crates in the hold of the *Servia*. Here is his rough copy of the drawings. Our experts in the Royal Navy are convinced that the crates contained sections of a new type of submersible vessel. There are questions about how the crew can obtain breathable air in such a vessel. Dr. Bell, kindly look at this sketch and give us your expert opinion as a man of science."

I peeked over his shoulder as Dr. Bell examined the drawings. "Incredible," he said. "The Americans have solved the problem of travel beneath the sea." The vessel was pointed at either end and powered with an electric motor. If the batteries failed, the crew, with a system of pedals, chains, and gears, could turn the propeller. "But, sir, how can the crew obtain oxygen? I asked.

"These two pipes extending above the water have manual pumps to draw in fresh air and to discharge the used air. When totally submerged, they have canisters of sodium hydroxide to absorb carbon dioxide, and a cylinder of compressed oxygen. The most incredible feature is this system of mirrors within a tube, which allows the captain to see above the surface."

"But what is the use of such a vessel?" I asked.

"Think, boy!" Colonel Beachy-Edwards replied. "This ship will revolutionize naval warfare. Furthermore, the Americans have improved upon the Whitehead torpedo. It has an effective range of three hundred yards and, if used with this submersible vessel, they would instantly become unbeatable at sea. Unbeatable!"

219

Bell studied the drawings. "Ah, yes, the firing mechanism uses compressed air to start the torpedo on its way, and then, a small electric motor turns a propeller that propels the torpedo to an enemy ship. The Germans and Americans have created a most diabolical instrument of naval warfare."

"You are quite correct. The torpedo has a plunger, which strikes a detonator to explode on contact with another ship." the colonel said.

"Why are the Americans involved? Dr. Bell asked.

"Some Americans think a Russian anarchist killed their President, Garfield." I said.

"Either way, things don't look good for the tsar on Sunday." Dr. Bell jumped to his feet. "I tried to convince the tsar to let young George rest, with cod liver oil and sunshine to complete his cure, but he insists on taking his entire family on board the *Nakhimov* when he reviews the fleet on Sunday."

"Good God, man! A single torpedo could sink the ship and kill the entire royal family in one fell stroke!" the colonel exclaimed.

"The Germans killed Tatum when he discovered the submarine boat between the two German ships. We must report this to the Russian police at once," Dr. Bell said.

"No, the Queen insists that the matter be handled quietly. She does not want to precipitate a full-blown European war," the colonel said.

"Well then, how can we prevent this atrocity?" Bell asked.

"I might have a plan," I said. "It is a bit risky, but …"

"I'm sorry, son, but I have to say your reliability is questionable, at best," the colonel said.

"I can vouch for Mr. Doyle, but if O'Grady, a well-trained practitioner of espionage, met his death in this crusade, I fear that there is little a common citizen like Mr. Doyle or I can do," Bell said.

"My lack of credibility with you might just be my strength. You see, the student anarchist groups trust me. I can talk to them tonight and learn if they are involved in the plot." I said.

The colonel was not eager to follow my plan, but he had little alternative. That evening, I went in search of Vera or Ivanov. My friends weren't at the Beranger or the Idiot's Café. The whole time, I kept thinking, *was Penelope involved*?

I could not forget her lips, her body, her passionate embraces … I knew that Vera and Ivanov must have means to contact her. She must not be hunted down and shot as a traitor to the Queen. If I could just get to Vera or Ivanov…

After a few hours, I dejectedly approached Dr. Sechenov's home, when a dark figure emerged from behind a tree. "Doyle, we must speak." It was Vera. I had spent all night looking for her, and only when I had given up did she find me.

She held me close, and I put my arm around her. We walked as lovers do, and like lovers, we whispered in the night, but they were not whispers of love. Rather, Vera asked if I was still sympathetic with their cause.

I hesitated for a second. Where would this lead? "Yes, I would like to help. Have you heard from the English woman?"

"We will meet her tomorrow, Saturday night."

"Where?"

"Alexander's Column at midnight. Bring warm clothing."

From my wanderings about the city, I knew the impressive column with the cross and an angel atop a great red granite base. It was in the open Palace Square, safe from surprises. So, I felt certain it wasn't a trap…

Or was it?

9 October 1881

I did not sleep well yesterday. Too much was riding on my shoulders. It was Saturday, and if I failed to do my job, and the Germans killed the tsar, the next day might explode into a huge European conflict. It was hard to believe; I could be the only person standing between the tsar's death and a disastrous war.

I did not feel confident, but I could do nothing less than carry on. The odds were against our small group, but then, Dr. Bell and I had saved the American president from a Confederate plot during our journey to America. The thought renewed my confidence.

Early in the morning, I dressed in a dark sweater and high boots and took Bell's telescope in a leather case. With Sasha, I loped along a path leading to the harbor. When the great fleet came into view, I dodged into a clump of trees and tied Sasha to a branch.

The Russian cruiser, *Nakhimov,* was on the far side of the harbor, perhaps five miles from the German ships. The Queen's royal yacht was anchored a quarter-mile off the cruiser's stern, and other ships were arrayed about the harbor.

According to the colonel's informants, tomorrow, the ships will pass in review, firing salutes to the tsar on the far side of the cruiser. Short of a long, cold swim, I could see no way to get near the German ships or the submarine boat. If there was a plan to kill the tsar and his family and set Europe ablaze with war, I had no idea how I might prevent it. I got Sasha and returned to my room.

Later, I had a substantial supper, alone, since Bell and the colonel were at the embassy. It was with some misgiving at my rather hasty decision to join the students that I ventured into the unknown for the midnight rendezvous. It wasn't until then that I wondered, with great anxiety, *Great God, what have I done?*

I was to meet with both Vera and, perhaps, Penelope. I hesitated, unsure whether to brave the love — or was it the wrath — of two women. But then, a deeper emotion, a sense of duty, won over. I went ahead, not knowing what to expect, but with the full knowledge that I had no choice but to continue walking down a potentially deadly path.

The streets under a fine, misty rain were deserted. I stood in the shadows, observing the Palace Square. A few minutes after midnight, two figures and then a third strolled past, turned back, and huddled on the side of Alexander's Column facing the Winter Palace. I eased forward and joined the group.

I did not recognize Penelope, who wore a dark, wool cap that obscured her face, a shapeless sweater, and trousers. "Why is he here?" she hissed.

"You requested four crewmen to help the count," Vera said.

"Damn, why didn't you bring a Russian student?"

"The reliable ones are all dead or in prison. Dr. Doyle has aided us in the past. I trust him," Vera said.

"It will be very dangerous. We might all die." Penelope said.

I listened to the exchange, totally flummoxed. Neither woman cared a good damn whether I lived or died. I called on my Irish backbone. "It is a good cause," I said.

Vera shook my hand. "We are all together. Wear this."

I put on a dark student's jacket and pulled a visored cap over my eyes.

"Excellent," Vera said.

We walked towards the Neva where we met a four-horse carriage coming along Dvortsovaya Street. "Get in, quickly," Penelope ordered. I hesitated but climbed into the closed carriage.

The two men wore naval uniforms. When my eyes adjusted to the gloom, I recognized the German, Count von Wittenberg, and Gritz, the American engineer. We clipped along, in silence, for over an hour, turning into one street, then another, apparently to avoid followers. It was a dangerous mission, but there was no other way to see the submersible vessel.

The driver doubled back to the square and paused for long minutes. "Good, we are not being followed," the count said in English, which I presumed was for the benefit of Gritz.

At the wharf, the guards came to attention, saluted the count, and waved us on. We alighted from the carriage, crossed a gangway to the cargo ship, and climbed down a ladder to a landing stage where the submersible was hidden. I immediately noted how three sections were bolted together and recognized the breathing tubes and the periscope.

We descended through an open hatch into the belly of the beast, which was dimly lit with two Edison electric bulbs. I quickly scanned the interior, which was truly an engineering marvel. The navigation station was near the center, just forward of a huge electric motor connected to a series of batteries. Further aft, there were gauges, levers, and electrical devices I could not recognize. There was no doubt, however, about the rack containing new Mauser repeating rifles next to the navigation station.

When we reached the bottom of the ladder, Penelope gave the count an enthusiastic embrace. "This time, we must not fail," she said.

The count pushed her away. "If we prepare properly, we cannot fail. First, we assign stations, and then, we practice for the final run."

"We shall test the motor, but must save electricity. Hans, Fritz, Adolph, show this young man how to pedal," Gritz said.

Ivanov joined the German sailors at a series of pedals that turned the propeller shaft. The count led Vera to the forward-breathing tube pump and, for a moment, left me near the navigation station.

I peeked through the periscope for a minute and noted the steering wheel and depth control levers. While the count and Gritz were busy demonstrating the various pumps and pedals to the students and Penelope, I studied the compass. Whether or not the American, Gritz, was as much of a drunk as he appeared when we had first met, it was clear he was an experienced engineer.

Evidently, the captain navigated with the compass while submerged below periscope depth. It was a larger version of the simple magnetic compass I had used during hikes in the highlands. The black end of the needle pointed north, while the white aimed south.

Gritz came aft, pulled a switch, and the electric motor started with a whine. The deck vibrated, and immediately, the compass needle reversed itself. After the test, when he switched off the engine, the compass returned to normal.

"You," the count ordered. "Man the aft breathing-tube pump."

My job was to sit on a sort of saddle and turn bicycle pedals that, through a chain, ran a pump which brought in draughts of fresh air. *This will be hard, monotonous work,* I thought. The count seemed satisfied with my efforts, then took Penelope by the hand and went forward to what I deduced to be the torpedo firing station.

"Penelope, dear, you may have the honor to press the trigger to fire the torpedo that will kill the tsar," the count said. Would Penelope go with their plan or was she playacting? It was hard to tell. I had no choice but to let things play out.

The hatch remained open, and after the practice session, the count ordered us to rest. Meanwhile, he had turned the steering wheel and worked the lever, which moved a rod near my station.

I dredged up a memory from my brief look at the diagram. When the rod moved forward, the fins turned downward, so the boat went deeper. Moving it backward made the boat return to the surface. Could I move the rod by hand to control the boat's depth? There had to be a better plan.

Hours went by. I hated this ship, but tried not to let anybody see my distress. It was impossible to stand erect in the horribly cramped space. The atmosphere was hot and dense with humidity, even with the open hatch. I had been in dangerous situations during our American trip, but being entombed in an iron coffin was far worse. To make matters worse, I was far away from home and family and, not for the first time, yearned to return to dry land and lovely Edinburgh.

Then, I thought about how even Dr. Bell was unaware of my whereabouts. Sweat rolled down my face, but I shivered with cold fear. No one would know if I died.

I had been such a fool to meet these lunatics at midnight. What was I thinking? It was the day of the Naval Review. I was in this crowded space, close to Vera and Penelope — once, or perhaps, still, the love of my life — but visions of being in the open air with Ferguson on his yacht beckoned. The rascal would be sipping champagne with a couple of ballet dancers while he watched the parade of ships.

225

Then, I kept reminding myself that my comfort was of no consequence today. My task was to save lives at all costs. These people hated the tsar, but I knew him to be a good and kind father to little George, and the lives of everybody back home might be at risk if I failed.

Then, with a start, I thought of Sasha. Would someone care for her, or would she be returned to Pavlov's dreadful laboratory?

I felt sluggish and developed a headache. The air smelled stale. Nine people used a great deal of oxygen. I pedaled and, immediately, there was a breath of fresh air. I sucked in several lungs full and my headache cleared. The others sagged or held their heads in their hands.

In a flash, I realized that I controlled the amount of fresh air in the boat. If I pumped slowly, there was enough air for me, since the vent emptied out close to my head, but not enough for the others. The chemical, sodium hydroxide, would take up carbon dioxide too slowly to clean the air breathed out by nine people. This might turn out to be a valuable bit of knowledge.

Hours went by until I judged the sun to be nearly overhead. "Start the pumps and close the hatch," the count suddenly ordered.

In the dim light cast by the Edison bulbs, I watched the German crewmen and Ivanov pump pedals that turned the propeller. The boat moved sluggishly, then gathered speed. The count was glued to the periscope with his hands on the steering wheel. He moved the lever forward and the deck inclined downward.

"Five feet, continue to descend. Ah, good, maintain ten feet. At this level only the tips of our tubes are visible," Gritz said.

I pumped for all I was worth to maintain fresh air in the boat.

"Course, thirty-two degrees to the *Nakhimov*," the count said. He turned the periscope one hundred and eighty degrees and watched intently for several minutes. "Ah, right on schedule, our cruiser is following us. After we fire the torpedo, she will provide cover for our escape."

Gritz went forward and tapped a gauge connected to a large steel cylinder. "Good — two thousand pounds pressure, enough to fire the torpedo."

The count and Gritz kept up a steady patter. "Clear of the wharf. Five miles to target," the count said. "You fellows, more speed."

The big German sailors and Ivanov pedaled furiously. Sweat dripped down their faces and they gasped for air.

"Let us start the engine," the count said.

"Not yet. We must conserve electricity for our escape," Gritz replied.

I gradually slowed my pedaling until there was only a soft draft of fresh air on my face, but hardly enough for the others. Vera's head drooped, and the German sailors took in great gulps of air. All of them sagged and lost great quantities of sweat in the hot, closed space. Hans, one of the German crewmen, stumbled and nearly fell.

"Damn, the air is stale in here. You, British boy, pump harder!" the count shouted.

I pedaled furiously for a few minutes, but when the count went back to the periscope and attended to steering the boat, I slowed my pedaling and the intake of fresh air diminished to a trickle.

"Ah, my dear Gritz. Come, see a beautiful sight. There she is, less than a mile away," the count said.

Gritz took the wheel and put his eye to the lens and system of mirrors. "Ah, yes. Very good. The tsar's cruiser is anchored, broadside to us. The other ships are passing in review on the far side. At a range of six hundred yards, go deep and navigate by compass. No one will see us."

Gritz shook hands with the count. "Our approach is perfect. When we close to three hundred yards, fire the torpedo."

"Penelope, dear girl, see for yourself — the fruits of all our planning."

Penelope was pale and stumbled when she went to the count's side and peered through the periscope. "I feel ill," she said.

"The air is rotten. You, boy, pump harder!" the count glared at me. "Pedal, pedal, pedal faster. We need oxygen."

I went through the motions and pumped furiously, but when he turned his back, I slowed.

"Close the breathing tubes. It is time to descend to twenty feet," the count said.

Gritz studied his depth gauge, and the count pushed the lever controlling the fins. The deck inclined downward. The Germans and Ivanov pedaled furiously to maintain speed.

"We are below periscope depth!" The count shouted.

"Level the ship," Gritz said.

"Target, three hundred and fifty yards."

Gritz opened the oxygen cylinder. The gas hissed but the air was still dank.

A long two minutes elapsed. I waited, furiously thinking of a way out, but it seemed helpless. My mind was foggy, but when the count shouted "Fire!" I reacted by instinct and screamed. Penelope had both of her hands on the firing mechanism. Her eyes were glassy with fatigue and lack of oxygen. "NO, Penelope! Don't!" Penelope dropped her hand from the mechanism and turned those lovely eyes on me.

I left my post and lunged forward, down the middle of the crowded boat, brushing against the count. He swung a clenched fist that grazed my head. The violence of his attack knocked away my visored cap. I nearly went down but regained my feet and continued plowing ahead.

There was no escape. "You damn English! Curse you, Penelope, for bringing saboteurs on my boat!" he shouted, between ragged breaths.

In an instant, the count pulled a Mauser rifle from its rack and pressed the barrel against my chest. I kicked him in the groin. He fell backwards, but the deadly rifle was still aimed at my chest.

"Stop! Don't shoot! You will put a hole in the boat!" Gritz yelled.

The American lunged forward and pushed the rifle barrel upward. The count's features contorted into a dreadful mask of hatred and fear as he pulled the trigger.

A terrific *boom!* reverberated inside the iron hull. The powerful blast drove the bullet through the hull over my head. There was an immediate trickle of water, which increased to a stream the size of my finger.

"Hans, the plugs, get the plugs. SURFACE, SURFACE!" Gritz yelled.

Hans gazed at the thickening stream of water and drew his finger across his throat."Kaput," he said.

Gritz pointed at the hole. "HANS, THE PLUGS!"

Hans smiled. "Ah, Verstopten."

Hans fumbled in a tool box, found the wooden plugs, and, with dull German efficiency, hammered a wooden bung into the bullet hole. The leak stopped, but the deck inclined upward so rapidly, I rolled in a heap against the air pump. "Surface! Surface!" Gritz cried.

The count lunged forward and struck Penelope across the face, grabbed her hair, and pulled her head back.

"You damned traitor! You brought him and the others. Saboteurs!"

"No! No! NO! They are loyal to the cause," she said.

"There isn't enough air for all of us if we descend again," said the count. "When we surface, leave the damn traitors to freeze in the water. We can still fire the torpedo and be gone," Gritz growled.

The count peered through the periscope. "We have surfaced. Open the hatch."

Fritz leaped up the ladder, twirled the opening bolts, and in a moment, we had air and sunshine. Vera and Ivanov, dull from lack of oxygen, slumped in the arms of the German sailors who carried them up the ladder. Penelope was next, then me. I offered no resistance when the three muscular German sailors dragged me up to the deck, barely awash with the sea.

In a moment, I was sprawled on the deck and gasped for air. Gritz slammed the hatch, and the submarine started its slow slide beneath the waves. Instantly, the four of us were floating in the freezing sea. We couldn't last long. I prayed for rescue.

My first thought was to shout and wave at the Russian cruiser, only three hundred yards distant, but sailors at attention looked to the starboard side where ships passed in review. Their backs were turned, and the booms of saluting cannon drowned my feeble shouts.

229

The cold penetrated my flesh like deadly, icy daggers deadening my limbs. I could only think of death by freezing; the blood congealed, the heart slowed to a standstill, and the brain became a lifeless pound of flesh.

I was on my back, nearly covered with arctic water, when Vera's face floated into view. Her lips were blue and she seemed lifeless. I struck out and slammed my open hand into her face. "Wake up, damn you! MOVE! Don't give up!"

She opened her eyes. I rubbed her arms and legs with as much energy as I could muster until she moved both arms and feebly kicked with her legs.

Ivanov had the good sense to grab the periscope tube and was making feeble efforts to stay above water. The effort brought life back, and I vigorously beat the water with both hands while taking great gulps of fresh air. But the icy water was so frigid that I feared I couldn't last long.

It was like a blow to the solar plexus when I again realized the Russian cruiser with the tsar was within firing range of the submarine.

Penelope started off, thrashing the water with strong strokes as if she planned on swimming to the distant shore. Her efforts soon diminished, however, and she paddled back to where the three of us clung to the periscope tube.

Penelope sucked air. "Damn, you Doyle! We will drown or be killed by the blast. Do something!" Her voice dwindled to a pathetic whimper but she was right. The others could do nothing to save themselves, and I was the only strong swimmer.

"Everyone, keep moving! Kick and hold on to the periscope tube with one hand."

It was difficult because the boat was slowly picking up speed as it headed directly towards the Russian ship. The count intended to destroy the tsar and start a European war. He would escape and no one would know of the German and American involvement.

We clung to the periscope tube, with water over our waists, but the boat was diving deeper. The cold penetrated into my bones, and for a moment, all I could think of was a warm fire. Then, I thought of the count, down below, peering at his prey and ordering Hans or Fritz to fire the deadly torpedo.

I gulped icy seawater and, in a flash, thought of a solution. Without the periscope, the count would be blind.

"Ivanov, hold tight. I have an idea. Just try not to move."

I stepped up on his shoulders, which were just above water, and clung to the periscope tube. I hoisted myself up, like a monkey on a coconut tree. "Ivanov, help hoist me up."

Ivanov gave me a great upward push with as much energy as he could muster, and I grasped the very top of the periscope tube. Somehow, I found the strength to tear off my student's jacket and wrapped it around the lens.

I slid in a heap down the tube, but now, even standing on tip-toe, the water was nearly over my head. We could not survive the cold for more than another five minutes. Vera was already blue and scarcely breathing.

I desperately slapped her again until she roused. The boat was diving deeper, so the breathing tubes were just breaking the surface.

Penelope again struck out, paddling and treading water. I grabbed her and held everyone together, hoping to conserve any last remnants of body heat.

I gasped and spit out a mouthful of salty water. "Stay together. Hold onto one another. Keep moving. Our only chance is to stay close for warmth," I spluttered.

We were now floating and drifting away from the periscope tube. I forced everyone to kick and to hug one another. Ivanov felt the vibration first. "They've started the electric motor," he said.

I felt a commotion in the water. The submarine turned erratically, first one way, then another, as if lost. For a moment, the boat came to its original course towards the *Nakhimov,* then made a one hundred and eighty degree turn.

In my mind, I could see the compass. When Gritz started the electric motor, the electro-magnetic field caused the compass to swing a complete half circle, one hundred and eighty degrees from north to south.

The count must have been confused, but, trusting his compass, came to the new course, away from the Russian ship. We had all been concentrating on staying afloat, but by chance, I raised my head and looked over the waves.

To my great amazement, the grey hull of the German cruiser was no more than three hundred yards away, directly in the path of the submarine. I remembered the count saying that the cruiser would cover their escape. For a moment, we floated, holding one another under a sunlit sky on a calm, cold sea. There were many ships and smaller pleasure boats about, mostly in the distance toward the Russian cruiser and the tsar. I idly remembered Ferguson's invitation to watch the review from his sailboat. If only we could stay alive long enough to be rescued ...

Suddenly, I felt a mild a concussion — like a gentle punch to the gut — when they fired the torpedo. Bubbles rising to the surface were on a course towards the German ship.

"That would be the compressed air," Ivanov said.

There were more bubbles, then a small wake, heading directly towards the midsection of the German cruiser. The count depended completely on the accuracy of his compass, not realizing it was completely reversed.

It was a rather pleasant thought that we had deceived him. If we died, at least our deaths would not be in vain.

I treaded water and, with one hand, held Vera and Ivanov afloat as we watched the bubbles rising from the torpedo streaking directly on target. It hit dead center just below the water line.

There was another *boom!* and flames and black smoke rose from the German ship. We were left rocking on a great wave, stunned by the concussion.

When the shock wave receded, I waved my arms wildly, hoping someone might see us. But, alas, all seemed lost.

We were destined to die from exposure at sea. It was just too cold and we'd been in the water too long...

As I gave up the last shreds of hope, I caught the welcome sight of a white yacht with twin masts flying in our direction. It rounded up with sails flapping in the mild breeze.

Was it possible? Aye...

Dicky tossed a rope with a life preserver.

"Old boy, what a show, eh? Best fireworks of the day!" Dicky shouted. "Grab the lifesaver!"

Ferguson, along with Dr. Bell and Colonel Beachy-Edwards, dragged us, one by one, aboard the little yawl. I had never before been so grateful to see my dear friends. I was still sprawled on deck, vomiting sea water, when one hundred yards away and, not far from the flaming German cruiser, the snout of the black submarine shot to the surface, like a breaching, wounded whale.

The periscope tube and the breathing tubes were torn away. It must have taken on water after the torpedo blast. By some miracle, Gritz, the engineer, had saved the boat.

In a moment, the hatch opened and Hans, the huge German sailor, pulled himself on deck. He lay, face down, perfectly motionless.

"If you please, Mr. Ferguson, let us pick up the survivors," said Colonel Sir Beachy-Edwards, hardly raising his voice.

Dicky put down the tiller, and I helped bring over the main sail. We went tearing down towards the submarine and drew alongside.

Hans was a mass of bruises, and there was a huge gash on his head. "Gott mit uns. Alle tot. Alle tot," he said, with a final gasp.

I recognized his words, "All dead. All dead." He then slipped away beneath the waves.

Then, before our eyes, a bloody hand came up out of the open hatch. With what had to be a tremendous effort, the count's blonde hair, then the rest of his head, appeared just at the level of the hatch opening. The submarine was slowly sliding beneath the waves.

Penelope sighed. "Oh, please, save him, please," she said in a weak voice.

I had no intention of diving back into those frigid, heart-stopping waters. I glanced at Dr. Bell for support. He shook his head and seemed to indicate to me not to risk my life. His face remained impassive; he was no longer a teacher-mentor.

Yet, it was my decision, and time was of the essence. *A life is a life*, I thought, and dove overboard. With a few thrashing strokes, I reached the submarine, sliding slowly beneath the waves. Another inch and water would pour down the hatch. I managed to kneel, grasp his hand, and drag Count von Wittenberg's dead weight to the deck. He lay on his back with those cruel, light blue, Prussian eyes that for the past thousand years had stared straight through common people.

The submarine commenced its last fatal dive. I slid into the water with my arm across the count's chest. It was then I realized his massive injury. The blast had stoved in his chest. Every broken rib on his right side grated with each of his torturous breaths.

"Take care. He has broken ribs!" I shouted.

Ferguson and Dr. Bell leaned down from the deck and, as gently as possible, heaved him to the yacht's deck. He was on his back, having his last glimpse of the sun and sky, when I pulled myself, hand over hand, into the cockpit.

Penelope cradled the count's head on her lap, stroked his forehead, and shed tears.

"Schatzi, mein liebling," he whispered.

She put her mouth next to his ear. "Carl, Ich liebe dich," she said.

So, they were lovers, a perfect match. It was still difficult to believe that lovely Penelope, woman of gentle English blood, was a traitor to the crown. I felt sick to my stomach, yet the worst was still to come.

With great effort, he pulled a packet wrapped in oiled silk from his jacket pocket. "Dear Penelope, the money is yours." He coughed and blood splattered on Penelope's face. With his last effort, the count withdrew a small, glass vial from an inner pocket and pressed it into her hand. "Take it. An honorable death is preferable to a life in prison."

I watched in horror as Penelope took from him the deadly vial of cyanide, the suicide poison chosen by spies. Count von Wittenberg drew in a long, lingering breath, turned his head to one side, and was dead.

Penelope's lips drew back in an ugly rictus — was it of fear, anger, or did she say "Good riddance?"

She tossed the vial over the side just as another ship passed the Russian cruiser and fired a noisy salute to the tsar. Amid the great firing of guns, Colonel Sir Beachy-Edwards removed the packet from Penelope's hand and, with great care, opened the water-proof package.

Inside was a stack of fifty pound Bank of England notes. "Ah, how unfortunate," the colonel said. "The Secret Service provides these notes to our operatives. Dr. Bell, may I see the note you recovered from the Chinese Cook who killed Asquith?"

Dr. Bell opened his wallet and passed the crisp new note to the colonel.

"Ah, yes. The serial number of this note indicates it was the first in the series that the service provided to Miss Walshingham."

Penelope shivered, but wrapped her arms around my neck and planted a hearty deep kiss on my lips. "Doyle, you are magnificent. You saved us from that fiend."

"Young lady, you are an accessory to murder and guilty of traitorous and duplicitous conduct. A prison sentence will be your just reward," the colonel said.

Penelope smiled. "Actually, you are mistaken," she said.

"No, Ma'am."

"Yes, colonel. I have a friend at court."

Dicky had brought the yawl on a new course, and within minutes, we passed under the bows of Her Majesty's yacht, the *Victoria and Albert*.

Penelope set up a shout and waved at a portly figure on deck. "Yoo-hoo, Bertie! Bertie!"

"Penelope, dear, is it really you in those dreadful clothes? You are just in time for Tiffin. Come, dear girl, I have an extra frock just your size," the Prince of Wales replied.

The colonel and, for that matter, the rest of us, were stunned. But Penelope just smiled as if all that had occurred over the past few hours was nothing but the events of another ordinary Sunday afternoon.

Dickie dropped the sails, and we glided up to the landing stage at the base of a ladder leading up to the port side of Her Majesty's yacht. The portly figure — with a spade beard and dressed in perfect nautical attire — descended the ladder, took Penelope in a great bear hug, and cooed at her. "You dear, sweet girl. It has been so long."

Before any of us could say or do anything, Penelope and 'Bertie' were gone. She did not even look over her shoulder as she departed. For once, I was not upset to see her leave.

A few minutes later, we went off with tight sails and passed near enough to the *Nakhimov* to see the tsar and his family happily waving to the passing ships.

Colonel Beachy-Edwards sadly shook his head. "Imagine, calling the Prince of Wales, the future King of England, 'Bertie.' The foolish sod does nothing but gamble and chase women. I pity the future of our homeland."

Dicky brought the yacht on a course for home and gave me the tiller while he opened a magnum of champagne and a hamper filled with glorious edibles. We all set about devouring the picnic, and I tried to shake off the cold and the memory of the past twenty-four hours. I tossed off a tumbler of bubbly but was overcome with a shaking chill and pain in every muscle.

"Such a pity. We may never know if Walshingham or the count paid for the murder of poor Asquith," said Colonel Beachy-Edwards, between bites of smoked salmon.

236

14 October 1881

I am now on the night train to Paris and have completed my report to Colonel Sir Cameron Beachy-Edwards. It's been days since the submarine boat episode, and things have settled down quite a bit. My thoughts have returned to the start of this adventure, when the Colonel identified Uncle Declan. I had regretted our failure to save his life, but would he have wanted to live without legs? Would he have wanted to be a half a man? He had endured suffering, but his search for truth and justice never ceased. His teaching during our visits to the museum was similar to Dr. Bell's. He told me to observe carefully before deciding on a course of action. It is essential to gather facts in order to know the truth. Uncle Declan courageously gave his life in honor of that noble pursuit. I am proud of that legacy in our family and hope it will help lessen mam's grief.

David Campbell is reading a novel by Dostoevsky while Sasha sits at his feet, twitching and whining, as if, in her dreams, she is chasing a rabbit.

After the near-catastrophe on Sunday, Dr. Bell had convinced the tsar to take his son south for fresh air and sunshine and ensure that the royal family was well out of danger.

And in the end, since Vera and Ivanov had committed no crime, I convinced the colonel and Dr. Bell to stay mum about their involvement with the plot. They were chastened and vowed to be good citizens of the tsar. Pavlov even agreed to employ both in his laboratory.

Ah, Dear Dr. Bell. At present, he is with Sir Cameron Beachy-Edwards in a separate compartment. The two of them have become quite companionable while they enjoy a tot of single malt and compare notes on criminal investigation.

Sadly, he still uses cocaine, but his use seems to be in moderation.

And Penelope? Dear, unfathomable Penelope returned to England on the royal yacht with Bertie. It is rumored that he has taken her as a mistress. I may never hear from her again. I will miss her, but perhaps that it is just as well. Who knows? Maybe one day, she will marry the prince and be the next Queen of England. Perhaps, instead, she will continue her dangerous double life. Or maybe — just, maybe — she might miss me and come back to cover me with her sweet kisses. Is that even what I want?

Oh well. At least with this adventure over, I am free to go back to my beloved Scotland and focus on my medical career. If I am lucky, and it is not Penelope who is destined to be Mrs. Doyle, perhaps I will fall into the arms of that pretty Scottish nurse back home. Even if those plans don't work out, Sasha will certainly be my faithful companion for many years to come. After all, dogs are said to be man's best friend…

Perhaps, someday, I will publish the stories in this journal so the world can learn about how I, in a small way, assisted Dr. Bell. It was really through his keen mind that we saved Europe from a great war!

In the meantime, last night I had a dream that gave me a glimmer of an idea for a story. I imagined a great detective in the very image of Dr. Bell who solves the most difficult crimes. Of course, he would require an assistant, perhaps a rather bumbling physician, such as myself . . .

Dr. John Raffensperger is a surgeon and medical historian who received his B.A., B.S., and M.D. degrees from the University of Illinois and was a medical officer in the U.S. Navy Reserve. He has served as staff surgeon, acting director of thoracic surgery, and chief of pediatric surgery at Cook County Hospital in Chicago, chief of pediatric surgery and surgeon-in-chief at Children's Memorial Hospital in Chicago, and visiting surgeon in Haiti and St. Lucia. "Dr. Raff" was a clinical instructor/associate professor of surgery at University of Illinois College of Medicine and an associate professor/professor of surgery at Northwestern University's Feinberg School of Medicine, where he remains a professor of surgery emeritus. He has been a visiting professor in Alabama, Connecticut, Texas, Bolivia, Canada, Cuba, Ecuador, Germany, Japan, Mexico, Poland, and South Korea, as well as a case report editor for the *Journal of Pediatric Surgery* and founder and editor of *The Child's Doctor*, a journal of Chicago's Children's Memorial Hospital. Approximately 300 of his articles have been published in the medical and surgical literature, and he has written book chapters on topics ranging from pediatric surgery to ethics and medical history, as well as non-medical essays on sailing, the environment, and art. Raffensperger has authored several books, including *Principals of Nursing Care for the Pediatric Surgical Patient* (Little, Brown & Co.), *The Acute Abdomen in Infancy and Childhood* (Lippincott), *Swenson's Pediatric Surgery* (Appleton, Century, Crofts), *The Old Lady on Harrison Street, the History of the Cook County Hospital, 1833-1995* (Peter Lang Publishers), *Ward 41, Tales of a County Intern* (Discovery Association Press), *Two Scottish Tales of Medical Compassion* (Cosimo Classics), *Children's Surgery, A Worldwide History* (McFarland and Company, Inc.), and three self-published works.

Richard Krevolin is a teacher, writer, and director. A graduate of Yale College, he earned master's degrees in screenwriting at UCLA's School of Cinema-Television and in playwriting and fiction from USC. "Prof. K" has been an adjunct professor of dramatic writing at USC School of Cinema/TV, UCLA, Pepperdine, Emerson, Ithaca College, University of Redlands, and The

University of Georgia. During the last decade, he has taught the art of communication and storytelling to international executives, creatives, lawyers, and brand managers. The author of several books, including *Screenwriting From The Soul* (St. Martin's Press), *Pilot Your Life* (Prentice-Hall), *How To Adapt Anything Into A Screenplay* (Wiley & Sons), and *Screenwriting in the Land of Oz* (Adams Media/Writer's Digest Books), he has also written several young adult novels and over twenty stage plays. Krevolin has several scripts in development in Hollywood, including *SAFER,* with Tom DeSanto Productions, which will be produced in 2017. He was a documentary writer for *Fiddler on the Roof: 30 Years of Tradition.* He wrote, produced, directed, and starred in the documentary, *Making Light in Terezin*, which aired on PBS. Krevolin also wrote, directed, and co-produced the feature comedy film, *Attachments,* which stars Katharine Ross.

Also from MX Publishing

MX Publishing is the world's largest specialist Sherlock Holmes publisher, with over a hundred titles and fifty authors creating the latest in Sherlock Holmes fiction and non-fiction.

From traditional short stories and novels to travel guides and quiz books, MX Publishing caters to all Holmes fans.

The collection includes leading titles such as *Benedict Cumberbatch In Transition* and *The Norwood Author* which won the 2011 Howlett Award (Sherlock Holmes Book of the Year).

MX Publishing also has one of the largest communities of Holmes fans on Facebook with regular contributions from dozens of authors.

www.mxpublishing.com

Also from MX Publishing

Our bestselling short story collections 'Lost Stories of Sherlock Holmes', 'The Outstanding Mysteries of Sherlock Holmes', 'Untold Adventures of Sherlock Holmes' (and the sequel 'Studies in Legacy') and 'Sherlock Holmes in Pursuit'.

Also from MX Publishing

"Phil Growick's, *'The Secret Journal of Dr Watson'*, is an adventure which takes place in the latter part of Holmes and Watson's lives. They are entrusted by HM Government (although not officially) and the King no less to undertake a rescue mission to save the Romanovs, Russia's Royal family, from a grisly end at the hand of the Bolsheviks. There is a wealth of detail in the story but not so much as would detract us from the enjoyment of the story. Espionage, counter-espionage, the ace of spies himself, double-agents, double-crossers . . . all these flit across the pages in a realistic and exciting way. All the characters are extremely well-drawn and Mr Growick, most importantly, does not falter with a very good ear for Holmesian dialogue indeed. Highly recommended. A five-star effort."

The Baker Street Society

The characters return in the sequel, *The Revenge of Sherlock Holmes.*